For Philip
B...

Do...ty

2'ston 2019

GHOSTLY

DEMARCATIONS

STORIES

❦

JOE TAYLOR

Sagging
Meniscus

ISBN: 978-1-944697-75-4 (paperback)
ISBN: 978-1-944697-76-1 (ebook)
Library of Congress Control Number: 978-1-944697-75-4

Sagging Meniscus Press
saggingmeniscus.com

In memory of Galen King and Joe Stearns

Acknowledgments

Some of these stories previously appeared in the following publications:

"Madonna on a Country Road": *Steam Ticket*
"Galen's Mountain Child": *Red Dirt Forum*
"The Mansion, the Chandelier, the Belle": *Jitter*
"Faithful Companion": *cleansheets.com*
"Tit for Tat": *Red Dirt Forum*
"A Red Phase": *moonShine*
"I'll Be Home for Christmas": *Weird and Whatnot*

Thanks to Tom Abrams, Anne Kaylor, Sarah Langcuster, Christin Loehr, Nick Noland, Tricia Taylor, Amy Susan Wilson.

Oh! Blessed rage for order . . .
The maker's rage to order words of the sea,
Words of the fragrant portals, dimly-starred,
And of ourselves and of our origins,
In ghostlier demarcations, keener sounds.

—Wallace Stevens, "The Idea of Order at Key West"

Contents

GHOSTLY DEMARCATIONS

GALEN'S MOUNTAIN CHILD

"I KNEW IT WAS A GHOST because he was more afraid than I was," Galen said about his sighting. "There was a kid, up on this mountain—" Galen jerked his thumb toward the attic's sole window— "years back. He was kept chained in a cellar and got burned alive. It was him, I'm sure."

The house we were staying in was a two-story farmhouse. In its basement sat an ominous, rust-brown coal-heating unit, which would occasionally clank or pop through all the vents. The house was built on the side of a mountain near Irvine, Kentucky, and the mountain itself sat half a mile from Red River, where Mr. and Mrs. Moore—the house's owners—kept bottomland to raise corn, mostly used to slop their hogs. Situated near the mountain's foot, this house was the first of three. The other two were spaced about four and then five hundred yards as you climbed. I'd walked up to the second house once when I went to visit with Galen, but I never saw the third, for it lay on the mountain's far side, away from the river. Back then, Kentucky had a good deal of snow in the hardest part of winter, especially in the eastern coal part of the state. Back then, there was a good deal of unreported child and wife abuse, especially in that same region, so Galen's comment about the chained kid seemed . . . well, normally awful.

We were supposed to be sleeping in the unfinished attic, a huge room that topped a third of the downstairs area. What all was stored in the remainder of the attic behind a plywood partition I never learned. It was winter and it was snowing, large flakes that softly nipped at our bedroom's single window like lonesome, misplaced summer moths. Usually, Galen visited his grandparents then, in summer I mean, when school was out, but this time was different. I got invited as the semi-orphan, since I had a single mom just like Galen, or maybe I was there as someone to keep Galen out of the way. I think his mom was having money problems, which was why she visited in winter, and maybe she needed to talk with her parents alone.

"Over there is where he stood," Galen continued. "By that little iron bed. He was staring at the crib in the corner."

"How'd you know it was a he?" I asked, checking the crib, which struck me as creepy enough already, since its white sheets had cradled nothing but dust for well over a decade.

Galen gave a soft snort. "If it was a she I would have invited her here to my bed." Galen patted his mattress, extending his arm and crooking a finger in a come-hither gesture. Even at our ages, thirteen and almost eleven, Galen was over-developing into a sex fiend. No wonder he wound up in the Navy five years later.

Wind picked up outside and snow pelted the window beside us. Galen's arm was still raised, his finger still motioning a come-hither crook.

"Shit," he whispered.

"Damn," I said.

A sheaf of fog hung beside the crib, its coldness swirling slowly toward us. Someone rattled a pan downstairs—Mrs. Moore washing dishes? Two black eyes from the sheaf snapped open, and the fog filtered upward to soak into the bare wood slats of the roof. Snow still pelted the window.

"You think it was him?" I asked.

"Shit, I was just making that mostly up."

"Well, do you think?"

A crash erupted from downstairs. We used that excuse to hop from the bed we sat on and run down the steps.

When we rounded the corner, we saw Mawey—that's what everyone called Mrs. Moore, Galen's maternal grandmother—standing in the kitchen slack-mouthed. She was staring toward the enclosed skinny run that led along the back of the house, behind the bathroom and the bedroom Galen's mom slept in. About thirty feet long, this run also crossed over the cellar and the furnace. Mawey's husband ran into the kitchen behind us, with Galen's mom not far behind.

Mawey stood at a counter and pointed along the enclosed run. "A little boy. I was setting out the coffee for percolating tomorrow. He must have opened that screen door, but I didn't hear." She returned to staring. We four walked around the refrigerator to look. The plastic tacked up for winter to cover the dogtrot's summer screening flapped in cold wind, but that distant outer door remained shut. Then a calico kitten jumped onto the hip-high balustrade, a low tongue-in-groove barrier painted chalky blue that separated the dogtrot from the steep steps leading down to the cellar. Its purpose must have been to keep people from falling, but the Moores used it as a catchall for harnesses, kettles, and boots. The kitten balanced atop a harness, and then jumped to hit the dogtrot's green linoleum with a soft thump. The kitten looked at us, then back toward the screen door's flapping plastic, then hissed and jumped again on the balustrade to disappear down the steps. The door's plastic covering snapped hard from a gust of wind.

"I'm going to check that latch," Mr. Moore said. He reached back to pick up a piece of kindling from a pile beside the refrigerator before heading to the door.

"It was just a boy." Mawey's voice was quiet.

"I just want to make sure."

"Maybe he's lost out in this snowstorm," Galen's mom said.

Galen made a screwed-up face. His mom had been dating men starting the year after Galen's dad died and she hadn't been the gospel of kindness. Or maybe she was the gospel to the men, but not even the epistle to Galen.

Mr. Moore came back after calling outside several times, rousing the rooster in the hen house to crowing for his efforts.

"You know who he looked like," Mawey started. She heaved a sigh. Mawey was as considerable a woman as her husband was wiry.

"Let's all go to bed," Mr. Moore interrupted, rapping the kindling on the breakfast table. "Enough for one night. You boys latch that stairway door."

That was nearly as much as I'd ever heard him say. Though Galen's grandfather lived on for several years, I never heard his voice again after that night. If we humans could always recognize the last words we were ever to hear from each person we knew or even met, our lives would perch as fragile indeed, gathering tragedy every listening moment to lean over a dark cellar, of dark farewells.

As the plastic covering the line of windows and the door continued to snap, Mr. Moore and the other two adults hurried us toward the stairs to the attic room. Galen and I hesitated at the steps, considering what we'd seen up there moments before, but the door got closed behind us, and Galen obediently dropped the feeble latch into place.

"As if that'll keep him out," Galen's mom murmured on the other side of the door as the latch clicked its little click.

"Hush," Mawey retorted. The three of them shuffled off. Galen and I climbed the creaky wooden steps but stopped when we heard the two women speak again.

"The mountain child hasn't been around for nearly two years, since Weldon died."

"Momma, you . . ."

Their conversation shuffled into silence, so Galen and I climbed on to again sit on his bed. We weren't about to sleep.

"I wasn't really making all that up," Galen said, staring into the corner at the iron crib. I stared there too, aware of the wind and snow buffeting the window to my right.

"Weldon was your dad's name, wasn't it?"

Galen nodded. "My grandmother thinks that the mountain child kept coming to call him home. She's said it before."

I'd learned about this type of messenger ghost in something I'd read or maybe heard around my single Cub Scout campfire, so I nodded wisely. Galen and I had left a table lamp on, by the window. Galen had dark, almost Cherokee skin from his dad. Now it looked as pale as mine in the bulb's glare, since there was no lampshade. A noise sounded by the crib in the far corner and we jumped. But it was nothing. The only real sound was the wind and snow pelting the window.

"I wasn't making it up," Galen said again. "There used to be a fourth house near the top of the hill, on the far side. It burned down. I climbed to see it last summer, but everything was overgrown. It took me an hour to find what was left of the chimney. Grandpa and the other folks living around here filled in the cellar because that's where they kept the boy roped up, chained up. They found his burned body after the fire. Some say maybe he was retarded, some say he wasn't, just made that way because of his father and mother and the chains. Mawey says they were the ones retarded."

I'd been there three days and was used to the old house creaking and shifting with the winter cold, the furnace popping in the middle of the night. But no sound came, except Galen's voice. Even the snow had slacked off, so there was mostly just silence.

"My mom says she was lots younger even than me when this happened. The man and the woman just disappeared.

Someone claimed they'd seen them in town at the Greyhound station. No one knew about the boy.

"Then the Masters, they're not the ones farthest up, but the ones with some green apple trees, then they started hearing whimpering. They thought there was a dog lost, or maybe a bear cub, which scared them, because momma bears can be mean when they have cubs."

Through the heating pipe—Mr. Moore had enclosed old chimney pipe in bricks and cement—we heard a high noise.

"One of the kittens?" I asked. I was supposed to stay five days, and Mawey said I could have one from the litter to take home.

Galen shrugged. I felt this from the bed and saw it in the shadow he cast on the wall.

"Mr. Masters and his two sons took shotguns and went with a dog searching, but couldn't find anything. They stopped at both houses farther up. The very top one with the people who'd left was empty, but no one knew they'd gone at that time, much less that they'd left the mountain child behind—that's how people call him now."

Another meow—that's what it was for sure—through the heating pipe. But Galen said,

"That's not a cat or a kitten."

We listened. We heard nothing.

"Soon enough, the people on up the other side of the mountain heard the noise too. The man there joined the Masters and his sons, and this time they spent half a day looking, and again went up to the highest house—remember, they still didn't know about the mountain child—but it was locked. By this time, rumor'd spread about the couple being at the bus station, but you need to mind your own business, so they called at the locked door and went away when no one answered."

The cat—or whatever it was—started up again through the nearby pipe. This time it sounded like a voice to me.

"It's saying 'Help me.' "

"It's a kitten," Galen said, contradicting his earlier self and coughing.

Galen had started smoking on the sly. I think it was to irritate his mother, who was ignoring him for all the men hanging around. She had a job in a dress shop that sold mostly patterns and fabric, so I don't know where she met the men, looking back on matters. Where there's a need, there's a way, I suppose. Galen reached under his mattress for his pack of cigarettes and some matches, which he shook. He gave me a look.

"*Help me.*"

"There, did you hear it?"

"It's a kitten," Galen said.

Something else came through the pipe, several times, a boy's voice for sure. Years later I told Galen that the voice was calling out in French and Spanish and other languages. "You're full of bull hockey, college boy," was his answer. "Drink your beer."

But back then, in the lamp's light on that cold night, I looked at Galen and shook my head, even as the voice repeated its plea. *Help me.*

"A kitten. I'll prove it." Galen put the cigarettes and matches in his shirt pocket. "Get your coat and walk down on the left side of the steps, except when I pull you to the right for three of them that squeak. No noise that way."

We put on our coats and walked down the stairs, quietly enough to still hear the voice echoing from the heating pipe above. Why weren't the Moores and Galen's mom up? Couldn't they hear this voice calling through their vents?

By the refrigerator Galen stopped to pick up a piece of kindling, just as his granddad had. Kid see, kid do, so I picked up one also. I'm left-handed, so Galen and I balanced in an odd fashion. We went through the kitchen and then out onto the enclosed run, a walkway wide enough to be partly used as storage as I mentioned. Galen nimbly avoided a couple of boxes and some leather harnessing. His grandfather used a mule for plowing the corn and beans. I leaned over the balustrade to listen to the cellar, but heard nothing, no meows, no hisses, no voices.

We sneaked open the screen door, the wind flapping its plastic and disguising the sound of the door's unlatching and creaking. It had stopped snowing and the temperature had dropped ridiculously. A strong moon lit the fallen snow. The rooster was still crowing, though not as often.

"Let's light up. It'll calm our nerves."

I had no idea what movie Galen got this from. Or maybe it was a TV western or detective show.

"If you're going to cough, don't inhale," Galen told me.

"*Ayuadame! Hilf mir! M'Aidez! Pomozite mi!*" The voice was a whisper, it was high whispers, low whispers, rolling whispers. I looked to Galen, but he was only watching the glow of his cigarette and shivering. I don't mean to say that I heard these distinct languages then, or even held them in my memory when I told this to Galen years later after he'd returned from the Navy. Sometimes you just know things. I will say, however, that a crackling of cold skipped across my shoulders later when I sat at a faraway desk in a faraway high school studying, *¿Donde es la biblioteca, Isabel?* and spotted the word *ayuadame*.

A physical blast of cold hit both Galen and me standing outside. We stood staring at the henhouse thirty yards away. The rooster had at last gone back to sleep, maybe lulled by the wind, which seemed to be playing a weird symphony, crashing now through the clacking, half frozen pines, simpering now with frosty sibilance through the snowy mountainside. My fingers stung with cold. *Help me.* Galen lit another cigarette. I had a gag reflex when he offered me one, so he put the pack in his shirt pocket. *Ayuadame.* My body was shivering now, and so was Galen's. The wind picked up to play a Tchaikovskian finale of Napoleonic grandeur, sweeping across Russia and the frozen corpses of French infantry, just simple, gulled men who'd been promoting egality. The tip of Galen's cigarette glowed without cease. The backs of my hands stung, my ears burnt. Somewhere up the mountain a large limb cracked under accumulating snow.

Help me.

There, I heard it for sure.

"As soon as I finish this fag, let's go look at the kittens," Galen said.

"Maybe we should just go back upstairs."

Help me.

"We need to get something cleared first." Galen flipped his cigarette toward the line of pines heading up the mountainside, but a gust blew it back at his face. He slipped aside and it hit in the gravel drive. He flipped it again, more effectively this time. The wind turned to a steady howl, like it can in the mountains.

"Let's go."

We went back in, latching the door. The plastic covering kept still now, respecting the steady howl outside.

Help me.

"Damn kittens never sleep."

"It's not kittens," I replied.

Galen didn't respond. Instead, he picked up a flashlight at the head of the basement steps and started down. The stairs seemed a mix of concrete and earth that completely muted our footsteps. A third of the way down Galen turned on the flashlight, when the reflective light from the outside snow faded.

"Kitty-kitty," I called when we neared the bottom.

"Shh," Galen hissed. Rounding the corner, we flipped on the single electric bulb that hung overhead away from the furnace. Its low wattage glowed. All the kittens scattered, even though they weren't feral. *Where's the mother*, I wondered. *Out chasing a tomcat, like Galen's mom?*

The floor of the cellar seemed to be the same mixture of concrete and dirt that made the steps. One kitten's mew came from coal piled in the corner, another from wooden crates in the opposite near corner. A pair of long iron pincer tongs fell, clattering.

"*Help me.*"

A screak and a bang, then a yellow light glowed from inside the furnace, as if the overhead bulb had stretched its wires and now dangled in there. But it was the furnace's somehow opened door creating that light. A low, droning roar emitted from the exposed bed of coal, and a child sat in there—yes!—a child sat inside, atop those live, softly burning coals—keeping its back to us.

"Shit."

"Damn."

The child, a glowing young boy, turned at our voices, clanking a chain. When he saw us he stood and fiercely tugged at the chain. Chunks of glowing coal popped up from the orange bed as he kicked and tugged, his eyes widening terribly, his mouth opening in a silent but horrible scream. He fell onto the bed of coals and then stood, staying in a panic and pulling at the chain, which seemed to be connected to the furnace's inner wall. A chunk of white-orange coal hopped from the furnace's mouth. The boy leaned backward at an impossible angle, frantically tugging the chain around his ankle until somehow the furnace door got slammed shut.

The hunk of coal lay smoldering where it had landed. On a mat? A slat of wood? A small fire ignited.

"Shit," Galen said. "Go put on those gloves from on that crate." While I ran and donned the fireman's gloves, which engulfed my hands, Galen himself grabbed the tongs that had fallen. With them, he picked up the coal, stomping the mat at the same time. I helped until the fire went out.

We both then stared at the closed furnace door. A kitten mewed. Another batted something across the floor. We stared.

"This coal is heavy and hot," Galen said, nudging me.

I nodded and opened the furnace's door with the gloves. A white-orange bed of coals was all I saw. Galen tossed in the chunk with the tongs, and I looked in again. After sparkling from the chunk, the coals returned into one evenly burning hypnotic orange bed.

"Close it," Galen said.

I did. A kitten rubbed my leg, the jumpy calico from earlier that I'd wind up taking home. We made sure the mat was extinguished, then walked up the steps and outside for one last smoke to calm our nerves.

Galen spoke true: Just drink my beer and shut up. And I suppose that one way or another I concocted all the foreign language business. But just four nights ago as I pulled my record player from storage to listen to Eddie Arnold's "Cattle Call"—musicians are right, analog beats digital hands down—I realized something about that burning kid's voice: he wasn't calling out 'Help me' in *any* language; he was singing, merrily singing to himself, amid those fiery coals. So I will shut up now . . . but here's one last thing I want you to riddle me . . .

what kind of damnable world is it where a child's singing ghost turns around, only to get thrown in a panic on seeing the living?

I Am the Egg

ALEN TOLD ME that the old guy who did all the magic at the downtown hobby shop was "queer as a three-dollar bill," in the vernacular of the times. Despite that warning, I was drawn to the mustachioed guy, who would grimly perform the three-cup trick, the disappearing coin trick (complete with faux glass coin that the mark—me!—dropped into a glass of water and heard clink but could never, ever see), and assorted flashy card tricks. He'd do just one trick per visit, leaving kids leaning against the counter for more.

He was grimly innovative too: he'd rigged up a life-sized witch with a most terrible pasty and warty face, a ragged black robe, and gnarled and bloody hands grasping a broom-stick painted virgin—or bone—white. With a clank, she would emerge from the shop's back storage loft to clatter and wobble underneath a track mounted in the ceiling. From up there she'd perch on her broom and screech out Latin, different Latin each time, or at least different each of the dozen or so times I heard her. Except one.

"The crone. I don't bring her out when girls are in here," the grinning shop owner told Galen and me. "They'd pee their panties and leave nasty puddles I'd have to clean up."

"See, I told you," Galen said when we walked outside the shop. "The old fart hates women. He's banana queer."

Galen went to the shop for modeling clay—he'd yet to find his lifelong niche in woodcarving. I went there because Galen did and because I was weaning off my last stage of model trains. So I'd buy a magic trick to branch out. Most of those came from a company that packaged them with a slyly grinning red dwarf for its logo. The shop owner would cover the dwarf with his palm and look away when he rang them up.

"As if I don't have enough trouble in here already without this one," he'd say whenever I bought a trick from that company. And here would come the crone, spewing her Latin, rattling overhead, a talisman, I supposed.

"Is that your falsetto voice in the recording?" I asked him once. I was so proud of myself for that Italian word.

"What recording?" He made a face at my pretentiousness.

I pointed upward to the crone. Now and then she'd smell really terminal, and whenever she did the owner would tug his large brown mustache, giving a worried glance toward the storage loft over the back room, or the back room's fire exit, or the far wall's bare bricks crumbling behind robin's egg blue shelving that held layers and layers of dolls.

The old guy—looking back I figure he was only in his late forties—may or may not have been gay, may or may not have hated women, despite that half a wall filled with dolls and sewing paraphernalia, which he actually used to sew doll dresses. Myself, I avoided that section of wall as if it were a pustule. Did that mean I was gay or hated women? No, I think it was a simple growing phase, for eventually I followed Galen's penis prints and became a womanizer, though not nearly as successful. But back to the shop owner—Mr. Howard, Mr. Max Howard—well, was Galen right about him? I'll never know, for Mr. Howard died prematurely and awfully.

It must have begun the evening before I went to his shop that Friday. School had just let out for summer, and when I walked in the crone was hovering over the cash register, quivering but not really moving. This was odd, since I'd also spotted a woman and her two daughters in the store one aisle over, looking at the dolls, and Mr. Howard had repeatedly made his silly proclamation about girls "peeing the floor." The girls weren't peeing; they were oohing and aahing over a particular doll from what sounds I could make out.

I was going to ask Mr. Howard if he'd have to clean up pee, but his face was contorted with worry and he was tugging fiercely at his moustache. Besides, I smelled something awful drifting down from the crone. When I covered my nose Mr. Howard leaned to whisper, "Garlic, white vinegar, and blood from three fat rats. There was a sword storm last night that passed directly over this building." He pointed to the storage loft where a blue glow pulsed.

Again, I heard the two girls giggling.

A drop of red—rat's blood?—dripped from under the crone's witchy black dress onto Mr. Howard's forehead. He reached and smeared it, then made a tiny sign of the cross with his thumb. "Praise Him," he called up to the crone's robe. I looked and saw that she was wearing a garland of green with white bulbs mixed in. My mother planted flowers this way, but these bulbs were way too big.

"Garlic and poison ivy," Mr. Howard leaned across the counter to tell me. "You might want to at least sleep with this garlic tonight." He pushed a large bulb toward me, so I obediently dropped it in my pocket. "And don't come in tomorrow, whatever you do."

The mother, a black-haired woman with a pale, stunning, movie-star face, peeped around the corner and held up a doll in a glowing white silk dress. "Are there two of these by any chance?"

Mr. Howard tried to answer, but only crackling and choking came from his mouth. He glanced at the storage loft.

"Max? Max, are you okay?" The woman evidently knew Mr. Howard. He grabbed under his chin and pulled his head down in a nod, expelling a final cough before he was able to answer:

"Another. There is. I sewed it a bright red dress, though. It's . . ." he faltered again, then looked at me. "It's up in the loft.

Maybe my assistant . . . here . . . would be willing to climb and retrieve it for your daughters."

The two girls were about my age, and they were likely just saying *adieu* to their I Hate Boys stage to match my *adieu* to my I Hate Girls stage. They both crinkled their noses unsurely. *I'll show them*, I thought. Irrational, illogical, of course, but what else is new?

After brief directions from Mr. Howard as to where the doll was stored, I climbed a wood ladder whose rungs were smoothed from his many trips. I heard a low buzz overhead in the loft, like something electrical. From below I heard girl giggles and admonishments from the beautiful mother.

Mr. Howard had sent the crone clanking back toward the loft before I started climbing. He'd told me he was doing this so she could "cast a shield of protection up there." Her smell now wafted over me, and of course it was even stronger since I was halfway up the ladder. I noticed the girls had stopped giggling. One of them let out a "Pee-you," again to be admonished by her mother.

Nearing the top rung, I heard snaps coming from the loft, like dozens of mousetraps going off. The crone stopped directly over me. Her stench was awful since I was just three or so feet away, on the ladder. "*Benedicite*," she whispered, then continued wobbling to her landing near a back corner of the loft.

Mostly what the loft held was boxes, of course. I could see them as I neared the top.

"That witch spoke," one girl below me said.

"No," her mother answered.

"Yes."

"I heard it too. She's alive and she stinks. I'm scared. Can we go?"

"I'm scared too. Something bad is going to happen."

Both girls began whimpering and the mother let out a sigh.
"Max, I'll just come back tomorrow for the two dolls."
"NO! I mean, don't come tomorrow. Monday, come Monday. I'm going to be closed tomorrow."

I was up in the loft now, squatting and looking down on the conversation. It was like there were four puppets on the floor below. I could see how soiled the place was: paper, torn box tops, candy wrappers, fallen toys that Mr. Howard hadn't re-shelved, and what looked like a crumpled argyle sock. And those four talking puppets down there, moving mechanically.

"Okay, Monday, then," one puppet said.

I raised my right hand and twittered my fingers to make the woman and her daughters leave. They headed for the front door.

"That's right, that's right." I heard this whispered, so I turned. It hadn't come from the crone's corner, but from boxes directly behind me.

The front door's shop bell tinkled, and the woman and her two daughters left. Mr. Howard kept watching them walk away on the sidewalk, even standing on tiptoe to lean and follow them. I raised my right hand again to get him to look at me and he did, seeming surprised to see me staring down.

"What . . . what are you doing?"

I didn't answer, but just stood to find the doll with the red dress, in a bright red gift box, just like Mr. Howard said it would be. When I opened the lid to make sure, the doll's face iced over like a windowpane on a wintry morning.

I raised my hand and it defrosted immediately, expelling minty air from its Parisian-lipped mouth, which turned a terrible whorish red once the ice had gone.

"That's right, that's right." This was whispered again in the dusty dim. I twisted to see a red blur jumping off one of the

larger boxes. The crone no longer rattled and shook, though her face had turned to stare at me in an anxious, pale tilt.

"Did you find her, Billy?" That was Mr. Howard, shouting up to me. Billy wasn't my name.

I raised my right hand and heard him grunt. Something thumped below. I raised my hand higher and a blue shaft spiked down from the ceiling. Mr. Howard gave out a yell.

And when I looked back at the large boxes in the middle of the loft, I spotted a foot-tall red demon, just like the miniature on all the packaged magic tricks: "Throw Your Voice," with its tiny metal cylinder that tasted like rust; "The Disappearing Coin," with its piece of invisible glass sized like a quarter; "The Whoopee Cushion," with its heavy inflatable rubber pouch that simulated farts when "your unsuspecting victim" sat on a pillow or sofa; "The Pocket Funhouse Mirror," which contorted faces when you twisted a knob. The small red imp emblazoned on each trick and prank seemed low-class and not all that inventive. But this foot-high red demon struck me as the real deal.

"*That's right, that's right,*" he whispered. Was he shifting from foot to foot?

I thought of the raven-haired mother and her Hollywood blue eyes, I thought of Mr. Howard's brown mustache and his long, thin, magician's fingers. I thought of the two sisters, who were just developing breasts that I'd seen protruding from above. Did they wear bras yet? One had blonde hair, one dark red, both curly. I'd woken up with several hard-ons in the spring, and they hurt oddly, so I wondered all this.

"Did you find her, Bobby?" Mr. Howard yelled up again. His voice was creaky and wet, as if he'd caught a sudden and nasty summer cold. Bobby's not my damn name, I thought, and I raised my right hand again. Mr. Howard coughed wetly, wheezing and having to catch his breath. The red demon nodded and grinned, thrusting forward and rubbing his crotch with both hands. His teeth were sharp and very white, like a young snarling dog's fangs. A cool blue emitted from the crone in the corner. She was still staring at me, though her brows were crinkling now. In disapproval? In wonderment?

I looked to the doll and realized it had tiny pointy breasts. I touched one and thought of the sister who was blonde. I was getting a hard-on.

Mr. Howard coughed and I again raised my right hand. This made him start gagging. I carried the doll in its red box to peek over the edge of the loft to see that he was on his knees, holding his back and his chin. "Tommy," he called out. But that's not my name, either. "Tommy, did you find her?"

"That's not my name," I hissed.

The back corner where the crone perched began to flash a low blue. Her tatty black dress was crackling like it was electrified and she was rattling under her ceiling track, staring at me. Another woman—staring—like my teachers, my mother.

"That's right, that's right," the red demon seemed to coax, his hands still rubbing his crotch.

I raised my own hand—

"Timmy," Mr. Howard called. "Mike," he added weakly, phlegm extending the K in that name into several rasping syllables.

"Paul . . ."

I twirled my fingers and a glittery blue sword crashed down from the ceiling to jam into Mr. Howard's right leg. He screamed, pinned to the floor. The crone rattled and shook her track, pulsing blue. "Mr. Howard," I yelled. "Are you all right?"

At the same time, my right hand lifted and my fingers twirled.

"That's right, that's right."

"*Quid est bonum?*" It was the crone, who had scuttled forward to the edge of the loft to gaze down on Mr. Howard. She was bouncing under the track that held her, as if trying to break loose. "*Puer!*" she yelled. "*Desiste!*"

Her yell shocked me. I dropped the doll and its box. I had enough altar boy Latin to know the word for *boy*. And, *What is good?* I lowered my hand and Mr. Howard let out a groan. I could see him crumpled on the floor. He was near the HO scale train engines, fancy locomotives with tall smokestacks. But wait . . . *Desiste?* Who was she to tell me to stop? But then, if I should raise my *left* hand, would it help Mr. Howard? I looked to the crone, who just stared down, ignoring me. And the red demon behind me had shape-shifted more into an imp, flaccidly dancing on a box's top to his own silly rhythm.

Tentative, I raised my left hand. Mr. Howard groaned. The blue sword that had pinned his leg stopped glowing and crumbled into blue diamonds that clattered onto the floor, then turned to steam to vanish. He moved his leg and reached upward toward me.

"Johnny," he pleaded.

"That's not my name!" I shouted and raised my right hand. This time two swords slashed down in a single blue blaze. Mr. Howard was knocked on his back. One sword hit his left shoulder, the other pierced his groin.

"*That's right, that's right,*" the demon called out, now dancing a happy jig.

The crone let out a scream that didn't need to be translated. She shook and came free of her track, clattering onto her side. She righted herself and started for me, but changed her mind and swooped down for Mr. Howard, spreading her black cloak over him for protection. Protection? From me?

Up in that all-seeing loft, I was even angrier than when he'd misnamed me so many times. Who were these people to tell me what to do? But then, just what was it that I wanted to do? A panorama of images sped through my head. Raven-haired women in violet silk bras, a pale man holding a long black and white wand, one sister with her curly blonde hair and blue eyes, Galen giving me his angry Cherokee look, the other sister with her curly red hair and blue eyes, my black and silver bicycle, my sprawling HO train set racing in circles, my comic books, the red imp humping air with his crotch, the stinking menstrual crone.

Behind me, I heard the red imp's feet tapping on the box. "*That's right, that's right,*" he sang. Below, the crone seemed to be humping Mr. Howard, not protecting him.

I raised my right hand, slashing it down, again and again. Fluorescent blue swords clattered throughout the store, knocking train sets onto the floor, dislodging dolls from their shelves, ripping at the shelves themselves. Five blue swords stuck in the crone's black dress, but she kept humping. I looked back to the red demon, who was clapping and grinning while all his sharpened white teeth ripped at a red box—the one with the doll I was supposed to fetch for Mr. Howard and the movie-star mother. I lunged and snatched it from him and scuttled down the steps. Something tickled my left leg, causing me to miss a rung and fall the last three feet. Left arm outstretched, the virgin white doll lay turned over on a shelf, where I supposed the Hollywood mother had left its open box. Its eyes stared at me in wonder, and I caught my balance on the shop's floor. Turning, I raised my left hand. Mr. Howard sighed and the crone gazed at me: "*Quid est bonum?*" she asked, with a smoker's rasp. It was the only time I'd ever heard her repeat anything. I ran by her, slipping on blood, Mr. Howard's or the crone's, or both. I could hear the red demon up in the loft, slashing other boxes and cackling. At the front door, I remembered the doll and dropped her shiny red box on the floor. The entrance's bell tinkled when I hurried out. Overhead, heavy thunder rumbled. Hot air blasted down on my head, and then cold, making me inhale sharply. I ran to a bus stop.

I never went back. Galen told me that the entire building, bricks and all, had collapsed, that a tornado had touched down, hitting only the magic shop and the owner within. Local Baptists claimed this was God's right hand of judgment, since Mr. Howard scandalously had sawed a nearly naked woman in half at a Lion's Club function. More grist for Galen's he-hates-women-mill . . .

Mr. Howard's favorite card trick was the force, akin to pushing up the short straw so that the mark has a tendency to pick it. I think about that now and then, whenever I wonder why he called me his assistant and sent me climbing into the loft, neither of which he'd ever done before. And to do so right after the previous night's sword storm—whatever such a thing was, though I guess I have a clue, don't I? But why send me? Fear for his own safety? But to endanger a child? Hatred for that child, all children? Was he a pederast and not gay? A sadist? Was it guilt? General malaise? Was his downtown business failing because of the new shopping mall? Was he trying to commit suicide? Was he having an adulterous affair with the movie-star mother and longing to talk privately with her? Was he avoiding a death even more torturous than what I'd witnessed? But then, *had* I witnessed his death—even any death? Was it some mystical illusion brought on by not so mystical hormones? All these questions have roasted inside me in a tiny hard golden kernel, kept secret almost from myself.

These many years removed from Mr. Howard and his magic shop, I teach at a small college where faculty members from varied departments actually interact. I once made a comment about Jung and Freud to a colleague in Psychology and received her scoff in reply. And I truly do get it: The Id, the Super-ego; the Shadow Aspect, the Other—all those theoretical mentalisms and their worrisome ephemeral apparatus just begging to be sliced away with Occam's Fine Razor. But what gets left? Minute and oft-repeated experiments under strictly controlled situations, blinds, double-blinds, carefully selected (!) random participants informing a statistically significant population, $P<.05$, chi-square significance, and the omnipotent experimenter . . . all these myriad, wondrous, tangible (!) things expanding, even bursting, the nitrogen, oxygen, argon, and carbon dioxide mix we blithely call air.

But that recipe doesn't hold. Egg is missing, so it doesn't hold. The crone, the red demon, the twin dolls, the three rats, the garlic, the poison ivy, the two young sisters, their moviestar mother, Mr. Max Howard and his brown moustache—all thrash disparate and lifeless like silent movie frames, without a binding egg. Was I? . . . Yes. I *was* the egg. I *am* the egg. We are *all* the egg. That is what magical Mr. Howard and his moustache knew. That's the final illusion that wasn't an illusion, which he acted on. *Quid est bonum?* What is good? The egg. The egg is good. And . . . must not the egg be broken to accomplish any good?

KIDS KNOW

THE AMERICAN LEGION's Man o' War baseball stadium ordinarily was conflagration waiting to happen, being surrounded by empty, weed-ridden lots and poverty-level shanties with wood-burning stoves—not to mention its own wooden bleachers and weathered half-roof built after World War II. But this night was rain-filled, the steady type of rain lasting two or three Noah's ark days, this being the third. Speck, the Post's team manager, fit perfectly with the rain: spaghetti-thin hair, snaggled right tooth, milky blue eyes, and an everlasting two-day beard. He smelled of whiskey as he spat a dark wad of tobacco into a puddle growing underneath the bleachers. The wad sank, then floated. Lightning flashed and the rain stopped, which left Speck's voice to echo under the bleachers:

"Ten years ago, a man and woman was murdered here."

There were six of us listening. We were in the Legion's Color Guard, and marched in parades and shot off blank imitation cartridges from real rifles at real funerals. We were all teenagers, and all more or less impressionable, though four would soon be in some branch of the Armed Services. A clap of thunder shook both our soles and the bleachers we stood under. Their wood leeched amorphous dark stains, much like Speck's chewing tobacco. Shuffling three times I bumped into Terry, who if anything was more impressionable than I was. He moved away.

"They was killed by a husband, who found them under here, drinking and doing some heavy stuff." Speck looked knowingly at the four older guys, though I'm not so sure the oldest, Denny, knew much more than I did.

I pictured Terry's mom, who always wore her wool skirts tight enough to scare teenagers, leaning by the ladies' room, smoking a cigarette and letting some tall man rub her butt. This was something I'd seen when Terry's dad was up in D. C.

"When it rains hard enough, their blood pulls up through the packed dirt, right over there, next to that concrete buttress. They say people back in the bar in the bottom of the post heard dogs howling when it happened."

"Dogs?" This came from Roman Budzinski—'Bud' because we all tripped over his last name and because Roman sounded just too formal for everyone but me. Roman was one of the four who would soon be in the Armed Forces.

"Don't make sense, does it?" Speck said. "But dogs is what people over there heard, though a couple of them argued that they heard the goats from the front lawn."

For several years, the five long, sloping acres in front of the post held goats, since some bright Legionnaire claimed they would cut down on mowing and double as barbecue for the Post's July Fourth picnic. Then two got out on the highway and nearly caused a wreck.

"The husband stabbed the guy eighteen times in the stomach and back, and he strangled his wife. He danced around her six times, then bent and cut off the guy's dead dick and stuffed it in her mouth, told her if she liked it so much, she could have it for keeps."

"How'd they know what he said?" Galen asked. Galen would soon join the Navy, so he was expected to be cynical.

A door banged over by the post's bar, which was located, like Speck indicated, in the cellar, and we heard a woman calling a man a son-of-a-bitch. I felt Terry tense—he'd moved back closer to me.

"Eighteen is older than all of you are right now," Speck said. "They knew because two boys were out sneaking smokes in the bleachers up there. Those kids saw it. They saw it all."

"They didn't scream or anything?"

"Kids are too scared to scream or tell. But they know, all the same." Speck spat again. "Didn't matter, because those two kids—they died a year later, drowned face down in a puddle of water not much bigger than some of these around here for the past day. Some folks say they come back haunting too. The two kids. When there's enough rain. Play around in the bleachers up there." Speck jerked his head and we all jumped, maybe hearing running footsteps echoing off the wood.

The cellar and the legion bar were fifty yards away. We heard more arguing, the woman's voice, the man's voice.

"Just like back then," Speck commented. "It don't never stop."

Headlights from two cars swept the bottoms of the bleachers. A ten-foot length of twine hung down from a row of seats, and two drink cups sat up above it. The cups glowed in the headlights like a pair of eyes, and then both cars topped the small rise and pulled into the graveled parking lot and things went darker than before, though we could hear tires crunching gravel. The arguing man and woman moved toward us. Speck tittered, lowering his voice,

"The murderer, the husband, squatted down and talked to his dead wife for a long time after he killed her. He told her he was leaving for Florida, that she'd have to stay, but that he'd send her up a Greyhound Bus ticket when he found a job and got settled."

Car doors shut. The arguing couple walked closer to us, away from the cars. There was a covered woodshed where the post kept firewood for cookouts and for the big fireplace they had on the second floor—the building was three stories if you counted the basement. The woodshed housed a copperhead that ate rats, some greasy fat man told me. I didn't believe it, but I avoided the shed just in case. I looked back up at the twine. It was jiggling from a wood bleacher, like maybe from the wind, but there wasn't much wind right then, just rain starting up again and falling straight down. I thought I saw a pale hand yanking the twine in a spiral.

"Come on," Speck whispered, moving to the other side of the concrete buttress.

"We keep quiet, we get to watch these two fuck," Roman whispered. Roman always had a grin on his face, which was pink and boyish with big lips. He was bony and walked like he was still growing too fast for his legs to coordinate.

"That's the idea, get bit by the snake," Galen said.

"You two keep quiet," Speck told them.

We moved behind the concrete buttress and Speck lit his lighter and bent to study the ground, damp and dusty despite the rain.

"Is this where it happened?" Roman whispered.

"Where what—yeah, this is where it happened. Or maybe by that other one over there." Speck clicked his lighter shut.

The couple had rounded the woodpile now and stood under its jutting roof. The door to the basement bar screeched. The post kept the hinges rusty since they kept a row of illegal one-armed bandits in a back room for gambling and they wanted ample warning if cops showed.

"Come on, Laney. You know I didn't mean what I said," the man whined.

"Sure as hell sounded like you did," the woman replied.

She had a hard, clipped voice like Terry's mom. I only knew his mother as "Mrs. Bryan," so the name *Laney* didn't mean anything to me. Terry had moved into the dark now. The rain started back up crazy.

"He was still yapping to her about Florida when the cops came, squatting right next to her and yapping. Nutty as a loon. The two kids finally sneaked off and ran into the bar to tell people. No one believed them until the woman's husband went out and found the bodies."

"I thought the woman's husband stayed squatting and talking about Florida." Galen of course, snapped this out.

"Yeah he did. It was her brother come out."

"They're gonna do it," Roman said. "Look."

"The kids said that's right where they started, over by that woodshed, and then they came in here, under the bleachers. He backed her up against this concrete and she knelt down and started undoing his belt."

"That's right, that's right," Galen said.

"The ol' cornhole," Denny said.

"Lord, son," Speck commented. "Get in tune."

Terry stood next to me. I could smell him because he always overdid the English Leather cologne. His mom made him do it, said it was her favorite. She also, one time, on learning that he wore pant size 32 x 32, laughed and said her son was "square."

Another car came up the grade and headlights again bounced under the bleachers. The twine had a noose at the end, which I hadn't seen before. The drink cups weren't there now. Had I imagined them? Terry's warm breath was hitting my right ear. The car stopped on the grade, so I tapped Terry and pointed to the noose, which had started to twirl again, though I didn't see any hand above. Terry didn't even look. Rain returned in torrents, and the drainpipe on the buttress gurgled.

"The police said they had to haul the husband off the body because he was kissing his wife and holding her."

"With the guy's dick in her mouth?" I just knew who said that.

Speck spat in response. Water was puddling at our feet.

"Blood's gonna come up soon," Speck said.

Roman did two skips, but instead of getting out of the puddle he splashed himself. The rain now blasted in steady, heavy sheets, and the drainpipe was spilling from rusted seams. Overhead on the roof, sheets of rain were making a racket like someone beating drums. The car on the slope stayed where it was, like in a murder movie.

"Good holy fuck," Galen commented. "She's going down on him right there in the woodshed."

It was so.

"Be weird if it all happened again, wouldn't it? I mean with us watching and a crazy husband running out, maybe from that car stalled on the drive," Speck said. "Anybody smell something odd?"

"He hasn't cum yet, so that's not it," Galen offered.

I tried Roman now, nudging him and pointing at the noose. We both caught our breath, for the twine had grown into a rope. One cup had returned, squatting shiny and mean.

"Laney, you're the best. The best, the best." We heard this even over the rain.

"He's getting a rhythm," Galen noted.

Terry had moved to the other side of the pillar. I edged a bit and could see his dark outline, his hands lifting to his eyes and rubbing them. The drainpipe was going crazy with rattles, and a weird bird called, half between an owl and a . . . I don't know, but it scooped an up-down note. I thought of Indians surrounding settlers and whooping out secret codes before attacking. Now the roof sounded like baseballs were hitting it. Lightning struck beside one of the shacks and thunder blasted immediately, pushing against our ears and faces.

"Oh Laney, oh Jesus," the guy was yelping.

"It's about the right time. I bet their blood's coming up."
Speck lit his lighter and Roman screamed, jumping again. His
tennis shoes were spattered with red. He bent and touched
them and his hands became spattered red too. He and I looked
from them to the rope, which had a naked male body twisting
from it, covered in rivulets of dripping blood. Two pale faces
stared down at us, grins on their bloody teeth. They tugged
the rope, and the body twisted to reveal huge purple lips and
a skinny, high-cheeked face just like Roman's. A large gash
slowly opened, making its way from the forehead, by the right
eye, then along the cheek, and blood gushed out. There was
plenty enough wind now. I grabbed Galen to look, but the car
that had stalled moved off and there was nothing to see in the
remaining dark. Then the rain let up as if swatted away with a
huge palm. I felt Roman shivering violently. He was gagging,
and I was afraid to touch him.

"What the hell's wrong with you kids? It's a ghost story, a
little red clay."

"We better get back on in before your husband misses us."

"He's too busy bragging about ammunition stored at the
depot."

The two walked off. Terry's dad worked at Bluegrass Depot, a storage facility then for the Army. Speck pulled a flashlight from his back pocket. "A ghost story, a little red clay."
He shined the light and sure enough at our feet lay orange-y
clay.

"Shine it up there," Roman said, halting his spasmodic gagging.

"What, you saw the husband sharpening his knife?" Galen
asked.

"Go on, I thought I saw something too." This came from
Richard, who hadn't spoken yet. Soon he was to get some

weird government job carrying a pistol on flights to keep sky-jackers from heading planes to Castro and Cuba.

Speck shined his flashlight under the bleachers. The twine was still there, innocently dangling, but both cups were again gone. The man and the woman lit cigarettes. Terry moved forward, then quickly back when Speck shined his flashlight on his face. Roman was still shaking when Speck's light hit his face. He must have wiped his right hand on his cheek, because it looked to be deeply bleeding. I yelped and skittered, Roman stared at his bloody-looking hand, and Terry sniffled, standing apart. Roman started gagging again.

"Last ghost story I tell this bunch," Speck said.

So what did Roman see, what did Terry hear? Roman joined the Army a year later, and was dead half a year after, mangled in a rainy night wreck on the infamous G. I. Blues highway leading from Fort Knox to Louisville. Terry's mom and dad divorced, but Terry stayed Terry—well not quite—I met him for a beer when he was managing a pizza place, and he tucked a small .32 into his pocket in his tiny back office. "You can't ever tell. Too many stupid kids these days. They don't know a thing."

His office light was dim. He still wore entirely too much English Leather, just as if his mom lurked around the corner, saying her son was a sweet-smelling square. I looked into his eyes, which were so light brown that they were almost green. He looked away.

"No," I said. "You're wrong. They know too much, they know way too much."

ANGEL'S WINGS

I N THE SUMMER BEFORE HIGH SCHOOL I built a crystal radio set. In case you don't know much about radio components, such a set has around five parts, so don't be impressed. Crystal radios, as the name suggests, use a crystal's structure to pick up and resonate AM radio waves, which get magically amplified into a headset. *Boo.* Ghost voices. The result for your ears may as well be ghost voices, for it's mostly scratchy static, except on a very, very clear night.

My older and best friend Galen had shipped off with the Navy, and I wasn't really looking forward to high school, since I too would be shipped off—understandably—to a boarding school. I wrote 'understandably' because my mother was a single parent in a time when being so was neither common, casual, nor cool. I received nasty looks from scout leaders when I mentioned I had no dad, and from department store clerks when I tried to use my mom's credit card in her maiden name, me having retained my father's name. I received these looks enough to remain well aware that my situation clearly was not—common, casual, nor cool.

It was late July and ridiculously hot for nighttime. I was lying in bed, listening for some future message beyond the static, maybe the Nobel announcement of my pioneering work in electronics. A Reds baseball game must have trickled through, or maybe a horse race was being called. The novelty of my crystal radio hadn't tarnished, else I would have fallen asleep at either. Suddenly an explosion burst through the tiny headset (the fifth of the five pieces, remember). I heard what seemed to be Galen's voice screaming, "Fire! Fire! We need help down here!" Then a man calling, "It's a fast, dusty track tonight for this tenth and final race under the lights here at Keeneland."

I popped up in my bed, a maple headboard, single mattress deal that I had nearly outgrown. Outside my screen window the lawn's grass glowed moonlight silvery. I could see our clothesline to my left and the golf course behind our back yard, with the course's four black walnut trees standing as ominous, towering sentries to whatever lay behind or ahead.

"And they're off! Brown Beauty jumps into a lead from the gate!"

Kentucky racetrack radio announcers both then and now adopt a whining, high nasal voice much like Bill Monroe's bluegrass music, *the high, lonesome sound.* This announcer was no exception: "And now it's Step-toe pressing Brown Beau-ty near the first turn, it's Step-toe and Brown Beau-ty neck-and-neck in-to the turn." A feminine sobbing hazed over the announcer's voice. "Why? Why? Why?" she repeated endlessly. My stomach quivered. I knew the voice, I didn't know it. My bed sheets were sticky from the heat.

"We need help down here!" came Galen's voice again. "Why? Why? Why?" the woman's voice continued. A cricket under my screen window chirruped its existence importantly. It was joined by human voices, a veritable chorus, both male and female, child and adult. "Why? Why? Why?" they all were pleading. The cricket paid no mind. My eardrums banged, my stomach quivered.

"And now they're in-to the straight-a-way. It's Brown Beau-ty and Step-toe, neck-and-neck, with An-gel's Wings just half a length be-hind."

"We need help down here fast. This fellow's burned bad." Galen's voice again.

"Why? Why? Why?" Back to the solitary feminine voice, the one I seemed to know and seemed not to know. Pressing the headset to my ears I tossed off the damp sheet and stared out my screen window into the silvery back yard. The chain link fence that the golf course erected two years before wavered, pale in moonlight. I'd received a gash in my arm climbing that fence the year before, hanging by flesh momentarily. The scar is still there, though it needs searching to find in these adult times. The cricket, judging from its diminishing scritches, had shipped off toward the corner of the house. "Why? Why? Why?" Straining to peer into the yard I saw not people marching and shouting an endless chorus of "Why," but a line of black bears lumbering along the golf course, emitting from the third golf green and those walnut trees to my right, dutifully heading for the fourth green's tee-off to my left. As their muscles and bones rippled with every step, moonlight turned their fur silvery blue, to match the yard and the fence. And what? Were babies riding atop those silent bears? I mean human babies—but not crying or wailing, just passively riding. And behind, atop more lumbering bears, were there women? Non-smiling, though they didn't seem angry or even grim, they seemed . . . intent. And then . . . men, atop yet more bears? Then children? An endless parade of silent, silvery blue bears carrying silent, silvery humans, riding in the silent moonlight, their only defined goal to hang onto their bear and maybe follow the bear before them.

"Why? Why? Why?"

"Get help down here now! The damned fire hose has split!"

"Now they're a-pproaching the fi-nal stretch. It's Step-toe and Brown Beau-ty, followed closely by . . ."

And then, static. I pulled the sheet up and threw the headphones on the floor. The four walnut trees stood solitary and alone, the cricket had shipped off.

When Galen came back three years later I told him about this dream, this vision, whichever it was. I mean, I didn't tell him the moment he came back, but after we'd moved in together, him living in the basement that he'd turned into a partial woodshop, me upstairs in a weirdly constructed two-story house that wasted every imaginable space in every imaginable way. When I told him the parts of the dream that I remembered, he gave his high Cherokee brown stare. "That happened. I'd been aboard ship for a week. The guy, Billy Knight, died two hours after. They had to transfer me to bridge from then on. I couldn't take the machinery and the heat down below. I felt trapped." I opened my mouth, but Galen gave a wave of his hand and poured more wine, even though we didn't need more in our glasses. Galen loved to talk about women, and he'd also talk on and on about woodwork. With much else, though, he'd shut down pretty quickly. Still, even in Galen's terms, this presented an unusually abrupt conversation's end.

Ten years after the crystal radio dream—if it was a dream—I finally recognized the woman's voice who was shouting, "Why? Why? Why?" It was my wife, Linda, when she lost our child on the birthing table. We'd hopefully named the unborn "Maxine Ellender" for a girl, "Max Allen" for a boy. That night, sleeping in the hospital room near a deeply sedated Linda, I dreamed that Max Allen was riding a bear under a silvery grove of walnut trees. Max stared ahead, clinging to the bear with his chuffy baby legs, while holding his chuffy baby palms up in a Buddha pose, not glancing toward me, though I waved and jumped in daddy-joy. Of course, I never mentioned this dream, for Linda took matters badly. We divorced not a year later, and she overdosed three years later, following the footsteps of her father, who had killed himself by carbon monoxide when she was six. She remembered his hair color, a wavy black just like hers, that was all, she told me.

"Why? Why? Why?"

So many voices. So many silent trundling bears and people.

About the time I constructed the crystal radio, I read a book investigating soap bubbles. Did you know they cleanse by what's called titration, the lifting of particles with osmosis? Amazing, eh?

I wonder: Is death a soap bubble lifting particles too dirty, too tired, too disillusioned, or simply too untimely, out of life with a cleansing motion, to ship out on its silvery back?

And then this: what if that single crystal I'd bought at Electronics Unlimited had been an anomaly? What if it had been perfectly wrought in some dark prehistory cave, so perfectly compressed that its vibrations attuned to global, timeless grief? But why only grief? Why not resonate joy? For joy's there, isn't it? Well, the crystal wasn't really perfect, after all . . .

If what I'd heard that night—Brown Beauty lost by a nose to the horse that had been running hard third—if what I'd heard was all humanity's flesh, bone, blood, and plasma shouting its grief and bewilderment across time, well then, my voice must have floundered in that mix, too. So at my demise will I emit only grief, will my silvery bear lumber and plod dully, blindly as my spindly legs clutch its rough-haired sides? Is there no chance that a fast-moving angel's wings will lift me from the mire onto a fast, dustless track, just in time to form one brief smile?

"Why? Why? Why?"

HEY-HELLO/HEY-GOODBYE/HEY-WEEP-NO-MORE

"SOMEONE HAS TO BE FIRST," Galen admonished. We were bumping over double railroad tracks with a spur that serviced Lexington's GE Plant. Galen had just informed me that Charles "Lucky" Grayson and Emily Louise Johnson were the first Lafayette High School students to die by drunk driving after a prom, killed upon the very spot we just bumped over. "Lafayette was built only three years before, in 1939," he continued. "The parents had bought Lucky a brand new Ford Fairlane. He likely would have bitten the big one anyway, since he'd signed on as a Marine to fight the Japanese, who as you know from being a smart valedictorian had just bombed Pearl Harbor and sunk the USS Arizona."

Well, Galen had some of his facts straight, so I let the Ford Fairlane go. It wouldn't see a production line for another thirty years. And I'd only popped in second, a salutatorian. Which was fine with me because my speech was expected to be a much shorter hey-hello/hey-goodbye/hey-weep-no-more.

"Thirteen kids since then have been killed at that same spot back there, and there's not even a curve, just that dip. See if you can keep this little Austin-Healey Sprite of yours on the road three weeks from now."

"Yes, Daddy," I replied.

I was going to Lafayette's prom because I was held in thrall by a girl from there who was a senior. I was a senior too, but was graduating from a Catholic boarding school in Bardstown. I held no love for that place, so no prom for me over in western Kentucky. But Paula and I were going to be the hit of central Kentucky, and we would indeed need to cross these treacherous double tracks on Lane Allen Road to get from her house to the prom.

37

"They ought to exorcise those two off this road," Galen commented.

"What do you mean?"

"I mean those two ghosts are jealous of the living kids and try to kill them, ruin their lives, just like theirs were. You'd think the two of them would find something better to do in the spirit world." Galen snapped his fingers. "That's it. Get some fancy priest to go back there with holy water and vestal virgin candles and scoot them along into conducting other business." Galen giggled. I think he'd been smoking marijuana on top of his infamous red wine that he imported from his time in the Navy, which had been cut short only one month earlier because of his views on Vietnam.

I relayed his message to Paula, leaving out the vestal virgin part, since mutual virginity was becoming a sore spot. I, of course, was doing my hormonal male best to cure that problem, to Paula's consternation. And to the consternation of her parents, I'm sure.

"Maybe we could convince the ghosts to commit suicide," she commented.

"Um—"

"Our school counselor has been harping on drinking and driving. She says that getting killed in a drunken car wreck is like throwing your life away in suicide. She also says that sometimes suicide can be a logical choice, though. If there's no good future visible, she means." In Paula's advanced English class they'd been reading Camus and other existentialists, so this all wired together like a fancy seven-transistor radio.

"Do you think that's an appropriate thing for a counselor to tell students?"

My comment received a withering stare from Paula, something my zealous peter and I had become all too familiar with.

One Friday later, I was back from Catholic boarding school and Paula was beside herself in smiles. We were in my low-slung Sprite cruising the local drive-in hamburger joint, looking for our friends Gary and Frances.

"Miss Featherstone loved the idea of an exorcism. She's going to dress up as a nun and her boyfriend is going to dress up as a priest and take a bunch of students to those railroad tracks next Friday." There was no one monitoring matters back then to warn, *Naughty-no-no, you shouldn't mock those poor, misled Roman Catholics like that.* Can't you see? This is exactly what today's political correctness has cost us: a sense of frivolity.

Next Wednesday was my big moment to star as salutatorian, so I could easily appear for this high drama along the tracks on Friday. The GE plant was obligingly going to open its parking lot for the cause, and two city cops were going to direct traffic. So Saturday after a movie, Paula and I held hands, French-kissed, and did everything imaginable except the imaginable. Then, as we pulled into her driveway, her younger brother stood on their back porch staring me down, no doubt readying a pop quiz on the movie. If only I could exorcise him, I thought.

Three of my classmates had been caught drinking after finals, though they weren't even driving, more of a Wobbling While Intoxicated. In consequence, they weren't going to be allowed to graduate. *We let these three get away with this, the kids next year will drink too*, the Xaverian Brothers running the school argued. *You* don't *let these three get away with this, the kids next year will drink* regardless, we all knew. One of our main dormitories, Spalding Hall, had been used as a military hospital during the Civil War. That night, after this grand Brotherly proclamation, we all heard ghosts of dead soldiers cackling, disbelieving that adult men had nothing other to worry about than three drunken high school kids tripping over mossy dormitory steps. The ghosts went at it in full merriment: staid paintings were dislodged, mice were draped across heaters, buttons and Minie balls were left at the top of stairs. The entire building reeked of disinfectant, gangrene, and yes, Ulysses S. Grant's favorite whiskey. My roommate even swore he smelled cigar smoke by the window at the end of the hall. Lo! Next morning, the fathers of the three, who were prominent Lexington physicians, made convincing monetary propitiation. Result? When I climbed four steps to give my dinky salutatorian spiel, I looked down at the trio's sullen but smirking faces. I thought about the cackling ghosts back in Spalding, both Rebel and Union, to hear the dangling historical rumors. It was they who rendered the most resounding judgment in the end.

Months before, in the dead of winter, several of us had approached Brother Romuald about these ghosts. They whisper to each other at night, we told him. They snicker at us and pull off our sheets. They moan like they're dying from gangrene and wounds all over again. Their heavy military boots clomp. They knock things down. They curse Abe Lincoln, they curse Jeb Stuart. They knocked over Bug's guitar case and my science-fiction books. Can't we get the local priest to perform an exorcism on at least our third floor?

Know your audience is the key to life. Brother Romuald was a physics whiz who every summer won fellowships to study at Carnegie Institute of Technology. He had a thin smile and shiny black stubble. Giving us that thin smile and a dismissive twitch of his stubble, all he said was, "Gentlemen."

"I told you we should have asked Zmigrodski along," Bug huffed as we walked back down the hall to our haunted rooms. Zmigrodski was our *valedictorian*. A gibbous moon glowed through oak trees onto our windowsill. That night,

I'd heard the dead soldiers snickering, tossing what sounded suspiciously like dice against the hallowed plaster walls.

Friday came. Paula and I safely bumped over the tracks.

"This car is so low that I can almost reach down and touch the hot metal rails," she said.

"Once, I almost drove this car under a train stalled down on Broadway."

"Why didn't you?" This was asked in a tone I wasn't sure of, even though I'd kept my good friend Peter under control all last night.

"Ghosts," I replied ignoring her existential, suicidal barb. "Our dormitory served as a Civil War hospital. Sometimes we could hear them talking. Sometimes they screamed in pain. I saw one, one night, just staring out a window at the end of our hall. He was watching maybe the moon, maybe the high school basketball game letting out from the public school down the street. He was tall. I thought he was my roommate, so I called his nickname, 'Bug.' But he never turned around, he just stared, maybe wishing he could have been kissed good-bye before he died in battle, I guess, maybe."

"At times I really do love you," Paula replied, looking back from the railroad tracks to me.

Paula showed her Lafayette High School I.D., and the guard at the gate let us into the G. E. plant's parking lot. We parked and walked hand-in-hand like two high school kids—gee, imagine that!—toward Lane Allen Road and back to the tracks. I made a joke. Paula laughed. Paula made a joke. I laughed. It wasn't a bad teenage relationship, as they go.

We spotted Miss Featherstone and her boyfriend standing alongside the road, talking with a handful of students who'd already arrived, though we were early, since Paula adored Miss Featherstone.

"The boyfriend's name is Paul," Paula whispered to me, tugging my shirt with a pinch.

"Just like your brother? Is he going to—" I wisely bit off, *Try to preserve your virginity, too?*

Miss Featherstone was beauteous, even considering my late-teen hormones, even considering the nun's wimple surrounding her face and the cascading black gown hiding her figure. Paula introduced us, and I almost got to touch Miss Featherstone's hand, but her boyfriend intervened, readying to pop me with a pop quiz.

Within half an hour, over two hundred Lafayette High seniors had gathered. Miss Featherstone and her boyfriend organized half of the class on one side of the tracks, half on the other. If the Xavierian Brothers had been doing the organizing, virgin girls would have been facing virgin boys across that hot steel, I was certain. We were handed little filing cards with *"Abscedede, daemonia!"* printed in red ink. The teacher's pet, none other than Paula of course, got to hold a huge brass bell, which surely weighed four pounds. Paul, the interloper boyfriend, held a leather-bound Bible for Miss Featherstone to recite from. All the students were given small votive candles, which they were to light and then blow out at the ritual's end. As an honorary Lafayette student, I held one, too.

Miss Featherstone didn't bow to fashion. Today, she wore white sneakers underneath her nun's black garment. She and a Latin teacher had come up with some mumbo-jumbo that likely would have meant little to the spirit world, but tickled the funny bone of eighteen-year-olds. *"Lafayettus scola alta"* was one of the sillier phrases, standing, I supposed, for *Lafayette High School*. She carried on in this manner for about five minutes. Then she motioned Paula to ring the brass bell. Paula gave it a clang right beside my left ear, rocking me momentarily in the trackside gravel. Then all the students lighted their candles and chanted the bit on the cards, "*Abscedede, dae-monia!*," three times, giving the old college matriculation try.

There were no trains; Miss Featherstone had checked the schedule. But as we blew out our candles and as Paula clanged her bell three last times, I heard a locomotive's roaring whistle. One lightning teardrop flashed my right eye, one my left. I wobbled in sudden oppressive and inky darkness, both ears filled with two voices screaming in full-tilt anger. I felt hard nails pinching my right arm, a calloused hand shoving my left. I felt a hot, woolen car seat itching my back as the two yelled and pushed on my either side. Ahead in the windshield shown only darkness. Then a roaring whistle blew; then came screams of terror. I felt myself being spun about as if on a circus ride, I heard metal squealing on metal as the new red Packard was dragged along the tracks, as the engineer frantically applied brakes and reversed his engines, only coming to a stop one hundred yards down the tracks, just beyond the perimeter fencing of the newly constructed wartime effort G. E. Plant. Steam from the locomotive huffed in dismay. I felt warm blood pooling underneath my pants and on my hands, which were grasping the car's front seat. In black and final silence, two torn hearts palpated out one last bloody spurt. Heated, uncertain air couldn't decide which way to flow. Then katydids resumed their nighttime summer calls. A dog barked. Crewmen's boots crunched gravel as they ran back along the tracks, one of them tripping with a grunt. A watchman from the plant shouted and ran from his gatehouse. Steam, oil, gasoline, and blood filled the nighttime air.

With a flash, daylight returned. I stared up at the summer sky where I saw the blue eyes of Charles "Lucky" Grayson and the green eyes of Emily Louise Johnson blink down in wonder at the great crowd of students gathered around their long ago death scene. Heat from the gravel and the steel railroad tracks crept up my pants legs. Above, Emily nudged Lucky to point out a store that hadn't existed when they were kids. They both gave one last earthly blink.

Paula grabbed my arm as Miss Featherstone intoned, *"Requiescat in pacem."*

Who would ever think that a ghost—two ghosts—would or even could commit suicide? I suppose that is what happened that day, for after those singular blue- and green-eyed blinks, I gazed into a clear, beneficent, early June sky. No train in sight. The pin oaks along the tracks swayed: dry, hot, and somber.

Behold. It wasn't the bump that killed the two and totaled the new red Packard—not a Fairlane, Galen. No, they were drunkenly sitting one unlucky late prom night on these double-tracks in that fancy Packard, blithely screaming and shoving at one another. Had Lucky's hands or other bodily item roamed too far before he started up the Packard, or even as he drove it down Lane Allen Road away from the prom? Was Emily Louise panicking at the thought of an infant left fatherless, its teenaged Marine dad lying dead on some tiny Pacific island, with warm waves splashing his rotting flesh and bones? And just how could the two not have heard the monstrous huffing of an antiquated steam locomotive?

The pin oaks lining the searing tracks swayed. The sun hovering in that blue June sky tracked.

Paula and I broke up come fall, in late September, courtesy the postal service. Her parents had sent her away to a Midwest college before we had a chance to do the wrong thing and murk it further by doing the right thing. Galen once commented that not all good-byes are sad; in fact, he insisted, most are golden opportunities. He wasn't even drinking wine at this momentous declaration, but Turkish coffee, another Mediterranean import of his. What he said is true enough, I suppose. After all, my vision of Lucky and Emily's ghostly good-bye had conveyed seeming happiness, considering the preceding grinding steel and the frantic nighttime sparks that had just spun out, prohibitive of any romantic metaphor. I presume those two will never again witness other prom deaths to remind them of their own, I presume they now freely roam constellations in constant wonder. And steam locomotives have been replaced with more efficient diesel; that good-bye presented an economic opportunity, didn't it?

Though no seniors died drunkenly from Paula's hey-hello/hey-goodbye/hey-weep-no-more class graduation, four went down the next year in a single car crash on Lane Allen Road, right beside the G.E. plant, so maybe Galen was wrong about the ghosts of Lucky and Emily causing the wrecks. Maybe it was simple over-celebration and that prosaic dip in the road, which Lexington finally deigned to mend, spending with its local propitiation about what its three physicians had spent in Bardstown. Speaking of which, my own goodbye to that Catholic boarding school gratified me no end: books, brains, booze, beauty beckoned.

But what about the forlorn Civil War soldier, his forehead pressed to that high window in Spalding Hall, spying down on frolicking post-ballgame merrymakers? His eternal goodbye seemed not just sad, but tragic. Didn't he give the lie to Galen's comment? Don't we all eventually give it the lie? Don't we all eventually need some expunging rite of exorcism, even if mumbled in cheap Latin and uttered by glowing, ingénue poseurs?

Hey-hello/hey-goodbye/hey-weep-no-more.

MADONNA ON A COUNTRY ROAD

JUST OUT OF HIGH SCHOOL, just in college, seven of us packed into a Ford Galaxie for a nighttime country romp. Well, I'm lying on one point: Galen was recently out of the Navy, had never been to college. There were three girls and four boys salt-and-peppered throughout the huge car, though again, Galen surely counted as a man, having served nearly four years. He'd been released early because of his political views on Vietnam. He sailed on the sister ship of the USS Maddox, which wound up in some troubles in those Vietnamese waters, while his own ship cruised the bars and brothels of the Mediterranean to hear him tell it.

It was fairly on into this night, pulling close to eleven. No property lines as yet had been drawn between the sexes. You might say the surveyors were still working their transoms and plotting the lay of the land.

We were drinking Pabst Blue Ribbon and Boone's Farm, smoking cigarettes, saying all the silly things youth are up to saying, and driving on a country road that temporarily paralleled Elkhorn Creek on the right. Every road in Fayette and the surrounding counties sooner or later seemed to parallel this creek. It was winter and it was cold, with patches of snow remaining from a storm ten days before.

A house lay ahead on our left, its white outline glaring a death-mound of persistent, smothering snow. As we neared it, Libby and I screamed. The driver, Tim, stopped the car, and we screamed again, joined by Goldie, a tall blonde who fancied himself a poet.

"Go! Go!" Libby yelled.

She yelled because on the front porch of the Kentucky shack sat a figure this side of pale, emitting an actual yellow glow. Neither the bitter cold nor our presence on the road made the least impression on the figure. It sat rocking, rocking, rocking, staring somewhere that wasn't our where.

Tim sped off, spinning the Galaxie's rear wheels on black ice.

"I think he was nude," I said.

"In this cold?" Galen asserted.

"He had a rifle across his lap," Goldie said when we stopped a hundred yards away, where the road veered from Elkhorn.

"She was a woman," Libby said, "with yellow hair and a baby."

"In this cold!?"

"I'm saying what I saw."

A beer tab popped, two cigarettes got lit. Libby rolled down her window and looked back. *God, don't get out*, I thought, almost touching her tan woolen coat that smelled of kittens.

"I hear something."

We all listened. There was a high drone, like wind in trees, or tires on a long silvery road leading straight to the moon. But the sound didn't increase or decrease in pitch. A dark movement slipped through the winter-straw underbrush to our left.

"I once had a calico kitten," Libby said. I felt her breath on my cheek.

"Me, too," I said.

"I think it was a weasel," someone in the front seat said.

"Out of the water?" Galen commented. "The creek's on the other side."

The droning wind rendered all our statements true, as surely as it rendered all of them false.

"It's going to snow," Libby stated.

"It's been clear for three days," Galen countered.

"What's that have to do with anything?" This from Libby, who shifted, her right knee bumping mine. While Goldie pretended to be a poet, Libby led her life as one, for the motions of this earth never seemed to tabulate much with her: rather, her ears were always listening for some ethereal sound, her blue eyes always chasing some slanting light, her thin hands always twitching at some promised caress or threatened nip. It turned out that two years later she would declare herself lesbian. Of course, this made her all the more attractive to me. I think, though, her real reason for declaring herself so was that this drastically diminished any human contact she would need to make. I know, I know, sexual inclination is not a choice. That's exactly what I'm saying. Libby had no choice.

"A baby," she insisted. "Back there. The woman held one. I think she was nursing."

We just had to drive back on hearing that.

"I could back up," Tim suggested.

"Yes," Libby said, her face once more pushed out the window into the cold, her hair whipped with a sudden gust.

"What if I'm the one who's right, and he does have a rifle?"

The rest of us didn't need any hooting owl, keening wind, or flashing lightning to urge caution. The decision was made to circle around and approach from our original direction. This time Tim turned out the headlights before we neared the house. Except we never neared it. We all leaned forward, searching the ribbon of road, but only darkness reached into the car. Tim braked several times as black creatures scuttled on the road before us. Soon, we were back at the turn that led away from Elkhorn Creek.

We had to have missed it, Tim decided, because the car's lights were out. Libby again rolled her window down.

"There, hear it?"

48

The same drone presented, higher, louder. Tim again suggested that he could just back up, but he was once more voted down, even Libby joining in on the side of prudence, plus she feared we wouldn't see the black kittens going backwards and might run over one.

"They're not kittens."

Not weasels, not kittens, I thought.

So after circling, Tim drove even slower and kept the car's lights on. Maybe a hundred feet away, the house's outline showed through the trees.

"Douse 'em," Galen said. Tim turned off the lights.

We drove ever so slowly—I could have kept up alongside in a stumbling jog—but once more we found ourselves at the turn that led away from Elkhorn Creek, and once more there was no house. Libby fluttered her long-fingered pale hand out her window.

"Snow," she said, pulling her hand in. I couldn't believe that I reached to touch it, but I did. Of course, any snow that may have been there had evaporated. Libby recoiled at my touch.

"That cry, it's not kittens, it's human, it's a baby," she commented. "A tiny baby, a nursing baby."

Three more windows got rolled partway down, and we listened. The wind, the wind, the wind. Snowflakes as large as my thumb fluttered like Libby's fingers.

A third time we circled, with the same no-result result. Tim thought he saw rubble from a foundation, but it was just clumped weeds.

"Sailors avoid the Bermuda Triangle if they're smart."

But Libby opened her door and bounded from the car. Impossible thumb-thick snow swirled in a mad dance, already accumulating on the road in our headlights. My heart leaped toward Libby's retreating figure, as my surveyor's transom focused boundary lines hard and clear. I too scrambled from the car.

"Libby!"

In my mind now, these years later, she ran like an eight-year-old, her calves and arms flailing at odd angles. But I know that then she ran with intent, not slipping—I was the one who skidded on an ice patch—she ran with hard intent toward the spot where the house should have been.

Behind us, a mix of admonitory shouts and drunken hoots erupted from the Galaxie. My hand stung where I fell, but I righted myself and ran on toward Libby, who had left the road to jump a shallow ditch and enter a line of thin trees. Wet brush and twigs tore at my face as I followed. Snowflakes fell on my forehead and cheeks, melting or glancing off. Something dark flashed to my right.

"Libby, please!"

And then, in front of us sat the house, illuminated in wavering yellow as if rows of Edison's original filament bulbs lighted the wrap-around front porch. We both stopped. I had nearly caught up with her; she was within arm's length. I held back, though, from reaching out, remembering her reaction in the car. Black hunks and patches like repressed memories skittered atop the railing guarding the porch, while snow sifted through the trees, which grew thicker around the house, the opposite of what you'd expect. It was as if the trees were congregating and keeping vigil. A steady creak channeled underneath the moaning wind, coming from either the trees or the house itself. I looked to the porch and once more saw a figure, rocking, rocking, rocking. Libby let out a guttural yelp and stretched her right arm forward. I'll see her that way now sometimes before I go to sleep, all these years later: her long fingers splayed, her tan woolen coat straightened, smelling of kittens. I know that her cherubic cheeks are facing the house and the Madonna. I know that she is the Madonna.

Libby was right: the figure was a woman and the woman was cradling an infant. On hearing Libby's outcry, the woman protectively covered the infant, and, standing to turn from us, entered the house, giving us one last fright-filled glance from the door, which banged.

The snow turned incredibly thick, belying Galen's judgment about clear skies. Wind that had been moaning now howled. A back door to the house slammed. A tree or a heavy tree limb crashed to the earth. Off the house's back porch—I made this out through white railing that hung at my eye level—a woman leaped and began to run, shuffling side to side the way someone does when she is carrying a weight close to her body.

"No! Wait! Stay for me," Libby pleaded. She began running toward the woman.

I ran after Libby, looking back—that's what we humans always do, isn't it? Look back?—looking back to see if the others were coming to help. I could make out the Galaxie's headlights behind on the road. I twisted about, but there was no house now. I thought, *I must be facing the wrong way.* The car horn blared, pulling my glance again. I heard hooting and music. Then I saw the five of them in the car's headlights. They were dancing with abandoned exaggeration, their knees lifting to their chests, their arms akimbo. One of them pumped a branch like a spear in the air. Their dance circled around a slithering black weasel that writhed up into the freezing blackness and seemed to dance with them.

"Libby!" I turned and ran toward her. A vine snagged my right foot and I nearly fell.

The woman with the infant had advanced so far that she was hidden by the thickly falling snow, the trees, and the underbrush. Now only one figure ran ahead of me, Libby. I closed in, making out her tan coat and her bouncing yellow hair she had gotten up into a ponytail.

"Libby!" This time a vine did trip me and I fell hard enough that my breath left. From overhead came a vast inhalation, which turned into mortal gasps. The black branches, wintry and deprived of leaves as they were, bent inward, downward, and outward with each gasp. "Libby." This time my call seeped out weak and factual, as if I'd spotted the distant exhaust of a bus that was to carry me to midnight Christmas Mass, where I was to meet my true mother. The branches overhead were still swaying inward, outward, downward with their hugely gasping breath, except now the branches were clacking with ice and fright as they swayed. They sounded like the telling of rosary beads, the tabulating of an abacus, the last clatter of a baby's rattle as it rolls under a dresser to be forever lost. The wind whistled, the snow swirled.

I lay on the cold ground in that country of no-consciousness that a yoga practitioner would label no-mind meditation. Except that my mind struggled mightily to find its grip. The wind whistled, the snow swirled. *Two figures running, waddling heavily under their loads. Two figures becoming one, running under its load. Running under her load. A moaning that became gasping, that became howling, that became keening. The wind whistled, the snow swirled. A thud that became a falling limb. A thud caused by a vine or root. A beating that became so regular that I went to sleep. A beating that quickened, so that I awoke. Liquid—warm, life-giving liquid— filling and pumping through my lungs. Air—rushing icy air—filling and pumping through my nostrils. My nostrils that burned from cold, from heat.*

I gagged and startled, coughing, my head in Libby's lap. Her fingers skittered through my hair, which was sticky and wet. She peeled something from around my head. It was thick and moist, and it quickly transferred all its warmth to the open air. She tossed it on the ground, where it made a heavy, sloppy plop. My eyes felt glued, as if some kid had grabbed flour paste and smeared them. Still, I fought to open them and search.

"Where is she? Where's the baby?"

"My baby," Libby cooed, peeling another damp, iron-smelling skein of flesh from behind my right ear. This she also tossed aside. It made a wet plop and my eyes opened. I saw a black creature dart and gather the skin or whatever it was in its teeth, shake it viciously, and turn away.

I realized that I was shivering, that the only warmth was coming from Libby's lap. "How'd I get so wet?"

"My baby," Libby cooed again, giving a jerk of her fingers to pinch and pull mucus from my right nostril. I breathed much easier and realized that my lips had been puckering in a sucking motion. Libby touched a finger to them. I heard a button pop, and Libby placed it in my shirt pocket with a smile, her fingernail scratching my chest enough that I inhaled. Then she bared her breast in the cold and bent down. I sucked in thin liquid warmth. I felt Libby's heart and timed my suckling to its beating, beating, beating . . .

"How'd I get so wet?"

"You fell out . . . you fell into Elkhorn Creek."

"We need to turn up the heat," a voice interrupted.

"It's as high as it'll go," a second voice replied.

"The creek's on the other side of the road," I said.

"It's everywhere," Libby replied. "Everywhere."

Years later, at Libby's funeral—she had overdosed—when I was looking down at her pale face, her yellow hair, pristine in her blue-bronzed casket, I keened like the winter wind had that night, though it was mid-summer. I keened and I sucked in air, bending over. A friend of hers grabbed my elbow and put her hand behind my neck, pulling me outside the funeral home, into the summer sun.

There, after I was able to breathe and stand on my own, she told me that Libby had lost an early third trimester child when she was sixteen and had never . . . Some asshole punched her stomach. / Her boyfriend? / I don't know, probably, if you want to call him that.

This friend had been with us on that wintry drive. I asked her why they were dancing in the road. What do you mean, she replied. / Dancing. In the road. I saw you all in the head-lights. There must have been some dead animal you all were kicking as you danced around it in the snow. / Animal? Danc-ing? We waited in the warm car until Libby yelled. / You mean when she yelled at the woman carrying the baby? / What woman, what baby? There wasn't even a house, just a lean-ing shed. You were drunk and fell into the creek. That's why she yelled. When she got you into the car and the dome light came on, you were covered head to toe in blood and black crap that looked like afterbirth I've seen mares slough off, about five pounds' worth of the horrible, slick stuff. The friend then reached, just as Libby had that night, to pinch my nose.

I'd kept, through four wallets, the as-good-as-virgin white button that had popped from Libby's blouse. I pulled it out now and showed it to our mutual friend, who shrugged in con-fusion. There was no sense trying to explain. Behind her, I saw pallbearers carrying Libby in her casket, at rest at last, alone at last. "Libby," I called weakly. *Momma*, I thought. The world clogged about me and I once more swayed, then coughed and opened my mouth to breathe.

Faithful Companion

O N THE PARTY TRAIN and all but dropping out of college, popping a beer and tooling my restored Austin-Healey Sprite down Lexington's Main Street, I was driving toward a blind date, a promised beauty. Galen, who'd fixed me up with the date, was sitting at my side. Ha! Let UK's atomic clock click its loudest: what care I, with such a faithful companion close by?

Then a traffic light turned red and a scowling cop eased alongside. Galen lit what he swore was a Cuban cigar and I cradled my unsipped American beer. While we three obeyed the red light, I managed to open my door and ease that virgin beer onto the road's dividing stripe—antique Sprites being unbelievably low to the ground. Sans incriminating beer, I pursued my civic duty and nodded at the cop, the cop pursued his civic duty and frowned at a soon-to-be-ex-college punk—Galen, who'd evidently completed his civic duties with his stint of naval service, puffed and polluted.

Then we all pulled away. In my side mirror was reflected the can—blameless, full of itself, and alone. Galen gave a puff and said, "Slick move with the beer." He paused, studying maybe a bat skittering through the dusk. "She's hot, bud. I've met this woman, and She-Is-Hot. What else can I say?"

You could say, 'Even a once and future dropout like you can sweet-talk her.' You could say, 'Let me handle anything involving social graces, you just guzzle beer until she's lathered like a racehorse.' But I kept quiet, not from political correctness, but because I was the only one lathering, too young and too stupid to know what I was lathering about.

As we drove on, Galen wouldn't let up: "Are you going to try this time? I mean, I've set you up with three women. No excuses this time. If you can't make it with this one, even clam juice won't help." True to his nearly four years in the Navy, Galen's favorite aphrodisiac was clam juice, though hardly his only. I, on the other hand, spent nearly four years cooking pizzas and restoring this car, weaseling into college to major in physics or something stellar and smart. So far, women resided in another star system.

"Well?" Galen insisted.

"No excuses," I replied, imagining colliding nebulas glowing pink and purple, like silky undergarments.

"You promise?"

Hadn't my physics professor recently solicited just such a promise about my studies? The guy had adopted me for some reason. Did I resemble his lost son? He sure didn't resemble my father. He'd have to be an anti-neutrino to do that. Non-existent, as far as this flowing world was concerned.

"You just come on as slick with her as you did with that beer can . . ."

Galen's girl, Karen, shared her friend's apartment, though there was only one bedroom. Galen confided that when we arrived I should quickly motivate down the hall to the adjoining dentist's office with the roommate since he and Karen were going to motivate to said single bedroom and do what every twenty-two-year-old male and female do immediately upon convening. That was all right for the old folks, but at nineteen I needed prep time. How could a dentist's office help?

"She'll figure something out for you. Maybe laughing gas is an aphrodisiac."

"Maybe that squirting flavored water is."

"That's the spirit."

Galen indicated a driveway. We parked then lugged two fat jugs of wine and two six packs of beer inside the building and up a creaking staircase. As I glanced down I thunked one jug against the wooden railing.

"Careful! That's our key to a good evening."

Galen had pronounced Sneaky Petes an aphrodisiac comparable to clam juice, Sneaky Petes being a mixture of cheap sparkly Rhine wine and even cheaper bubbly beer. His concoction tasted like you'd imagine, horse piss, a taste that working part-time on a horse farm gave me ample opportunity to imagine.

A woman waited ahead on the landing. She was twenty-four or -five, an ageist conspiracy forming against me. Though old, she had the coalest black hair I'd ever seen—better than that, her breasts were slag mountains, her eyes eastern Kentucky blue skies, her lips western Kentucky wet lakes, her voice ("Hello down there.") a cardinal's chirp, her legs a thoroughbred's canter. *My God, my God, why hast thou forsaken me?* I quickened my climb, unsure why that New Testament verse resonated, maybe delusions of Appalachian grandeur.

"Sarah, this is my friend I told you about."

"Hi. Let me help." Taking a jug, Sarah was duly impressed with our drink selection. Some type of moth was also impressed, for it began banging against a bare overhead bulb. Down the hallway, then inside her apartment, Sarah offered containers that resembled spittle cups dentists give patients.

"That's what they are," she said, swaying her hips against her kitchen sink and its maroon countertop. This spurred me, a stud stallion roaming bluegrass, to heave into a sweat. Her sputtering window air unit prompted further sweat.

"Sarah, why don't you two hit Dr. Grey's office? We'll be over in a while. Take a jug and some beer with you."

Good ol' Galen. Certainly not one to wimp around when anything close to shore leave heaved-ho. I hadn't even said hi to his girl, a sultry redhead with the largest Paris lips imaginable outside a *Cosmopolitan* cover, because she was still in the bathroom performing nebula-like chores or swirling galactic spirals. When she did emerge, he shoved Sarah and me into the hall—even before his girlfriend nodded. He closed and locked the door to drive the point home.

Click.

Sarah tossed her black mane: "Kicked out of my own apartment." She took charge to hug a six-pack of beer and tote a wine jug while I carried our drinks, careful not to squeeze the fragile spittle cups too hard. We overlooked the stairwell, which seemed cavernous—all the cracked plaster must have given that illusion. The hall itself smelled of dust, mold, and termite juice. Its floors screaked, and that single bare light bulb dangled from cloth wiring to glare wantonly at the yellow-and-black moth still dancing around it.

"What kind of moth is that?"

"Dead, if it keeps that up." Sarah set down the jug and beer, then gave a life-saving jump and swat, but the moth ignored her warning. I gave her Appalachian hips a glance, planning my seduction.

Seduction? Who was I kidding? It was clear even from the way Sarah heaved the jug over her shoulder who would be this night's seduce-er and who the seduce-ee. *Pop! Pop!* My soulmate the moth was already back at it, drawn to scalding electrical love.

Sarah produced a key to the dentist's office from tight black jeans. Keeping pace with my thoughts, the opening door did a squeak thing. When we entered, an obligatory black dentist's chair dominated pink linoleum, which spun outward from that dental throne like gum disease. The chair's black leather was cracked, revealing yellowing foam rubber. Backed along two walls, chipped white ceramic countertops hung off-angle. Fluoridated water had evidently set this poor dentist back. I imagined his only customers being victims of sugar-laced chewing tobacco, and even they would lower his profits by stuffing stacks of his spittle cups into their pockets when he wasn't watching.

We talked for about an hour, Sarah showing me denture molds, trays of scissors, and enough pries, picks, and knives to resurrect the Inquisition. She kept the office door open, and occasional moans slid across the dank hallway, oozing from under her apartment's locked door. These gave us both a laugh, and in frolic I picked up a set of dentures and inserted my thumb to have them clamp down. Boldly phallic, I realized, amazed at my audacity. Was radiation from the physics lab skewing me?

Sarah giggled and led me into a cramped office with one filing cabinet, one desk, and one bright orange shag rug. Orange shag struck me as emblematic of contemporary love, so I tried my arm about Sarah's waist, pretending to reach for a paperweight. She eased aside, tingling my fingertips and electrically tugging me back into the larger room with the dental chair's cracked leather. Upon hearing the moth pop! pop! against the hallway light, I also observed emerald and yellow love plasma cascading from Sarah to me. Sneaky Petes, working their magic. I reached again, but Sarah deftly shifted to open a closet. My love-reach boomeranged to slosh my drink, for in the closet hung a skeleton, like a winter coat.

"What's he doing with that?"

"Come on, touch it."

"Is it real?"

"Of course it's real. He's a dentist, he can get things like this. He tells me he used to study chiropractic, but I think the skeleton's just his sickhead idea of a joke. Scare some poor kid into flossing. There's a tooth missing. Come on, touch it."

"No thanks." Hanging from its hook, the skeleton was taller than I was.

Sarah shrugged and edged her plenteous hips into the closet. "Excuse me, Francine." She reached for a box, sliding the skeleton aside with a frail rattle.

"It's so tall—are you sure it's a she?"

"A woman can't be tall?" Sarah pulled out a pair of thin, translucent ivory rubber gloves. "Go sit on the chair and I'll show you a glad surprise." She popped a glove by stretching it. The sharp noise reminded me of something, but I couldn't place what.

A button to her blouse had opened itself during her short stay in the closet and revealed to my glaucomic eyes a heavenly arc of the palest, milkiest bosom I could ever hope to see. By midnight would that bosom and I enmesh? I envisioned its relative, Nina Nipple, a raspberry atop a creamy mound, awaiting my anxious lips . . . ahem. You can see that Kentucky pasturage had given way to Vermont dairies, Maine backwoods, and my puerile *Penthouse* imagination.

Sarah closed the closet door. Clack-clack went her steps, even though she was wearing red sneakers. I mean, this was a woman's woman, maybe even a man's man.

"Go on," she said. "Sit. And keep your drink. There's a tray."

I did as I was told and set my drink on the tray, my body on the chair. A crack in the leather pinched my thigh, since I was wearing shorts. Sarah slipped the second rubber glove onto her hand, then bent to kiss me fully. Resting her right leg between my two, she began running a Latex finger along my lips, my teeth, my gums as she kissed—pressing until I could feel two luscious raspberries, firm, ripe and erect, imprinting my chest.

Another moan—from Karen, Galen's girlfriend. Unable to hear the moth's sharp pops, I laughed nervously for fear that the creature had died. Sarah eased aside the tray holding my drink and climbed over the chair's arm. The Latex glove was replaced by her swollen tongue, which had somehow acquired the wildest cinnamon flavoring. What? Was my mouth becoming numb? Panting, I wrapped my arms about her, hearing the rubber gloves snap. She reached for a lever and we were eased back, though the leather cushioning got in one more pinch.

"Get this." She grabbed what looked like a drill and flicked a switch. The drill started rotating, but it wasn't a drill, just one of those tiny rubber cups hygienists use to pick up gritty cleaner and polish grimy teeth. After rotating the cup in some paste and her Sneaky Pete, she told me to turn the thing off. I brushed past her breasts to hit a button—which incited an ominous whirring to my right— "No, the one next to that one," she said. I flicked the first one off then pushed the correct button. She went back to insinuating a deep, thrusting dollop of cinnamon and Sneaky Pete into my mouth. The chair moved us upward as she purred and ground her hips against my pelvis.

"Umm, it's like a dental drill down there," she commented, feeling my erection.

I didn't laugh, so she said, "Oh, this boy needs loosening." She continued grinding, then moved her blouse toward my mouth. One more button undone, and no bra! I searched for that elusive raspberry. Meanwhile, farther south where the banana trees grow, Sarah was unzipping me. Feeling her fingernails nip, I squirmed, but she only laughed. "Maybe not a dental drill but a big, gushy Texas oil derrick."

The chair hit top, shivered, then started down. "Automatic pilot," she giggled, pulling her breast from my mouth to drive her tongue deep, implanting more cinnamon and Sneaky Pete. I felt her wrapping something around my sac and stiffened, but she whispered, "It's only dental floss; that's the surprise; just wait, you'll like it."

She kept pressing her tongue like a probe. As the chair descended, I could hear Karen and Galen let out mutual moans, which Sarah echoed softly, comically. Or was she imitating the chair's electrical surge? She'd wrapped strands and strands of floss around the base of my sac and was now wrapping more around my penis. The chair hit bottom and started up. She squirmed and the lights overhead went out; a dull greenish examination light over the chair came on.

"That better?"

I didn't have time to answer, for she arched until her hair was silhouetted green, like an emerald angel guarding paradise. I began tugging her jeans; she kept wrapping my penis. My hand made a miraculous discovery: no panties! I felt her fur and she obligingly spread her legs.

Then the door downstairs squeaked. "Sarah?" a voice called.

"Shit." Sarah spit this out like a too-hot cinnamon ball, pulled me off the dental chair, and led me to the closet with the skeleton, shushing me with her fingers and giving me a rub where I needed it most.

"Sarah?"

"Up here!" She shouted then turned to me to hiss, "Be quiet. It's Dr. Grey." She ran to the chair and tossed me my clothes. Catching them, I squeezed next to the skeleton. Sarah licked her lips, smiled, and closed the door on me. Before she did, I heard the moth's *Pop! Pop!* in the hall.

Came a last squeaking step. He must be underneath the moth battering itself on that bare bulb. Would he shoo it off and save it? On instinct, I sniffed the skeleton, but all I could smell was the cinnamon dope Sarah'd rubbed on my tongue. I wondered if Francine really was a she skeleton. *Some svelte babe you must have been, Babe.* I swear I heard an answering clack of her mandible—*Listen!*—but the overhead lights went on, and then I heard Sarah toss something into a cabinet with a clunk. My shoes. Damn.

"Sarah?" the dentist called.

I scooted down to the sizeable crack between the door and the floor, from where I could see Sarah's bare feet walk toward the office door. She opened it.

"Sar—"

"Sh!" She giggled, standing there addressing a pair of shiny black shoes. My brow furrowed. Galen's and Karen's moans reached another plateau, near Himalayan.

"What the hell's that?"

"Sh. I loaned a girlfriend my apartment so she and her fiancé could be alone together. That's why I'm in here."

Good. Great lie. Now go home, Doc.

"That explains the lights. That's why I stopped."

A cataclysmic moan from Galen's girlfriend, followed by one from Galen himself.

"Fiancé? The two of them sound like they're on their honeymoon."

There was a pop, pop—oh yeah, the moth! Then a hiss, then a motor whirred. She'd forgotten to turn off the chair! But what was the hiss? Had the moth been fried? Was silent Francine getting sibilantly stirred?

"I was sitting in the chair listening. It's sort of kinky. Want a drink?"

After one galactic spiral came a boorish, slo-mo sip.

"God. What is it?"

"Sneaky Peter."

Sneaky Pete, damn it!

"Goes right along with what's going on over there, doesn't it?"

No answer. What the hell's she mean by offering him our booze? Get him lost.

Quiet.

"You're barefoot. I've never seen you barefoot. You have ballerina feet, strong and defined."

"I should run around barefoot more."

"You should."

Sneaky Peter! Sneaky Peter! Get him moving!

"My divorce is final next week."

"I know it's been hard for you."

Quiet.

I was getting cramped and I was getting tired of watching feet—ballerina or not—so I shifted to peep through an old skeleton key hole. *Sneaky Peter! Sneaky Peter!* Sarah was bent backwards over the counter under Dr. Grey, who wasn't gray but darkly around thirty. The old folks, crucifying me again. Her hand was rubbing his back, her legs were spread at an angle that allowed him to squeeze into her, her mouth was open so wide that her cheeks hollowed. All that cinnamon going to waste. The old fart was probably diabetic. The passengerless chair hit bottom, but they didn't mind in the least.

My nose pressed so hard against the door that I'd forgotten to breathe. Inhaling, I felt something tingle my scalp and thought it was a spider and turned, almost blowing my hidey-hole, for bony fingertips brushed my nose . . . Cinnamon, even Francine the skeleton was using it. I could hear the dentist and Sarah writhing, their mouths emitting sucking pops as vacuums suddenly created were just as suddenly filled. It was the fabled neutrino and anti-neutrino seeking one another for cataclysm. Then Francine's fingertips touched my lips.

"Nice," the dentist outside said. Was he already discovering the same lack of panties I had?

"Nice," I echoed, gritting my teeth enough to give a dentist some work. Not this one, though, damn it, I may have whispered. Francine seemed to appreciate my conversation, for her fingers caressed my cheek. "Nice," I told my sole companion. But my voice squeaked, while the dentist's damned voice floated suave and mature, like maybe he smoked imported cigars. *Nice.* Why hadn't I said that? Or even *ballerina feet?* Something dangled on my thigh, and my eyes widened in fear. But of course it wasn't a rat or even Francine being forward; it was the spool of the dental floss still wrapped around my drooping derrick. I tugged angrily and almost went through the closet door in pain. *You're going to enjoy this!?* Hadn't she said that? As I unwrapped inside, those two wrapped outside. I heard something drop . . . a damned belt buckle. I jammed my eye to the keyhole. Francine leaned with me, her thumb catching my hair. I guess it had been awhile for either one of us. I could see the other two moving into the chair, which was still going. Sarah took bottom this time. "Oh, ohhhhhhhhhh!"—Coming from neither Sarah nor the dentist nor the moth, but Galen. Evidently he'd brought a gallon of clam juice to accompany his Sneaky Pete. Francine kneed me, wanting a peep. Or was she offering companionship? Was it possible? Three lonely couples, passing like ships in the . . . tilting, I rubbed my hair in her fingers—she surely wouldn't mind post-teenage dandruff in all this dark. Oh, Francine . . . could we rent a raft and float the Ohio River to the Gulf of Mexico? Could we pile into an atom smasher and discover Einstein's secret universe?

The overhead lights once more went out, and once more the examination light over the chair went on. The trick had lost its shazzaam, at least from my vantage. The chair's motor hummed. More clothes dropped, and some change, one coin rolling to hit the closet door. All I could see through the keyhole was an ivory rump bumping like an ocean wave. Francine's fingertips nuzzled my cheek.

If you can't make it with this chick, even clam juice won't help. I leaned against Francine's hips to rub a finger over her lowest rib, wondering if she were ticklish. *You certainly are a slender lady. Would it be proper to kiss you here?* Her lowest rib—derived from Adam?—felt cool against my lips. "Ooh" drifted from outside. I turned to stare at the keyhole, its pinpoint shining like some ghostly light-wave experiment. Is it a wave? Is it corpuscular? Screw you, Galen. Screw your nubile Karen with her Paris lips, screw your damned Navy stories about whores in Spain, and screw your sure-fire aphrodisiacs too. Sink on a battleship—or better, a hospital ship, stuck in the dental hold beside an X-ray machine, why don't all three—four—of you? Francine's wrist rested against my left earlobe. My right, she knocked quietly with her wholesome hipbone. *Your origin and your resting place, lover. For eternity and a midnight more.* As she whispered this, dark warmth seared my packed brain meat. Meanwhile, outside my and Francine's noir boudoir, the two in the office began a tropical storm, now that Galen and Karen had finished their gale. Ah! Whir. Click. Oh! Um. Ah! Yes, yes. Whir. No more "ballerina feet"—the vocabulary had dropped to ur-syllables, maybe even pre-Big Bang.

Francine, ever mindful, tapped me again. *Lover,* she whispered, *It's me. I'll always be here for you.* My freshman comp teacher, a blonde whose husband raised thoroughbred mares, had taught me about seizing the day. Inspired, I kissed Francine's fingertips like a true gentleman caller, then dressed as quietly as I could, though I needn't have bothered, what with the Force Four hurricane building outside. I opened the door then lifted Francine off her hook—she was heavier than I expected, a real woman, Rosie Riveter, Carrie Nation. *No, just Frankly Francine*, I heard her whisper as her teeth gave my ear a nibble.

For a moment we danced cheek to cheek, our coming-out party to the world. Feeling her thin, thin breasts, her sturdy clavicle, I led lovely Francine toward the green examination light and the humping ivory that proved to be the dentist's rear end. *Slip-slide, back one, forward two, then spin.* Francine and I coasted the pink linoleum, which looked turd brown in the green light. *Your feet*, I whispered, *so articulated, like a ballerina's; your cranium, so capacious, like Madame Curie's.* She pressed eternally against me in response.

This dentist in the chair, he was some grey grinder. No wonder business was slow. As Francine and I completed a last spin and dip, either the dentist or Sarah accidentally kicked me. Francine and I held our breaths. Needlessly, for we were beyond the pale.

I want, Francine sighed into my ear, her teeth cool and smooth in the heat, *I need* . . .

Looking into her lovely, capacious eye sockets as she glowed mint green in the examination light, I nodded and rubbed my hand down her ribs, to where her belly button would have been. I tickled it through to her spine. She smiled, grateful. Then I hung her by that rude hook drilled into her skull, onto the swivel-arm for the dentist's drill. She tilted her head. The wallowing below must have brought back memories, for she grinned fully, though sexily gat-toothed. I wedged her fingertips into the drill's pulleys and moved the tray so she could comfortably lean. Ignoring the dentist's two huge, flopping anal molars, I used surplus dental floss to tie Francine's willing hand to the drill—not the polishing tool—aimed at his butt. Francine blinked flirtatiously. *Go home and study neutrinos*, she advised. *I'll attend the rest.* She was tired of being kept in a closet, miffed at the intruding hook in her skull. *I want . . . I need . . .* she whispered as her lovely eye sockets absorbed the ongoing scene. Her grin reflected greenish, just as her ballerina toe bones reflected the pink linoleum. I brushed her mouth with cinnamon-Sneaky Pete mix, fitting my little finger into a gap, the missing tooth. *Surely, Francine, no lover hit you there?* / *No, dear heart, it was too many sweets and chocolates, not enough kisses,* she sighed. As the chair hit bottom, I blew her a smooch to let her know her missing tooth offered no impediment to eternal love. *Goodnight Francine, I'll kiss you in my dreams.*

The chair had started its ascent and fetching my shoes would take too long, so I retrieved my beer and wine then hopped into the hall. The moth was still popping the bare bulb; taking pity I flicked out the light. I paused by Sarah's apartment to place my ear against the door and hear revived osculation from within. Behind, in the dentist's office, a hurricane was building: Force Three . . . Force Four . . . Force . . .

"AAAAGHHH!"

Yes! Skittering armloads of metal instruments and a heavy crash! Had the entire chair capsized? A scream, then the unmistakable vengeful clatter of Francine's lovely bones, at last getting what they needed. Out of the closet! Freedom!

Leaving the wine jug where Galen would trip over it in the dark, I hopped the fire escape three steps at a time, raising my beer in a thermonuclear toast, "Farewell, faithful companion, farewell!"

The Mansion, the Chandelier, and the Belle

WHILE WORKING FOR HIS OLDER BROTHER, Butch Collier was staying in a twenty-room brick mansion scheduled to be demolished for a subdivision. Since I also worked for his brother, I met Butch there one afternoon to pick up my paycheck. The mansion's opening foyer was huge and tall—it missed just ten years being antebellum, that was the rumor. Another rumor was that the original owners had made their money during the Civil War in growing hemp for the Union Navy's rope, and also in making charcoal for the Union Army's gunpowder. So the chandelier on the ceiling seemed hung not like a star, but more like a harvest moon, dangling finger bones of Confederate soldiers as glittering champagne pendants. I stepped on something and looked down to see a tooth.

"There's a big yellow dog hangs around here. Leaves that kind of stuff everywhere. They're going to sell that chandelier before they tear this place down. My brother says it'll bring two thousand bucks."

I nodded and glanced around. "My friend Galen used to come here and screw the owner's daughter."

The chandelier gave a tinkle that caught my attention, but which Butch ignored.

"This your friend I met who's screwed every woman in Lexington between the ages of sixteen and twenty-five?"

"Sixteen and forty," I corrected. "He's says the older ones teach him what he doesn't know."

Butch gave a grin. His teeth were small and even, and he was a stocky fellow who'd played football two years in our high school but had to drop out to work for his brother. Butch himself was one of those young people you occasionally meet whose hormones hadn't kicked in, might never kick in. Or maybe he just busied himself with other matters to avoid them.

I was a sophomore at the university, and Butch's brother was saving me economically, getting me out of shoveling pizzas into ovens for four dollars an hour. I even dropped weight from installing insulation, maybe because of all the itching and hot baths, which I learned later were just the opposite of what I should have taken, since heat opened my pores to let in the fibers. Maybe I should have slept with a forty-year-old to improve my knowledge base.

"The daughter you're talking about hung herself," Butch said. "That's why this place went up for sale."

"From that chandelier?"

"You've seen too many movies. How would she get up there?" Butch reappraised the chandelier. "It would have held her, though." He walked to a roll-top desk that was surely going to be sold also, retrieved my check, and handed it to me.

"No insulating tomorrow. Rick wants us to get some things here ready for auction. You want to spend the night?"

I looked up from my weekly check, which was larger than three weeks of pizza work, minus all the cheese calories and draft beer I could sneak, still being underage. Therein sat a second reason that I'd lost weight.

"If you stayed, we could get an early start." Butch's eye twitched. Butch was a pale fellow, from working inside all the time, I supposed. His haircut matched his name. "I'll pick up some pizza," he said. "Or something else, if—"

"Oh no, I still love pizza. I need to go home and get a change of clothes."

"Just be back before dark. There's a security patrol to keep vandalism down in the outlying property. Besides, this place turns creepy at night. That yellow dog's the least of the weirdness."

I nodded and drove home.

Galen was my prime source of beer since I was late nineteen and as yet without a fake i.d. When I asked him to buy some beer and told him where I was going, he looked up from the mask he was carving. "I need to get something from that place," he said.

"They've cleaned a lot of it out—"

"It'll be there."

I called Butch—the developer had left in a land line, which was all there was back then other than short wave or smoke signals—to let him know about the new plan. He chuckled and said that Galen would either need to spend the night too or leave before the security patrol started.

"I'll take my truck," Galen said, his attention back to the mask, which vaguely resembled a woman I'd seen around the campus's hippie bar. Galen had started woodworking just that year, but he was like one of those kids who picks up a guitar and plays like McCartney within a week. He'd already gotten a job in an antique furniture shop repairing or flat out re-creating broken newels, knobs, and spindles.

"What is it you left out there?"

"That woman was as hot as burning charcoal." Galen ignored my question. "Flaming red hair and freckles everywhere. Even on her ass."

It was hard to beat Galen for instant pornography. We drove to the liquor store for beer and a bottle of Medoc wine, which struck me as hardly compatible with pizza.

"I'm not planning on hanging around for pizza. I'm meeting someone."

Of course, I thought.

"That woman, the freckled redhead, she was wound-up crazy." Galen managed to open the wine and pour some in a coffee cup. "She wanted me to marry her and run the plantation. Thought we could raise goats and sell the cheese on those two hundred acres in the middle of Fayette County. Had a dog named 'Louie, Louie.'"

"A big yellow dog?" Galen looked up again and nodded. "He's still there," I told him.

Galen spilled wine and licked his fingers. After driving back to get Galen's pick-up we arrived at the mansion right after Butch, who was carrying in three pizzas. Galen held his bottle of wine in one hand, his cup in the other, and was staring at the house. I followed his gaze and saw it concentrated on a window with one pane missing.

"The crazy bitch threw my boot through that window."

Hearing this, Butch shook his head. A crow hopped on the bottom of the empty pane, from inside the room. It looked at us and then flew away with something shiny dangling from its mouth.

"Hope that's not what you wanted to get," Butch commented.

"It's not."

"That crow comes and goes in that room. What do I care? This place is gone in twenty days. I don't go to the second floor often. It's dusty and it's spooky."

"That was her room, her bedroom."

"Got any hot stories?"

"So how long did you date her?"

Butch and I asked our questions at the same time. I was surprised at Butch's: maybe his hormones were on the rise, or maybe that's how he kept them at bay: vicarious sex.

"Too long, seven months. And yeah, that redhead stayed one long hot story. Let's go in and I'll tell you some."

Outside, Galen had been jaunty and cavalier; inside, his mood changed when he spotted the chandelier, which began to sway when we entered.

"Wind from the door?" I asked.

"That damn things weighs two hundred pounds. No wind—"

Galen stopped Butch. "She hung herself nude from that. The handyman found her. We were friends and he told me. She'd gotten a ladder from the shed, then kicked it away. He took the ladder back out before calling the cops. They fussed at him for interfering with a crime scene. He also cleaned up what was underneath. She'd aborted a fetus. He didn't think it was anyone's business."

I popped a beer, which seemed the only answer to that tidbit. I handed one to Butch. The chandelier was still tinkling and swaying.

"Yeah, I'm here, Regina." Galen half-yelled this. He didn't have much of a yell, maybe his time in the Navy on saltwater took it out of him, or maybe being inside the mansion upset him. He stared at the chandelier. "She knew she'd get me back here," he told us.

"Was it your baby?"

Galen took a sip of wine, still staring at the chandelier. "Let's go up to her room," he said.

"Pizza?" Butch asked.

"You two go ahead. I have somewhere to be."

But we didn't go ahead; we followed Galen up.

"I don't come up here unless I have to," Butch repeated. "It gives me the willies."

"How's that?" I asked, since Galen kept mum.

"Things shift. Something knocks things over, that crow maybe. There are small grunts, like 'Ugh, ugh,' and then a long 'ooooh.'"

Galen stopped on the stairs. "She always made that sound right before she climaxed."

Butch and I looked at one another and rolled our eyes, figuring Galen was having us on. We bumped into him and he started up again. The chandelier below kept up its insistent tinkling. The Confederate finger bones were getting a workout.

"My brother Rick says the house is shifting. He thinks it might be because they've cut down so many trees and messed up the water table. I'm not sure where that big yellow dog manages to hide."

"Louie, Louie," Galen said.

"Huh?"

"That's what she named that yellow dog, like the Kingsmen song. 'Go way down low.' "

"That woman really was kinky, wasn't she?"

"Yep."

We reached the top step and looked across the hallway stretching to our right. Daylight still came in one window at the head of the steps, and from another at the end of the hallway, a good eighty feet off.

"There it is." Galen pointed to a closed door. "Her bedroom."

I grabbed his arm and nodded toward the crack at the bottom of the door, where a shadow moved back and forth. I thought I heard footsteps.

Butch moved forward. "Hey, no one is supposed to be up here!" He opened the door. The crow, its total blackness pervading the room, hopped on the windowsill with the empty pane. Once more, it clutched something in its beak.

"Shoo!" Butch said.

The crow stayed on the sill and just stared at us. Rather, it stared at Galen.

"Let it be. As you said, 'What's it matter?' " Galen tilted his head at the crow, which held a white feather in its beak.

Then he looked over to what I supposed had been her bed. "They left that fancy cherry poster bed?" he asked.

"The first workers freaked out and refused to go back into this room. They swore and told my brother that blood and flesh dripped from the wallpaper, that a baby 'haint' whimpered." Butch shrugged. "Superstitious hillbillies."

Galen walked to the bed and sat on it, putting a hand on the ripped pillow that the crow was evidently pilfering feathers from. "You wanted me to slap you when we made love once, remember? . . . And when I did, you screamed, 'What the hell are you doing?' And I answered, 'That's what you said you wanted me to do.' / 'The fuck I did,' you replied, throwing me off.' " Galen looked from the crow to us. "She was crazy as hell."

The crow perched motionless. Butch made a flapping motion, but Galen once more admonished him to let the bird be.

"Well, you got me back here. I want my ring, I want my necklace."

The bird shifted, hanging onto the feather it had filched from the downy pillow.

"I'm wise to your nuthead tricks," Galen insisted, now speaking to the crow, his voice cracking. He turned to us. "I carved a bone ring and necklace for her. She said it was an engagement set. Who ever heard of an engagement set made of bone?" He looked at the corner baseboard and walked over to it. "I made a hidey-hole for her there." He pointed with his boot. "You two ever seen that Hitchcock movie where the guy opens a safe and sets off a revolver rigged to fire in his face?"

We nodded.

"Wise to your tricks," Galen mumbled, bending toward the corner baseboard. He looked around, then opened the closet and took out a coat hanger, which he used to pry at the baseboard, but it wouldn't budge.

"You have a crowbar, a large screwdriver?"

"Downstairs," Butch answered, already turned and heading down.

The moment we heard Butch's creaking steps on the stairway, the room literally snowed dust. Maybe Butch's brother was right: the house was shifting. But it also turned cold and air exhaled through the broken pane, giving a moan that sounded, yeah, like someone having sex. I caught my breath.

Butch was about halfway down the stairs when Galen flicked at the floorboard again with the coat hanger. This time the board clattered and sprang toward him, slamming out a two-foot long one-by-eight plank, on tiny rollers. A pinecone held a bone ring and a necklace. But what lay in a makeshift cradle was what bent me over.

"Is it real?"

"Goddamn cunt," Galen said.

We were looking at a mummified fetus in the cradle, bedded in a gore-bloodied, white satin pillowcase. The fetus had a sixteen-penny nail driven through its heart. There was scuffling at the window, the crow flew at us, and then dropped the feather on the fetus's head. Galen kicked back from the board, and fetus's tiny arms jerked upward, as if to grab the feather. Mummified skin flaked onto the silk, and the arms fell. The feather was blue. That hadn't been the case, had it? Hadn't it been white?

Galen jerked up the pinecone holding the engagement set and threw them both at the crow, breaking a second windowpane. He leaned out the window and screamed at the crow flapping outside. "It's over, you fucking, bleeding cunt!" I heard a deep bark below. Then I heard Butch running up the stairs. He arrived at the top, carrying a crowbar painted red.

"Over, over, over!" Galen yelled again, running past Butch and down the stairs.

Not a minute later, I heard his truck start. Butch and I went to the window. A yellow lab—Louie, Louie—jumped into the truck's cab, and Galen rode off, the yellow dog sitting tall next to him. Butch turned and noticed the fetus in the tiny doll cradle. I told him what Galen had thrown out the window.

"No wonder the wallpaper runs blood," Butch commented.

We looked again at the fetus with the long sixteen-penny nail through its heart. We looked at the blue feather. Butch thought maybe that meant it was a boy. He said we should bury it, but I said this room was the only home it had ever known.

"He," Butch corrected. "We at least need to—" Butch nodded at the nail, and I nodded back. We both leaned to pull the nail out of the brittle little chest. To me, the nail looked wet, as if dripping fresh blood. I wound up holding it. I looked around, but then Butch said,

"Wait. That nail's the only thing it's ever owned. Just like this room."

I nodded and placed the nail inside the cradle, on the white silk, by the fetus's right arm, something like a sword to help it through the afterlife. To help him through the afterlife. We pushed the wood back in and replaced the floorboard. When we walked down to retrieve the pinecone with the bone ring and necklace Galen had thrown through a windowpane, Butch agreed that they made no kind of engagement set. I put the ring and necklace in my glove compartment, and Butch and I walked in to eat pizza, sitting close to the open door.

Despite what Galen yelled, it wasn't over. Around midnight, the chandelier fell with a huge crash. Butch and I ran from our separate downstairs rooms to find the mess. I thought I heard the crow upstairs, scratching at the window.

"Fuck," Butch said, hefting the red crowbar.

Next morning when we cleaned up the broken chandelier, we found a pool of blood underneath, which took a gallon of bleach to clean. The house remained silent: no crow, no moans, no tinkling Confederate fingers. And the glove compartment in my car, which had been locked at Butch's suggestion, held no bone ring, no bone necklace.

Eleven days from that morning, over a week ahead of schedule, Butch and I watched as the mansion, the belle's bedroom, the fetus, the sixteen-penny nail, and the tiny white satin cradle were all demolished. It was as if nothing had ever happened, none of it had ever been. By noon we headed to install new ductwork, in a new house, on a new street.

TACETE

HEN GALEN WAS TWENTY-FOUR, his older brother disappeared. I had known Wayne some: we'd drunk beer and wine together, he'd offered to manufacture a precise ball-bearing for this beater Austin-Healey I'd bought for $950 more than it was worth. You guessed right: $950 was what I paid. The point is that Wayne had a steady tool and die job in a Winchester manufacturing plant, and he'd held this supervisory job for five years. So why disappear? But disappear he did: the plant hadn't seen him for three weeks. They still held his last paycheck.

Galen said he was afraid to contact Salvation Army Services for information, afraid of what he'd find. One of his sequential girlfriends suggested that we four hold a séance. We four meant her and Galen, and me and her tall roommate, who'd been tolerating my bookish quirks for three full weeks longer than most. Again, you guessed right: three weeks was how long we'd dated. I could tell she was nearing her max, but held hope this séance might spark matters in the love, if not in the spiritual realm with Mel, the tall roommate.

All this happened several years after hippiedom had undergone some nasty turns: Altamont, Charles Manson, street overdoses, the race split after Martin Luther King Junior's assassination—you name it, flower power had taken a knee and broken both ankles doing so. Still, a séance sounded . . . well, groovy.

Friday night, and my cupola room seemed the natural place, since it had been painted a flat black by some misguided idiot, and another misguided idiot—me—thought it would make just the perfect Gothic bedroom and decided not to paint over. Even the floor, I should iterate, groped in flat black. That afternoon when Galen and I got off respective jobs, Galen from refurbishing for an antique shop and me from UK's bookstore, Galen insisted we temporarily move my mattress out into the adjacent storage attic. This was very un-Galenlike, since a four-way sex ride on a lumpy mattress would typically have pleased him down to his toenails. Me too, I must admit.

"No distractions," he insisted. "This séance bit needs to work."

So out the mattress went.

Galen looked about him. "God, this is an ugly room. How do you stand it?"

I shrugged. Galen began placing five red candles in the two windows that overlooked Limestone Street and a funky hotel across the street that was an antiquated mishmash of conjoined maroon-and-purple brick buildings. He lit the candles to check their effect. The one on the far left snuffed. He relit it and I turned out the overhead light. Once more, the candle snuffed.

"Not only a nasty, ugly room, but drafty too," Galen commented, scooting the candle a bit from center of the sill and relighting it. Again I flipped off the overhead light. My right shoulder twitched, for I had this ominous feeling that . . . and it did. The candle went out a third time.

"Hell, I'll let Frances worry about it. It's her idea. Let's open a bottle of wine." Frances was the girlfriend who suggested the séance in the first place. "Why's she want five candles, anyway?" Galen continued, searching for a corkscrew.

I figured that four of the candles represented us, the séance participants, and the fifth represented Wayne, the missing brother. Out of character, I stayed circumspect enough to keep this thought to myself, especially as that one candle had snuffed out three insistent times.

We opened the wine; the two women arrived with a bang at the downstairs door. Mel gave me a brief peck on the cheek at the top of the steps, while Frances hugged Galen and assured him that she had Romany ancestors and knew the ins and outs of conducting a séance. Frances was blonde and as fair-skinned as a bowl of heavy cream awaiting raspberries, though don't get me wrong, she was va-va-voom thin, pretty much *Cosmopolitan* cover material. But then, she did always wear a scarlet fingernail polish that outdid those candles, so that much was Gypsy, right? When she announced her supposed heritage, I rolled my eyes toward a tomcat that had adopted us. It stayed outside our second-story apartment as much as it stayed in, leaving and returning, it seemed, through some secret hole in the unfinished attic side, away from the main rooms. While my misgivings about Frances's genes might have been right, she unfortunately was all too adept at conducting a séance. And the tomcat, whom we named Houdini . . . well, you'll see.

The four of us carried the wine bottle and our fancy wine glasses up to my round, flat-black Gothic room, which, being in a cupola, was situated waist-high above the remainder of the upstairs apartment Galen and I rented.

"You got rid of your ratty bed," Mel commented. Mel, again, was the tall roommate. She had raven black hair and blue eyes—another Romany mismatch, though she at least had the hair-color down.

"We just moved it out for the séance," Galen commented.

"Oh." Mel buried several long sentences behind that disappointed word.

"You want to try lighting the candles?" Galen asked Frances. "One keeps blowing out whenever I do. Three different times, so I gave up."

"Oh."

It was going to be a night for abbreviated communications evidently, for Frances's single word seemed to hold at least as much import as Mel's had. But when Frances lit the red candles they all stayed burning, so I turned off the room's light. Frances moved the candle that had been snuffing out to the center of the floor where we were squatting, placing it on a low butcher's block that Galen had made two months before, a prototype to extend his capitalist wood-carving empire. Galen wasn't happy with her placement of the candle, so he left for the kitchen and came back with aluminum foil to serve as a drip-plate.

"That's good," Frances commented, "it will concentrate the candle's power."

It was dark enough that I felt comfortable rolling my eyes again. Mel caught that reaction and slapped at my forearm. Sort of hard, in fact.

"One last thing," Frances announced. "We must all take off our shoes. This opens our most daily used pores to the spirits. But—" she paused to catch each of our glances— "but we must leave our shoes in this room, for they have gathered the molecules of many dead souls in their travels."

"Barefoot? God, have you taken a bath?" Mel asked me, to Galen's scoffing giggle.

I waved her off and removed my tennis shoes and socks to scrunch my pink, clean toes on the flat black floor, which was warm from the accumulation of summer heat. The others followed suit and we adjusted our rumps. Then Frances recited some Latin—most credibly, at least to my altar boy ears—I mean she didn't even use the Catholic Church's soft Italian pronunciation, but hit those C's with a hard Roman K. As she recited she weaved her torso, and her lank legs slid about on the floor for several minutes, maybe up to five. She turned

high-wattage intense. I hardly expected this and was getting
chills. Then she switched to English:

"We ask the spirits to be kind. We ask the spirits to search
for Wayne Eunice Kingsbury, whom we love and want to contact. We seek information about Wayne Eunice Kingsbury.
We are worried about Wayne Eunice Kingsbury."

Maybe the inhabitants of the spirit world were a bit dense,
I thought, since she had to repeat Wayne's name so many
times. But soon enough the butcher's block quivered and coolness entered the room. The hairs on my neck and forearm did
a tiny dance. It was as if a gentle overhead air-conditioning
had just started up, and believe me, the apartment included
no such amenity. There was a bang on the roof. Galen looked
at Frances, I looked at Frances, and Mel looked at her. Something, somewhere, gave a pop.

"Plasmic transference from the ether world to ours,"
Frances whispered. Then, in a louder voice, "Are you Wayne?"
She gave us a nod and moved a silencing finger toward her
lips.

But no response came. As fast as coolness had entered the
room it left, leaving matters hotter and drier than before. Another bang sounded on the roof. Frances's shoulders rolled,
their non-Romany oil glistening. For this séance, she'd worn a
bare-shouldered gypsy peasant's blouse. My little mid-section
animal pal gave a little mid-section quiver. *One spirit departs,
another arises*, I cynically thought.

"Sometimes this happens. A spirit arrives, then decides it
cannot communicate. Or perhaps it is a messenger spirit and
must return to the ether world to seek a consulting spirit who
can further our requests. The spirits are anxious to communicate, mostly."

"Can we pour the wine?" I asked, mentally noting that
word, *mostly*. Again, a budding night for one-word communi-

cations. What would the *leastly* spirits be anxious to do? Yank human arms from their sockets? Slice living throats? Gash still-seeing eyeballs? Forcibly enter nostrils and explode lungs with atomic, plasmic force?

Mel let out a condemning sigh at my request for alcohol and shook her head. Galen came to his younger, semi-brother's defense by saying he was about to suggest the same thing. I don't think it particularly made Galen happy that Frances had taken the helm, so to speak. But he remained anxious about Wayne, and had turned a bit in awe of this new personality Frances was displaying. As had I. I glanced left to my nearby bedroom entrance and saw the tomcat that had adopted us, sitting on a step. He was almost solid white, and had pink, piglike eyes. I mean small and squinting. Had he made those noises on the roof?

"Yes, you may drink," Frances answered, "but do not contaminate the atmosphere with outward matters. Concentration is important to our success. No bookstore . . . no woodworking . . . no psychology." Frances glanced at each of us in turn, waiting for us to nod agreement, which we did. Then she noticed the cat and inhaled sharply. The cat ran off.

"Houdini's his name," I said, pouring the wine by candlelight. It was dusk outside. Red fluorescent lighting from the hotel created a patina on the windows.

"The real Houdini and his wife were not believers," Frances commented, pushing her palm forward to prevent my pouring her any.

This was certainly a night of surprises, insofar as Frances. I'd pretty much written her off as a sorority idiot, even though she wasn't in a sorority. Then she continued to speak:

"*Non summus divisa. Amor por Wayne est anima solus.*" She glanced at us as if we were the true idiots. "It means, 'We are not divided. Love for Wayne is our sole guiding spirit.' "

She repeated the Latin three times then picked up the candle from the cutting board. Now it seemed that same candle was impervious to drafts and snuffing out since she began swinging it rapidly through the air. I watched its motion then looked at the bedroom's windows. All our lights were out, as per Frances's Romany instructions, but the reflection of something in our apartment—maybe an errant appliance light—stared from both windows, like two eyes. Moments before, the outside had displayed a pleasant early summer's setting sun reflecting off the hotel's red tile roof and its red sign. Now everything was Arctic dark. Those eyes—I was certain they were meting out harsh, unforgiving bare truth—stared unblinking from each window. I looked away to concentrate on my wineglass on the floor before me. Frances's voice broke the spell.

"*Requiremus necessitatem, requiremus necessitatem, requiremus necessitatem.* We have a need, we have a need. I am imploring your guidance, o wise spirits who know this and all worlds. *Dona pro nobis.*"

The last phrase came straight out of a Catholic Mass. Another surprise. Maybe Galen would break up with Frances and take up with Mel. Maybe we could switch soulmates. I looked to the windows. The eyes were gone. I knocked my wineglass over, and of course it broke.

"Klutz," both Galen and Mel announced at nearly the same time.

"I'll go get a towel—"

"No! Stay! It is a sign." Frances huffed this out and began shifting her legs urgently, chanting, "*Dona pro nobis. Dona pro nobis. Dona pro nobis.*" She called this phrase out—I don't know how many times—until, out of self-defense, the three of us took it up. Then—

The same chill as before filled the room. There was rattling on the roof of the cupola, as if summer hail were suddenly on us. From the kitchen, Houdini gave out a yowl.

"*Galen.*" A voice that seemed to emanate from the walls filled the room and boomeranged off the backs of our heads. "*Galen, help.*"

"Billy?" Galen screamed this.

"*Galen . . .*" the voice faded. Another round of what seemed like hail hit the roof and Houdini again yowled.

Galen started to get up, stopped, started again, until Frances petted his forearm to calm him. "I recognized that voice," he said. "It was a guy I tried to save in a boiler room explosion on our destroyer. Billy. I just couldn't get him out. I tried. I tried."

"He knows," Frances said soothingly, still rubbing Galen's arm. And she repeated, "He knows."

Galen stood. "I need to go get my smokes."

The moment he stood, heavy boots began clunking up the stairwell leading to our floor. They climbed with exaggerated and total slowness, as if someone were carrying a bulky weight, or as if they were infirm. *Clunk.* Houdini ran into the room, hissing, and backed into what served as a corner since the room was octagonal, almost round. He stood on his toes, spitting and hissing. The boots kept clunking, ever so slowly, not even like a dying heartbeat, more like a drunken, rusty gong.

Clunk.

"Wayne?" Galen called, leaning toward the opening of my door.

No answer. The boots continued their laborious climb. *Clunk.*

"It is an approaching spirit. It will do no harm. Stay seated."

Who was Frances kidding? There were two bars not fifty yards from this place, one where the owner had shot off a pistol a week back to break up a fight. And that hotel with its red fluorescence across the street: drug overdoses laid up there weekly, hoping and searching for the final blessed break. I pulled out my knife, distracting myself from peeing my pants.

Now Frances grabbed my hand. "No, you mustn't."

Clunk.

I yanked away and grabbed a flashlight I kept by my door, then quickly skipped down my room's four tiny steps, barefooted and quiet. Halfway through the living room, I felt Galen's breath behind me. The heavy footsteps on the entrance stairway stopped.

"Wayne!" Galen's voice ratcheted an octave.

No answer, no noise. We passed the unlit kitchen and stood at the stairwell's head. The overhead light was less than useless, and though there was a small window at our eye level, it still showed the outside to be as inky dark as inky dark could get—that much hadn't changed. I shined my flashlight down the first flight onto a brief landing. Nothing, not even the scurrying of a mouse or rat, which was due more to Houdini's presence than any cleanliness on our bachelor part.

"Wayne?" Galen called again, leaning.

No answer. Or was there a shuffling? A whimper?

"Wayne, are you okay?" Galen pushed ahead of me.

"Here, take the flashlight and use it as a club if you have to," I whispered. Galen ignored me and rushed on down the stairs, so I followed.

Nothing, nothing, nothing. The steps held only nihilism to the tenth power. At the bottom I checked the door: bolted and locked. From the downstairs switch, I turned on the next-to-useless overhead light, a low wattage bare bulb hung from a short wire miles above. As I expected, the light revealed little more than my flashlight had. Except one thing:

"Wayne!" Galen's voice spiraled up the stairwell with echoing anguish, and I picked up a rabbit's foot dyed pink, a good luck charm Wayne always carried, though it earned him more fights than it did women or wealth. But Wayne didn't mind mixing it up, and he mostly won his brawls.

"Give it here," Galen said.

I complied happily, since the foot's metal clasp radiated so cold as to feel hot. Galen jerked in surprise from its temperature when I handed the foot to him.

"He probably dropped it here a month or so ago," I told Galen.

"Wayne!" Galen gathered his brow in angry concentration, not even bothering to acknowledge me. He turned to the entrance door behind us, took a step, and then turned again to run up.

I remained to look for anything else we might have missed. Nothing to the tenth power, so I walked on up, turning off the light when I reached the top.

I stopped in the kitchen for a new wineglass, a new bottle of wine, and a hand towel to clean my spill. I'd briefly flipped on the kitchen light, then flipped it off when I heard Frances yell that I was breaking the "atmosphere."

When I was again in the room, Houdini had calmed and was in Mel's lap, pretty much where I'd liked to have been, Galen was squeezing the pink rabbit's foot, and Frances was glaring at me, moving her hands in circular agitation.

I fumbled and offered everyone more wine. When I tried to clean my spill, Frances grunted out a sharp "No."

"It's a sign, remember," Mel said.

I squatted down, at least pouring myself a glass from the new bottle, a better vintage and origin than the previous. I switched off the flashlight when Mel gave a scratchy cough and hit my elbow.

Frances began her chant again. We all joined in, Galen quickly, Mel and I after a couple of minutes, again out of self-defense as much as anything. The pink rabbit's foot had taken its place on the cutting board beside the solitary red candle, which had remained lit, as had the four in the windows.

Frances kept at it five minutes or so. Houdini got bored and left Mel's lap, giving Galen a nudge and walking down the brief steps from my room.

"An unbeliever is keeping the spirits from returning," Frances announced. All three turned to me.

This didn't make particular sense, I pointed out, since the spirits had swam out of the ether half an hour ago when I was squatting around the campfire—oh yes, I may have even said something directly along those lines. Of course that phrase got me ostracized and booted down into the living room.

Where I sat. Keeping the lights off, under strict séance guidelines.

If I'd been cynical before, well now slouching miffed on an armchair, an outrider with fifteen feet of dark separating me from my three tormentors, my mind twisted their chanting and the flickering candles into low comedy. Still, I jumped when something bumped my leg. Houdini, of course. I leaned to rub his ears and surprisingly, he jumped into my lap. This represented a lot of human contact for him in one night.

Another bang on the roof. Houdini and I twitched, but the other three kept up their chanting.

Outside the building, squealing brakes sounded. Somewhere off, some time later, a siren, followed by a second siren. Then a large clock marking out the hour with bells. But wait, there weren't any public buildings or even churches anywhere nearby, not within a half-mile, I'd bet. The bells blended with the hypnagogic chants emitting from my room, a different Latin now, phrases I couldn't make out. And then quiet for what seemed an intolerable time. Houdini and I sat more than motionless—frozen, though without the accompanying cold. Paralyzed, I guess, but frantically so, like someone accidentally touching an open circuit while standing in dirty water. We stayed this way for what seemed an hour, two hours, four. Were my eyes closed? Open? I got my answer when I heard Houdini's eyelids open, followed by the quiet snip of my own, though this made little difference to my sight in the overwhelming darkness. And our breathing seemed to resume, though surely we'd been breathing all along, hadn't we? But where was the chanting? And this dank, total, cloying, enveloping dark . . . had the five candles in my room all blown out? I felt Houdini's tail twitch, my left shoulder twitch. I couldn't smell Frances's patchouli. The chants were gone, the street sounds were gone.

That clock again, telling a different hour. I counted. One, two, three strokes. Three A. M.? But it was barely past nine, at latest. From the distance came the whine of wheels from semis. Impossible, for this was the middle of Lexington and nowhere near the Interstate or bypass. But semis sounded. Houdini stood in my lap, tense, his nails gripping my thighs. I heard a metal door creak, briefly emitting laughter and shouts. Then it thunked closed. Those noises repeated: a metal door opening, laughter, a closing thunk. Misty rain began to fall. I looked up, as we always joked that the ancient roof would begin leaking any day. There was a moon overhead, glowing hazily through clouds and rain, so it must have been full. I shook my head at this reasoning: I was inside an apartment, so what did it matter whether the moon was full, quarter, new, or in eclipse—it shouldn't be visible at all. As if to underline my thought, soft rain fell on my uplifted face. Then I heard a bottle being kicked over rough pavement, and then someone belching.

"You fucking faggot!" I heard this slurred and I looked to its source. Not ten feet from me, two men were standing under one of the new yellow-glowing sodium lights that were supposed to minimize crime. Rain floated downward, steady and assured, in that same insistent, angry yellow light.

"Crap off, bud. The rabbit foot's a joke, given me by an old girlfriend."

"Faggot and liar!" This drunken speaker tilted a whiskey bottle in the air, finishing it off and then breaking it against a building, holding the broken bottle in his left hand and giving a swipe toward the second man, catching him full in the face. When the second man grabbed his cheek, the first lunged, giving a left hook with the bottle, catching the second in his neck this time. This effectively ended any fight, for blood gushed from the second's carotid. The wounded man staggered backward, his boots striking wet pavement with exaggerated, almost purposeful clunks. One. Two. A step forward. Then another. One. Two. Then he fell on his back. The drunk threw the bottle on top of the thrashing man and ran off in the rain, wobbling, slipping once. The man lying on the ground rolled and gurgled and then lay still. When his hands dropped from his neck, I saw the face I knew I would: Wayne's. The rain increased, cleansing blood from his face, so that the first gash in his cheek became visible, a rough half circle. For a minute or so, rivulets of blood trickled, and then the bleeding stopped. The rain turned torrential. Houdini and I stayed immobile and petrified. A small rat scurried over Wayne's left hand, which held the pink rabbit's foot. The rat, anxious to move out of the downpour, didn't even stop to sniff. Houdini stirred at the sight of the rat, but then the yellow sodium lamp went out with a pop, as if some kid had shot it with a .22 long.

I heard chanting again. Houdini shook off water and jumped from my lap. He was soaked, I was soaked. The armchair, the little table beside it, the stereo system, and the filthy rug were all bone dry. Shaking again like a dog, Houdini ran through the kitchen and into the adjacent attic to find his secret escape.

A trio of gasps came from my bedroom, which I could again see. The central red candle had just gone out. The room grew incrementally darker, to the sound of more small gasps. I presumed the other candles were snuffing out, one-by-one. Despite that we had no air-conditioning and that it was midsummer, I was chilled from being drenched, so I grabbed a throw off our couch and wrapped it about me. Feeling something in my shirt pocket, I pulled it out. In the complete dark, the fluff of Wayne's lucky pink rabbit foot tickled my fingers.

"Hush, be still. *Tacete, tacete.*" That was Frances's gypsy voice, coming from my room. They did *tacete*, for about five minutes. Then, shuffling started. While I was happy to stay *tacete* for the rest of the night until daybreak, shivering under the throw and holding what I knew was Wayne's pink rabbit foot, I could tell that the natives in my room were growing restless.

"Try just once more," Galen pleaded.

No, I thought, *don't.* Please don't. *Tacete, tacete.*

But Frances ceded and went at it once more, relighting the single candle. With my vision still burning from seeing Wayne lying dead, I saw Mel sneak a sip of wine, more of a gulp, so I guessed she was leading the unrest. I shivered, pressing the rabbit's foot and trying to block out the last I'd seen of Wayne, his skin pale, the three-day stubble on his face, and that semicircular gash in his cheek, darkly open in the rain.

"*Dona pro nobis, dona pro nobis . . .*"

"Wait! Where's my brother's rabbit's foot?"

Clunk.

The steps resumed on the stairwell. I was sitting ten feet from it, and I hadn't heard the downstairs door open. The clunks came with the same arrhythmia that had sent Wayne sprawling backward and forward on the rain-slick pavement under the sodium no-mugging light.

Clunk.

"Wayne?" Galen beat me to the head of the steps, though I was much closer. Mel and Frances joined this time, and this time one of us flipped on the overhead light. When it came on, the steps stopped. Galen had my flashlight and shined it down. Atop the lower flight sat a pair of tan lace-up work boots. I bullied past everyone and stood over them, dropping the pink rabbit's foot in one.

"Wayne!"

Galen retrieved the boots and carried them into the kitchen, where in better light it became apparent that both boots were soaked in water, oil, and blood. We stared so long that I became unnerved and grabbed the boots to turn them upside down, sending the pink rabbit's foot into the sink.

"He's dead," Galen said, picking up the rabbit's foot and holding it to his cheek, as if it might catch an oceanic, briny sailor's tear that would never fall.

Frances and Mel hugged him and I lay my palm on his shoulder.

"What did you do, go take a shower with your clothes on?" Mel asked when I brushed against her.

"It was hot," I replied.

"Hot?" they all asked.

"Hot," I affirmed, shaking and remembering Wayne as I last saw him . . . How did I last see him? When did I last see him? A puddle surrounded me on the floor and I spotted Houdini's wet paw prints leading toward the attic space, so I knew exactly when, if not the how.

"Hot?" Galen asked, now inspecting the pink rabbit's foot. "Hot?" He leaned toward me, squeezing water from the rabbit's foot.

Truthfulness. Sometimes it's not all it's fluffed up to be. I touched the scrawny pink foot and bit my lips. *Tacete, tacete.*

A Red Phase

ALEN WAS IN HIS red phase. This little resembled Picasso's blue phase, but meant that Galen had dated three red-headed women in a row, settling on a blindingly crimson one from Georgetown named Tracie. Of the three, I liked her most.

The phase wasn't just the redheaded women, for Galen's woodworking had taken on an odd quirk since he began dating Tracie nine months back: he started carving dolls. Mostly, and this was typical of Galen, he gave these to friends. Half-a-foot to two-feet tall, they would have sold for fifty to a hundred bucks even then, without the aid of today's e-Bay. They weren't happy dolls. Their eyes, which Galen had a miraculous ability to amplify using the wood's grain, bordered from angry gazes to disbelieving, stunned sadness—*weltschmertz* dolls, you might say. Their lips came out constant: thin and determined, almost fatalistic. Like *Grimm's Fairy Tales*, these dolls relayed a convincing message: *Look out, kiddies; things ain't so sugarplum as you've been told.*

Galen was also in an antique bottle-collecting phase. According with that, he, Tracie, Tracie's dad, and I were digging at an abandoned communal dump behind Tracie's dad's house in Georgetown. We'd found three Prussian blue bottles (beware of lead poisoning!), two bottles sealed at their bottoms by the antiquated glass-blowing process, and—best so far!—a Silver Wedding Rye whiskey bottle complete with metal cap. This bottle was intricate beyond baroque with its festive raised curlicues and its letter script proclaiming the whiskey. In addition: two Indian Head pennies, a broken rifle stock, what looked to be a key of some type to unlock a dream of some type, and an iron skillet rusted beyond even decorative use.

Then Galen dug out a doll, passing it back to me with the sardonic comment, "Control yourself." We were taking turns digging, and it was my time out in the fresh summer air, rather than under the moldy cave we'd created.

"It looks like one of yours," Tracie stooped to comment at Galen, leaving her red hair seductively obscuring her left eye. Tracie wasn't fond of Galen's dolls; she thought them too depressing.

I rubbed an index finger over the porcelain forehead to remove the dirt and noticed a ruddy-orange smudge. It looked like old blood and it wouldn't come out. The doll herself looked to be in wincing pain.

"Let me see that," Tracie's dad said, standing above on the bank. I handed it up.

Tracie's dad was a no-nonsense fellow. He'd served in Korea and worked as a diesel mechanic all his life thereafter. He told Galen how he'd first applied for a driver's position, but the supervisor told him that he'd "already seen how the Army drives trucks." Fortunately, a friend of his own father's took him on as an apprentice mechanic. So when this hardened vet recoiled at the touch of a mere doll, I was surprised. He quickly handed it back to me, looking away, his hand betraying a quiver.

"When I was just a boy, kinfolk lived over there." He pointed to three trees. One looked like a horse-apple tree, the other two just looked like squat trees with brown limbs and olive-green leaves—as non-descript as I felt.

Tracie raised her head to say something to her dad, but Galen interrupted.

"Here's another one!"

He passed this one back also. The same look on its doll face. I showed it to Tracie, who turned away, as did her dad, standing above us. I lay the dolls beside one another, near the Indian Head pennies, noticing a ruddy smudge on this doll too, though instead of being on her forehead, it was on her stomach. The dresses for both dolls were tatters, really just clinging pieces of nearly colorless cloth—dirt-gray, if I were pressed to name a color. With such scant protection on the dolls, I could easily assess stomach, buttocks, legs, whatever out-of-the-way parts a doll might care to have. I oddly leered at both and bent, thinking to give the last one a tit-squeeze, but shook that weirdness off. Where had it come from? Galen's silly suggestion? But then, where did *that* come from? I straightened and watched Galen's boots shifting as if to purchase a hold in the earth.

"When I was just a boy," Tracie's father began again.

Tracie bunched her brows but kept quiet, other than expelling air upward at him.

"When I—" He stopped, like a kid taking a run at a half-memorized poem. Then he started again. "When I was just a boy, there was a murder over there, where there used to be a house." He again nodded toward the three trees. "A young girl, woman almost, though younger than my Tracie." His Tracie was twenty-two.

Galen yelped, "Damn, here's another one! It's a regular doll factory!" He passed a third doll back.

"Did you cut yourself?" I asked.

"No. I don't think so. Why?" His voice slipped out as a thin echo under all that dirt. I watched his legs kick as if something had grabbed his neck far under that mini-cave. He was wearing yellow clodhopper boots—I guess to reaffirm he was no longer on saltwater and in the Navy.

This third doll had fresh blood on its right thigh. That was why I asked, but I simply answered him with, "Thought I heard you yelp." Tracie had seen the blood and was scrambling up the bank to stand near her father. I looked to see if somehow

I'd cut myself, but I hadn't. I placed the doll next to its sisters. Did they all turn to one another and squirm? I shook off that image.

"She was beautiful, red hair just like Tracie's. Same blue eyes." Tracie's dad laughed crookedly from above. "I guess I had a crush on her, though I was just twelve. She was my first cousin. That would make her your . . . what?" He looked to Tracie, who shrugged and blinked, as if holding back tears while forcing a grin. This wasn't an uncommon expression for her: she often looked as if the world pressed a bit heavily. Well, which of us doesn't look that way at times? I turned to the dolls: they certainly appeared as if the world had pressed on them. One's hands were covering its face, one's legs were spread as if stretched apart for a rape scene, and the last one with big eyes still appeared to be bleeding.

Galen mumbled something like, "Keep still, I'm coming." His legs spasmed again and his yellow boots kicked the earth.

Tracie was standing above, next to her father, gripping his arm.

"She had an older brother," her dad continued. "An ass-hole. She and I were both afraid of him. Their dad had fought in the Pacific, and when he came back, all he was good for was drink. The brother just got meaner."

Tracie moved her right foot forward, tapping the ground. I blinked. *Had she really worn those red high heels out here?*

"What would that make her, Lambkins? A second cousin? Some type of aunt? You know, you look and act so much like her. I've told you that before."

Galen said something that again was muffled by the dirt. Tracie recoiled and let go her father's arm.

"Murdered. Some things you just don't forget, they just hang around like these old bottles, waiting . . ." Tracie's dad didn't finish his sentence, for Tracie had edged from him, but he leaned toward her, as if appealing for her to stay close. "The brother was the one who murdered her, the police and everyone else figured. Beat her to death on a Saturday, they figured."

"Today," Tracie said.

Yes, today is Saturday, I thought.

Galen didn't even bother to pass the fourth doll back, he just kicked it with his boots. I bent to pick it up. There was fresh blood on this one too, and I again double-checked my hands and arms to see if I'd cut myself.

"Galen, I think you've cut yourself. You need to come on out," I said.

"I'm coming," Galen again mumbled. "Keep quiet, damn it, I'm coming," he repeated with vehemence and ridiculous heavy breathing. *Is he even talking to me?*

There were now four dolls lying together. The last one wound up on its side, observing its sisters. The sun overhead was August hot, the sky blanketing an Ohio Valley smog. All four dolls—even the one with its hands covering a good bit of its face—stared, their porcelain grins as insistent as the thin stoic lips of Galen's *weltschmertz* dolls. I vaguely wondered, *Why value wide-mouthed, toothy grins when they so closely resemble animal snarls and snaps?*

"He ran off and they didn't find her body until the middle of the week. After I noticed a smell around their house. I wanted to go in, but my mom made me stay on the porch until she called the police. A month later, they found his body up in Cincinnati inside some abandoned building. Maybe he'd killed himself, maybe someone had killed him. They did an autopsy on my beautiful redheaded cousin: she was pregnant, was the rumor. I wouldn't put it past the asshole to have raped her."

Tracie had taken a step forward, tapping the ground again with her high red heels, right, then left. Right, then left. Right, then left, faster. Right, left, right, left. Now punching, now digging those sharp red heels into the dirt with anger.

"I'm going inside for some coffee. Anyone want some?" Tracie's father gave the same nervous look at Tracie as he had at the first doll I'd handed him.

As I just noted, it was August hot, it was Saturday, and it was early afternoon. Coffee was the last thing on my or anyone's mind, I would have thought.

"Bring me some, Daddy. Lots of cream and brown sugar. You know how I like it."

Her father jerked at the lilt in her voice, though he just doddered off, seeming older than he'd ever seemed as he tracked toward their house. The moment his back was turned, Tracie began punching at the ground over Galen in earnest, actually grunting.

"Keep quiet, bitch. I'm coming," Galen called, coughing.

Then Picasso's blue phase took over. It must have been the August heat that gave everything a sudden sad sheen just like those famous paintings. Tracie's red high heels turned purple, and the dolls—Galen had kicked out one more to make five—looked blue-gray, corpselike. This last one had a huge splotch centered where a woman's vulva would have been, the splotch extending to the stomach and thighs, but that splotch wasn't red, it was more of a blue-black, even though it was glistening and wet to my accidental touch. As I bent, maybe the thought of hot coffee made me sway and blink my eyes like one of Galen's fabled semaphores. He was fond of telling how ghostly they blinked out over the water and through the sea fog.

Blinking, I watched Tracie punching the barren ground atop the entrance we'd dug. She looked to be dancing some voodoo ritual out of a *National Geographic*. Only half of Galen's calves were sticking out now—we'd dug back that far. And over him perched a full four-foot thick wall of compacted dirt and gravel. What could it weigh? A half-ton? More?

"Bastard! Bastard!" Tracie began shouting, emphasizing each kick into the earth with that word. She started to wheeze; from under the colossal slab of dirt, Galen returned her wheezes. I stood there, bent over the dolls and embarrassed, like when I'd ducked outside the basement door of our rental house as I heard them in the throes of hard sex.

"Tracie!" Her father's scream shrilled from the back porch. He ran toward us.

The blue-gray earth over Galen slowly shifted, like a wind-up mannequin bending from its waist with a large, insane grin, ready to entomb Galen with a bob of its head. Or maybe like reassembled DNA with dinosaur memory, set to avenge itself on the upstart soft-fleshed ones now treading the planet.

Tracie kept shouting and punching with those now purple high heels, sending them deep into the dirt. She was gashing herself, her ankles bleeding. The blue-gray earth shifted more, the blue-gray air wavered. I noticed a row of jagged glass protruding like fangs, directly over Galen's thighs.

"Keep quiet, bitch, I'm coming!"

"Bastard! Bastard! How could you?"

Another shift of earth, as slow as a cosmic yawn upon witnessing some primeval motion repeating, repeating, repeating, ad nauseam.

I lunged to yank Galen's boots, pulling him from under the congealed earth just as it fell. Above, Tracie's father grabbed and yanked her backward to safety, spattering coffee on her dress. Tracie heaved sob after sob in her father's arms. Galen stood and twisted to stare like a madman. The blue Picasso tint shifted, as if flung by a wind gust. Galen and Tracie simultaneously collapsed onto their knees, shaking their heads and looking about the dirt. Galen's face, arms, stomach, and hands were bleeding bright red. Tracie's ankles and calves were doing the same. The dry purplish leaves of the three trees where the long-gone house had stood returned to moist green. The Silver Wedding rye bottle was crushed, the dolls buried as a second hunk of dirt slabbed off to cover them, but not before I noticed that all five had turned their heads to stare at Galen.

"You two need tetanus shots," Tracie's dad volunteered.

Galen's red phase was over. He never again dated a redhead, nor did he carve another weltschmertz doll. Instead, they became big-eyed and happy. Tracie called one week later, wanting me to relay her confused apologies to Galen. They hadn't been in contact since that Saturday at the emergency room, where we'd driven separately. After she and I dragged out many assorted ellipses over the phone, Tracie laughed and asked if I'd watched any good late night horror movies, something she'd formerly teased me about with her beauteous blue eye-rolls. As flamboyant and enticing as her red hair and those blue eyes glowed, as lovely as her voice and laughter sounded, I couldn't rid myself of the image of her punching those red high heels into the widening fissure over Galen, possessed and screaming, "Bastard! Bastard!," and him underneath, possessed and mumbling, "Keep quiet, bitch, I'm coming, I'm coming!" Some memories are like bottles: they take geologic ages to dissipate.

"Uh, no, no I haven't. Sorry," I answered, hanging up. And I was, I truly was.

TIT FOR TAT

O N MEETING THIS ODDBALL COUPLE one late boozy night at the Paddock Club, Galen and I both became mesmerized for several reasons, first and foremost being that the young woman, Ashley, was "beautiful beyond repair" as Galen was fond of saying. And so she was, with the shiniest brown eyes I'd ever seen, complete with a filliping dance to them that normally gets reserved for hazel or blue eyes. And mellow Mediterranean skin, thick auburn hair, topped by a wry and spry smile. Her husband, Ray, though tall, hunched a bit and ratcheted out a chainsaw voice under blinding red hair. Together, they made quite the twosome. One could barely imagine the elf child they'd produce.

There's more. They were caretakers of a defunct Episcopal graveyard, whose last graves were dug directly after World War II. They received free use of a quaint cottage in return for this duty, but no pay. Ray confided in me one night that he and Ashley took turns working menial jobs, each for three months, while the other spent time in the spirit world.

"Just kidding," he said, "about the spirit world part, but the work part keeps true blue."

After I gave him my own true blue Protestant Work Ethic look, he added that they both read a good deal, he philosophy and far eastern texts, she Victorian novels. They both were toying with the idea of returning for a master's or a doctorate, and they'd both had small articles published. Publication was a key word with me at that time. I wanted to be like Herman Hesse, maybe.

"Yeah, far eastern like that," Ray added.

So Galen and I were drawn to that cottage in the middle of a graveyard, for disparate compelling reasons. But there was another, tertiary reason too. Ashley and Ray would tall-tale us about whatever ghosts they'd see in the graveyard. Murdered, murderers, suicides, brain-defective toddlers, shyster lawyers, octo-, nona-, and centenarians—you name it—they'd wisp up from the 300 plus graves surrounding the cottage, expelling yellow-green gasses and ectoplasm, swirling about to wail their pleas or rasp their threats.

"We're sextons, technically, even though we're not very good members of the church and Ray's an atheist." Ashley dug an elbow into Ray and gave a somewhat toothy, somewhat seductive smile.

Galen had never heard the word *sexton* before, so he made a great show of giggling in his Galen way and offering *Playboy Magazine* insinuations. I added my own variation,

"There were two sextons in Lexingtons who lived in a graveyard old . . ." I faltered pretty quickly.

Ashley looked from me to Galen as if we were benighted teenage boys. Not so, since Galen was entering his mid-twenties and I'd legally bought the wine we were drinking. Still, Ashley reached for the open bottle, exacting payment for enduring two post-teenage chumps. We were sitting on their front porch and the summer sky showed an evening blood red.

"Three nights ago, we saw a bobbing light over by those two pin oaks . . ." Ray began.

Oh yes, this is the liquor that brings us here, Galen and I collectively thought, leaning forward as Ray told of walking out that Wednesday night with his shillelagh—another new word!—to find two teenagers holding hands and whispering.

The disappointment in our faces must have shown, for Ashley interrupted,

"Tell them how they were dressed."

"Old timey white grave shrouds and barefoot. They were carrying an antique lantern that must have used whale blubber, for it stunk up the yard around them. We could smell it here on the porch even two hours later."

"Tell them what they said to you when you asked what they were doing.—Galen, did you bring your stash?"

So the tit for tat began early that Saturday, with Ray telling foolish ghost stories at Ashley's prompts, with Galen supplying the marijuana, and me supplying the wine.

Two weeks later, Galen and I were watching the place for the weekend, along with Louie, Louie, Galen's wonder dog. Louie, Louie was an old girlfriend's dog, and that old girlfriend could easily rank as a ghost herself, for she committed suicide by hanging from a chandelier worth two grand. Louie, Louie was a large yellow lab mix, something of a genius dog that knew about fifty words or more. *Publication* may have been one.

Ray and Ashley had travelled back home to Louisville, for a funeral: Ashley's aunt had died unexpectedly. Ashley wanted to support her mom and stay the whole weekend, so Galen and I had the job of keeping out looters and ne'er-do-wells simply by our presence. Ashley found it amusing that we two would have that job and she commented that Louie, Louie was the least reprehensible character of us three.

Not so, I wanted to respond. Galen had ended his bone-carving stage, and wood was becoming more and more his métier. I was reading French, thinking that I might actually get a B.A. on the university's dime, since I labored at its bookstore. And Louie, Louie was the wonder dog who understood at least fifty . . . well, maybe Ashley had a point.

Ray and Ashley kept a small grill on the porch and Galen had decided to slow-cook some ribs. I was busy drinking red wine to tune up my stomach for the same when Louie, Louie barked.

"Damn," I said, looking up, "two kids climbing the fence. I'll go."

They quickly spotted me and Louie, Louie walking toward them and hopped back on the other side of the fence and ran off.

"Maybe you should be a cop," Galen commented when I returned.

An hour and a half later we'd finished eating and were opening a second bottle of red, when Louie, Louie gave a low whimper. Galen figured he wanted more ribs, but that wasn't it: the dog turned hard-haunched, sitting with his ears forward to stare at a far end of the graveyard. The graveyard, I should mention, consumed a bit over three acres of land, with the sexton's cottage in the east corner by the main gate. Interspersed among the tombstones and a sprinkling of monuments were two bountiful apple trees, and two peach trees that rarely produced since we were too far north, plus the normal vines and crap that Ray made half attempts at cutting back now and then.

"There's a light moving out there."

I looked. Galen was right: a light was wobbling along among the tombstones.

"Your turn," I said.

"Shit. Not in this dark, and not in a graveyard. We both need to go."

So we did, taking Louie, Louie. Soon enough we spotted two people, bent as if elderly, walking along the iron fencing. As we approached, the couple sat on a stone bench I hadn't noticed before. The man lowered a lantern onto the ground—not whale blubber, but a reliable, fine Coleman. I could hear its hiss as we neared. The man was smoking a billiard pipe—the straight, no-nonsense kind you see scien-

tists in sci-fi movies pop into their mouths at some thought-
ful moment before the tangle-armed alien monster appears.
The pipe's smoke also smelled straight and no-nonsense: a ripe
Prince Albert tobacco. The woman wore a white hat with a
single lily bouncing on it.

"You're not the regular sextons," the man said.

"Yes, I hope nothing happened to that sweet couple," the
woman added, her lily bobbing.

"They're at a funeral."

"Oh my," the woman said. The man just took a puff of his
pipe and stared off somewhere.

"No one's supposed to be in here after dark," Galen said.

Their lantern hissed as if rebuffing him. An owl hooted.
Ray had told us that one lived near the graveyard, searching
out mice and occasional rats.

"Oh my," the woman repeated. "I hope it was no one dear
to them."

"An aunt," I said. Between their hissing lantern, our electric one, and Galen's flashlight, I could see that the woman and
man were in their 70's. Ashley's aunt had died quite young, not
even 50.

"You're not supposed to be in here after dark," Galen said
again, bulldog fashion as if we were playing good-cop, bad-
cop.

"We're not," the old man said. "We're not in here."

"Yes, we're searching for our son. He's only six."

"Almost seven."

"He was wont to play in here. Among the tombstones,
chasing cats."

Ray had mentioned that feral cats used to roam around
until the owl moved in. Then the cats left. Too many predators
spoil the broth, I supposed.

"Won't you sit down and help us look for him?" The man said this, leaving the pipe in his mouth and speaking through his teeth like Clint Eastwood facing desperadoes. There was a nearby stone bench facing at an angle. I shook my head in puzzlement at this second bench—well, the cemetery was large and I'd only walked it twice with Ray.

"Shouldn't we spread out and search?" I asked.

"You don't know children very well. He'll yelp any second now. That's how we'll find him."

We sat. I'd brought along our jug of chianti, half thinking that I could use it as a club—a mock shillelagh, if you will. I took a sip and offered the woman some, being a gentleman.

"Why thank you," she said. "See Frank, you complain about the younger generation, but they do have manners."

Frank, her husband I presumed, grunted. Louie, Louie whined, sitting ten feet away. Galen put the lantern between us. It was a battery-operated one with unnatural fluorescent lighting, but at least it didn't give off any heat. The owl hooted again.

"Remember what your mother used to say about owls, Frank?"

He nodded.

"Well, tell them, then."

It was as if this couple was an older version—a much older version, for I'd upped their ages to late seventies, even eighties—of Ray and Ashley talking. True to that scenario, Frank began to tell us what his mother said about owls,

"For every three hoots, someone is going to die."

"Well, that's just been two. So no one is going to die yet."

"You didn't listen very well, young man," Frank cum Ray said. "Who-whooo. Who-whooo. Four hoots."

Normally, Galen didn't take very well to correcting, but he surprised me and said, "That's true," not even making a wisecrack about one-and-a-third people dying if that count held. No, that observation was left for me to make, and I was immediately reprimanded by the woman,

"Death's not funny. It's the only thing we have."

I pondered the woman's words while Galen and the old man compared notes about their mothers. Galen had not been happy with his mother ever since she took a second husband and left widowhood. She was the primary reason he'd joined the Navy, I was certain. I looked to the woman, whose eyes had hooded, not in a bedroom or even a judgmental fashion as Ashley's sometimes did, but more in a sleepy, sad, world-weary Buddha fashion. I imagined her sitting cross-legged by the river with Siddhartha, watching it flow, flow, flow. Three times—did that mean death? I leaned toward her, ignoring Galen and Frank,

"We have life, too, don't we?"

"We only think we do," she replied, not even looking at me.

A great rush of feathers and a squeak sent Louie, Louie off on a tear. Mouse patrol on alert. Who'd win the prize of death? Their lantern hissed, ours tossed obnoxious white light. The woman looked up to the sky, where clouds scudded away from the moon, which shone nearly full. I pretended to feel my bones growing, my teeth extending in lycanthropy, like that king in the Old Testament, or like poor Larry Talbot the Wolfman over in Wales, just trying to reconcile with his poppa. That last word brought me back, since I had no poppa to reconcile with.

Now both Frank and the woman—whose name we'd yet to learn—were staring up at the moon. Galen lifted his shoulders in an exaggerated shrug and grabbed the chianti bottle to pour himself another glass. He always insisted on not being a rube, but drinking from a stemmed wine glass was something I rarely managed to do without tipping over the glass and breaking it, so I stuck with either the bottle or Mediterranean style from a jelly jar. The couple stared at the moon until Louie, Louie returned, once more sitting at a respectable distance.

When you're young, five minutes of silence comes unnatural, even ominous, so I broke in around four minutes to ask, "Are you two okay?"

"People say that the man in the moon is smiling. What did your mother say, Frank?"

This time Frank didn't need a second prompt. "He's laughing and he's crying at one and the same time."

"And why did she say that?"

"He's laughing at our dreams, he's crying because our dreams all die."

"Yes, that's all we have. Just as I said."

I grabbed the chianti. "There's life," I insisted.

The owl hooted, twice. *Who-whooo.* Galen held up his fingers toward me, to indicate six hoots. Two people. The woman reached for the bottle, and I tugged it momentarily. But ownership gave way to manners and unease, so I relented and gave it to her. I noticed how Frank never showed interest.

"We had a child," Frank said.

"The one you're searching for?"

"Yes," the woman said. "Tell them, Frank." She nudged him with the wine bottle and he jerked from it.

"We were driving to Cynthiana. To—"

"To see his mother. Tell them about the rain, Frank." She was still looking at the moon, waiting for the man up there to wink, or at least offer an empathetic blink.

"It was raining hard, very hard. I'd just finished my last class at the university. Psychology of Child Development for graduate students."

The woman whimpered but kept her face lifted toward the moon. "Tell them about your colleague. He works at the bookstore, maybe he knows him."

Galen and I glanced at one another. How did she know where I worked?

"My friend, Tom Harding, Professor Harding, stopped by my office and offered me a scotch—"

"Not just one," she said.

"That's right. I had two drinks with Tom, and then I drove home to pick up Sheila and the boy."

Sheila, so she had a name at last.

"Two drinks and hard rain and winding roads and our son. Tell them."

"Yes, two drinks, Sheila, our son, and I. And winding, leafy roads toward Cynthiana. No interstate as yet."

What happened, as the old man told us, was that a red fox ran across the road and he slammed on his brakes. The car spun around in the wet leaves and slammed into an oak tree on the rear passenger side, killing their son instantly, while the two of them were only rattled with a broken arm apiece. They each held up an arm, as if in proof.

"What was your boy's name?" I asked.

The couple remained silent.

"Your son, what was his name?" Galen asked.

"Death is the only thing we have."

"There's life," I insisted. "There's life *and* death. Tit for tat."

Time did a flip as if to prove or disprove or ignore all of us. Clouds scudded, hiding the moon. Clouds scudded, revealing the moon. The chianti bottle was nearly empty. Then another was nearly full. Louie, Louie lay down with a groan, as if his joints had aged from afternoon to evening to night. Clouds scudded. I had an ache in my side, a stitch as if some sorceress were casting spells. Galen popped his neck. The old woman never stopped looking at the moon during all this time—hours? The old man would motion with his left arm as if to reach for her, but would pull back just as quickly. Clouds scudded.

And then the owl hooted, three times, cutting short its last *Who-whooo*, instead leaving a prolonged and wobbly *Whooooooo*. The moon was shining fully. I looked at my hands in my lap, bending my right little finger down to leave nine digits. Three deaths.

"It is consummated," the woman said. "Tell them."

"No!" the old man replied forcefully. "Time unfurls at its own pace."

"Tell them," the woman insisted.

"No, we need to search for our son."

"He's dead. Death is all we have. Death is all anyone has. Tell them about their friends and the female belly-baby."

The old man leapt up and pointed toward the cottage. An ambient gray was running its fingers over it. He motioned for his wife, for Sheila, to stand.

"Tell them," she wailed, her arms stretched down toward the earth in anguish.

"No, darling, no. Time must work its own pace."

"It's not fair."

"No, it's not." With that the old man lifted the lantern and walked away from the coming dawn. Dawn, already? How? His wife stood, gave Galen and me a wide-eyed look of terror and followed her husband. Galen and I leaned as if to bring them back, and then we also stood. Louie, Louie began to howl like a wolf on a dark plain. When I looked from him to where the couple had walked, I saw only murk. A chianti bottle lay overturned at my feet. Both stone benches had evaporated in the dew and mist.

Around eleven o'clock the next morning, a Monday, Louie, Louie barked sharply. It was the Episcopal priest opening and walking through the main gate. I'd seen him playing warm-up folk-blues in local bars, a typical enough Episcopal priest. I waved.

"Bad news, fellas. Ray and Ashley were killed in a car wreck coming back from Louisville, very late last night." He glanced at his watch. "I mean, this morning, around five." He looked from the four wine bottles to Louie, Louie. Galen walked out the cottage's front door, and the priest repeated what he'd told me, adding,

"She was pregnant, you know. They were expecting."

"Three then," Galen said, staring at his hands.

"Yes, I suppose so. Three," the priest rejoined, staring at Galen's hands as if they held some mystery. "The service will be held in Louisville at Saint Andrews, I'd imagine. Three, yes three." He again looked to the chianti bottles. Galen said he'd offer him a drink but we were fresh out.

"Um, no thanks. I had to stop drinking a year ago. Um, listen, would one or both of you be willing to stay here for about a week, just until I can find a parishioner to move in?"

A sliver of pale moon still hung in the sky, competing weakly with the all-consuming, desiccating sun. Hadn't the moon been full last night? Or at least gibbous? Galen and I looked up, remembering the old woman, her husband, and the owl.

"Sure. We owe Ray and Ashley and their little one who never showed. Sure, however long it takes," I answered. "Tit for tat."

The moon clung persistently, though faded even from just one half minute, just thirty seconds before. I couldn't help but remember the old woman's admonition: Death is all we have. Death is all we have. Death is all . . . Three times, tat, tat, tat.

The Perfect Ghost Story, Plus One

"**T**HAT SOUNDS ABOUT RIGHT for you." Galen popped mallet onto chisel into wood. Since I caught his Cherokee mood in his brows, I could tell this was as much response as I would get and I was on my own. If Galen and I had been lovers, we might have been having a spat, maybe even on the verge of breakup, so I nodded and left the house, walking toward the new and improved retired hippie bar, High on Rose. Maybe the end to my summer's long search for love awaited me there.

It was early August, time to ready for fall rush at the bookstore. Evening sunlight strayed but weakly under all the trees along Rose Street—still, I wasn't at all surprised when an inky shadow started following me. This one wore a Sherlock Holmes hat. I could smell its felt, which let off a musty odor, though it hadn't rained for well over a week.

"That smells about right for me." I spoke this aloud, making a pert college student jerk and hustle to distance herself as she passed on the sidewalk. Her butch chestnut hair and zinc granny glasses looked familiar. *Galen's the one you want*, I thought to say, but didn't. None of this was her problem.

These shadow ghosts with hats had been what I was trying to tell Galen about when he cavalierly dismissed me. For over a week, since the last dismal rain in fact, I'd been haunted by them—morning, afternoon, night, it didn't matter. Sunny or cloudy, it didn't matter. Full moon or no moon, it didn't matter. Indoors or out, it didn't matter. Two had been skinny and inky, menacing. Two had been gray and oafish, cartoonish in demeanor. Two, including this new one, played out pretty much as innocuous mesomorphs, just like me. Imagine that. I looked back to the Sherlock hat behind me, which had acquired a silly Cavendish pipe underneath, its porcelain evenly yellowed from use. Accouterments were something new, so I stopped. The shadow mis-stepped and shuffled ahead on the sidewalk. As if sensing I'd stopped, the young woman picked up her pace even more and moved farther along.

"Galen's the one you want," I shouted.

"Screw Galen!" she shouted back, not even looking around.

Whoops. That's why she looked familiar. Returning to business, I lifted an eyebrow at this new shadow, who was waiting politely. His pipe jutted. Should I backtrack and follow the ex-girlfriend, see where she lived, report to Galen? But what would I say when she called the police about a stalker? My shadow made me do it?

"This is the stupidest hat yet," I quietly informed the shadow, stopping under a maple two steps from him to pack and light my standard but sensible billiard pipe—no fancy curves, no oversize bowl. After some comforting puffs I strutted on ahead. Public smoking laws weren't around yet, but they were in the air, so to speak. In just the last month, several people had coughed pointedly beside my desk in the bookstore. One woman had asked about a Germaine Greer book then sniffled at my pipe and commented, "Never mind, you wouldn't know," as if there were a connection between tobacco and liberal thought.

As I neared High on Rose Bar, I glanced to see the shadow's ridiculously oversized yellow Cavendish beginning to bob, either encouraging me onward or undergoing its own anti-smoking sentiment. But as long as Joe and Freddie owned High on Rose, tobacco would be welcome, especially by Freddie, a chain smoker.

Once inside, I ordered a draft beer, checking out a pair of legs in a booth to my right. Two nights before, on a Wednesday, I'd given a similar leer and my shadowy pal had made instant appearance, wearing a crumpled top hat similar to Dr. Seuss's cat. So I lied: the Sherlock hat really wasn't the stupidest yet. But tonight, the Sherlock hat and the yellow Cavendish had stopped at the bar's front door, unwilling to enter. There was still summertime light outside, and when I looked back I saw my shadow leaning against an iron pole supporting the stoop's awning.

"Come on in, the air's cool," I mumbled.

"More ghosts?" Joe grinned, clonking my mug on the bar. He'd not been receptive when I told him about the Civil War ghosts in Spalding Hall at my high school. His grin, in fact, had grown with my telling until his very face made a good candidate for a fiendish Jack the Ripper. I sipped my beer without response, looking through the glass door as my inky pal lit his pipe, using a coal black flame. Of course.

I toasted him.

Six songs later as sound system time flowed, Joe came back to set down another beer. "How about a Docburger and some fries, too," I said, giving a backward glance to the door.

"Want to order something for your friend?"

"You see him!?"

"He means me."

Her voice sent me jumping and I looked to my left to see the woman I'd passed on Rose Street.

"How'd you—?"

She nudged my leg with her foot in answer. She'd changed out of her heels into tennis shoes.

"Hello. She's been sitting there for two and a half songs," Joe said.

"Since 'I Can't Get No Satisfaction,' " she added with a wink.

Joe gave his patented laugh cum snort. "Buy her a damned beer. How often do you get a chance to do that?"

I lifted my hands in resignation.

"Why don't you tell her about the shadow ghosts following you?" Freddie called out as a cigarette bounced in his lips and he slapped down a yellowed wallet I recognized as Galen's. "He dropped this last night, called us about half an hour ago." Freddie slid the wallet down the bar.

"And warned us," Joe said, stopping the wallet with his elbow, "about the be-hatted shadow ghosts following you." He set down my beer and then the one for . . .

"I'm Stacy," Stacy said, holding out her hand to shake.

"I'm—"

"Galen's roommate," Joe interrupted.

"The bookstore guy," Freddie added from his end of the bar.

"I know his name. I know your name."

"Prove it," Joe said, his back turned to pull a draft beer for someone else.

"Non-believers," Stacy replied. She blinked underneath those zinc granny glasses. "Come on, let's get a booth. I have a real ghost story to tell you."

I looked out into the dusk. The Cavendish pipe was bobbing corncob yellow. I looked into Stacy's eyes, something of a green hazel. She was coming back to me. A history major working on her Master's. She'd had a letter published in *The New Yorker*. I'm saying that those zinc frames on her glasses bespoke of brains *and* looks.

Sitting in the booth so I could watch Mr. Sherlock, I snapped my fingers. "I remember. Swimming in the farm pond—"

"I'd rather not talk about that."

"Oh, right." An ex-Galen reaction, I guessed.

"So. You and that girl you were with, Robin?" she asked.

I motioned a no-foul with my hands. I also remembered this verbal quirk of Stacy's, beginning sentences with a declaratory *So.*

"I heard her play in the symphony, you know. I mean, she was third seat violin, so I didn't really hear her, but . . ." Now it was her turn to make a no-foul motion over the table.

Mr. Sherlock Shadow took that stupid Cavendish from his mouth and wound it in a circle, indicating I should get on with things. Had the entire bar turned to sign language? Even the jukebox became silent. Then Joe snorted a laugh, so I guessed not.

"Your ghost story?" I prompted.

Stacy leaned forward, taking off her glasses for effect and putting them back on. "When I first moved here six years ago, I collected dolls—I know," she said in response to my raised brows. "Still, that's what I did. Carrying a little bit of hometown Cincinnati down here to college. I had four when I came as a freshman. My mom and dad visited over Thanksgiving and they brought another one, a Cinderella that stood nearly two feet high, counting her wand. A gorgeous bridal silk gown, and of course glass slippers. But they weren't really glass, just a clear, hard plastic.

"So. First semester I made all A's and the President's list. I propped Cinderella on my breakfast bar. Neither Mom nor Dad had gone to college as such, though Mom went to R.N. school and Dad worked at the post office. They met in the Korean War, when Dad got wounded. Anyway, Cinderella stood on my breakfast bar to remind me of them. Well what do you know but this handsome Prince Charming moves into the apartment complex across from the house I was living in, and I thought for sure that—" More hand motions and we both paused to sip our beers.

"Girls can be just as stupid as guys over a pretty face. At least some girls, meaning me. Here's where the ghost part comes. I was dating Prince Charming for about two weeks when we started making the double-backed beast." Her hands began to shake, but when I noted that, they stopped. "So. One morning after he left, I walked to pick up a math book—basic studies still—and I looked to my little doll cabinet that Dad had built. The doll on the bottom shelf, she had both her eyes gashed out. Nothing but black holes left. I looked to the cabinet's tiny gold padlock, which was still intact and still closed. I pulled the lowest right hand drawer of my desk all the way out to find the cedar cigar box my father'd given me. And still inside that box still sat the key to the doll cabinet. I unlocked the cabinet and took out the wounded doll. Now her sweet doll smile seemed evil, her teeth showing even, ivory panic. I touched her right eye and dark goop like tar—or like sticky old blood—clung to my finger."

My shoulders hunched at this, and Stacy looked at me. "I'm not into screaming, so I didn't. But a shiver ran through my own shoulders and I spun about so fast that the room's colors tumbled like one of those kids' kaleidoscopes. My head was tumbling, too."

Her hands began shaking again. "So. When the spinning stopped, I was on the wood floor. I looked at the doll, which was lying facedown beside me. Some red blood goop oozed onto the floor. I left the doll there and got up to brew hot tea. I stood by the stove calculating people who'd been in my apartment for the last couple of months. Prince Charming, of course. The three girls who lived downstairs and who were music majors. Their nightly practicing was comforting, especially as they played mostly classical music. My girlfriend from high school. She'd come over and we'd taken the dolls out. She'd admired my rag doll so much that I almost gave it to her, but it was my only one. But her visit firmly set the last date I'd really looked at the dolls: March 20th, the day before her birthday. Four weeks back. Then I remembered a handyman about a week before, fixing a dripping faucet. He was the last person I could think of. I remembered being glad I had a class to go to because his pasty skin and oily black hair creeped me out."

The bar crowd was picking up. My inky shadow stepped politely aside as each group entered. Stacy caught my focus and twitched.

"So. I called the landlord—landlordess, really—and asked about the guy. She in turn asked if I had something missing from my apartment. When I told her about my doll with its gashed eyes, she became quiet." Another jerk of her hand and Stacy took a deep breath. "So. I finally had to ask if she were still on the line. She said she'd buy me a new doll, which was weird, you know?"

I nodded uncertainly.

"I mean, she's a lawyer and all." Stacy made a motion with her right hand of grasping money. "So. Two days later she really did leave an expensive Spanish doll outside my door. I heard her there, but when I opened the door she was already down the steps and backing up her fancy white car. I picked up the doll, which rivaled Cinderella in her beauty."

I could see from Stacy's body movement that she was jiggling her right leg, hard. She continued,

"When I called my landlady later, she said she didn't think the handyman was the problem, since she'd known him for over ten years. She wondered if there was . . . I thought of Prince Charming. But I couldn't see how he had any opportunity." Stacy sighed, I sighed, someone bumped the jukebox, and Freddie yelled.

"Anyway, that weekend, Prince Charming and I went to a movie. Movies and eating out, that was our dates. The Prince wasn't all that imaginative, and I was a silly freshman uninitiated into feminism and speaking up. After the Prince ate breakfast and left the next morning—he supposedly had a nosy roommate, so our trysts were all at my place—I went to the grocery, since the Prince had finished all my eggs and eaten a pound of sausage. When I got back I decided to change the bed sheets because the Prince had gotten rough with his nails and I'd bled from scratches. He sort of choked me too." Stacy rotated her beer mug at that, coughed, and then continued after inhaling,

"So. This time, when I saw this second doll, I did scream. She lay under my pillow. Both her eyes were gashed, just like before. I screamed and I screamed. All three girls from below ran up and beat at my door. When I showed them the doll— it was the Dutch girl I bought myself as a graduation present from high school—they all three hugged me. It was like the Weird Sisters in *Macbeth*. I yelped out 'Don't!' when the violinist leaned to put her finger in the Dutch doll's eye. She pulled back a bloody goop. It was my turn to hug and console, because she started screaming too. This roused a history professor—maybe this is one reason I majored in history, even though he retired—who owned the house on the other side of our rental. He stumbled up and beat on my door with a large cane. He came in and took charge, made tea and coffee for us all, finished 'stowing'—his word—my groceries and settled us down. Then he began the gauntlet of who had been in my apartment, who might have followed me from class, who the girls downstairs had seen—a real Sherlock Holmes."

At Stacy's words, I glanced out the front door. It was dark now, and a couple was entering the bar. My inky shadow actually tipped his ridiculous hat for them.

"I have a story too," I said.

"I'm almost finished," she said.

Joe stopped by, and I motioned toward our nearly empty mugs. "Twice in one night," was his surprised comment. "Soon you'll be a ladies' man just like your wretched roommate."

Stacy twisted her nose at that, then picked up her story after Joe walked away:

"So. When I told the professor and the girls all the people who'd been in my apartment, I said, 'That handyman. He could have made a duplicate key to my apartment and the doll case both.' / 'Tommy?' the professor replied. 'I've known Tommy longer than I've known your landlady. I recommended him to her, in fact. He married a widow with a child, and now they have two kids. Besides, he's been in the hospital for the past three days. You can't always tell a book by its cover.' Then the professor went on to talk about the guy I was dating, Prince Charming, saying he'd seen him hanging around. Had I called him that, I wondered. I supposed I had. Prince Charming, the professor said, had been in his American History class the year before, and co-eds had complained that the Prince would touch them as he walked down the aisle. A huge crack came from my doll case when the professor said this. The pianist walked over, but came back with a shrug.

" 'Well,' the professor said, standing, 'you could call the police, but they really wouldn't do much. You four ladies need to watch out for one another, is my advice. And here's my phone number.' He laid a card on the table. 'Maybe Liz will break her rules and let you get a little watchdog. I'll talk with her.' Liz was my landlady.

"So. With that, he left. Two of the girls left too, saying they had classes. The pianist, a milky thin blonde who looked like a ghost herself, stayed. She was the only one who ever departed from classical music. I told her I loved it when she played Dave Brubeck, that he was my dad's favorite. She ignored my compliment and said she had something to tell me. Her blue eyes shifted, searching the robin's egg blue, tongue-in-groove ceiling. 'I heard a rumor about your—about this—apartment,' she said."

Stacy stopped to sip her beer, sat it down to tap my mug with a clink. She didn't wear fingernail polish, I noticed. At the bar, Joe laugh-snorted and Freddie lit a cigarette. I opened my mouth to speak, but Stacy persisted:

"Things get really weird here. The pianist told me that right after World War II a G.I. had gone nuts and raped a woman in my apartment, choking her and gouging her eyes. He left a penned note saying that no one ever should have seen what he saw in the war. You know, it was one of those stories so nuts that it made sense."

I looked away from Stacy's own eyes to the bar's front door. It had started to rain. My inky friend was no longer there; maybe he went to exchange his hat for raingear. I thought about the Viet vet I'd briefly had as a roommate. He could get pretty hairy, but not . . . Stacy nudged my hand with hers:

"You were funny that night at the pond. I liked you. I hoped we'd meet again. It took me a minute to recognize you on the sidewalk. You've gotten bigger."

"Lifting weights," I said, nodding absently, still watching the door.

"Are you expecting someone?" She turned around.

"No, no, not at all. Was that the end of your ghost story?"

"Ha. Mine is a legitimate ghost story, complete with doll motif, haunted house—well, apartment—mood, moral, warnings, turning point, and climax. That afternoon I skipped class and went to the library to check old city newspapers on Microfiche. It took me four hours, but I found that what the pale pianist had told me was true. The murderer had been at the liberation of Dachau, where there were Jews still alive, but starving and looking like skeletons. It was in the fall of 1945 that the guy began taking classes under the new G. I. Bill. He wound up in my apartment on a football Saturday, when he killed the woman living here while her roommate—my apartment used to be a cramped two-bedroom—was at the football game. Three days later, he was shot and killed in my hometown, Cincinnati. I didn't know which one to feel more sorry for, her or him."

I again started to speak, but Stacy motioned me to wait.

"I told you mine is the perfect ghost story. Motif: dolls. Setting: lonely apartment, lonely young female. Mood: dark as hell. Secondary motif: the classic three warnings."

I shook my head. "Three?"

"Wait. My Cinderella doll, the one my parents gave me, carried a wand that she could wave. And she was one of the first singing dolls, too. She sang 'When You Wish Upon a Star.' " Stacy waved her hand: "I know, I know, Pinocchio and Jiminy Cricket. We do our American best to confuse even fairy tales and popular history. So. A few days later, the girls downstairs and I watched *Bullitt* with Steve McQueen on TV and drank an awful drink called Purple Balls. I awoke Saturday, the next morning, to that sappy 'When You Wish' song playing. My Cinderella doll was standing on the window's ledge, staring at me, waving her wand, and singing.

" 'No! No! No! No!' I shouted.

"You see, her eyes were gouged too. Blood was leaking from her sockets, even as her mouth moved and her wand kept beat to that silly song. As I watched from under my covers, blood rolled down her cheeks. I ran over, more concerned with my precious Cinderella than myself, and I almost fell into the window. Through the blinds I looked down and saw

Prince Charming. It was early morning. He had a girl pinned against a balcony support post, choking her with one hand and just staring at her. Another girl ran out of a nearby apartment and began hitting him with a book. The girl he was choking slumped down and he just walked away, unlocking his apartment door as if nothing had happened."

Stacy was shivering now. She stared at her second beer. She hadn't drunk much, and I'd finished mine. She poured most of hers into my empty mug, clinking the glasses. The rain outside had turned steady. My friend, the Sherlock shadow, still wasn't there. I steadied Stacy's hand and she nodded thanks.

"I wonder if Rita was happy after her last successful warning."

"Rita?" I asked.

"Rita Denise Gadsen. She was the coed strangled by the World War II vet in my apartment." Stacy had been focusing on a spot on the wall behind me. Now she turned those hazel eyes to me. "You see what I mean?" she asked. "The perfect ghost story. Three warnings from beyond, from a troubled spirit haunting its murder locale. So. Exactly two moon months later, Prince Charming—God, he was caught strangling another girl. This one he finished, but not before he raped her and left her body in a construction site on campus." Stacy bit her lips, rubbing them with her teeth. "There were four witnesses: two couples making out had seen him and the girl sneak behind the fence. He'd come out alone. His picture was pasted on the front page. A week later he was connected with a second murder-rape at the University of Louisville."

She continued rubbing her lips with her teeth. "Without Rita and those three blinded dolls, I might have joined them. Ghostly warnings taken. Boo."

It was a weak 'boo,' more of the beginning of a boo-hoo than a taunt. Still, Stacy nudged my mug. "So. Tell me about your shadow ghosts."

I mumbled, since my ghost or ghosts seemed silly in comparison. My hands were under the table, but I still motioned a "what the hell" with them. Then I ran through all the hats my ghosts had worn: a John Wayne cowboy hat, a World War II Nazi helmet, the Dr. Seuss Cat hat, a tam, a beret, and the recent Sherlock Holmes hat.

"Is he still outside?" Stacy asked.

"No—I mean yes! He's back!" For when I looked, the inky shadow had returned. "But now he's wearing a rain slicker and a rain hat."

Stacy turned to look. I caught a glance of her milky breast as she did. The yellow Cavendish pipe bobbed, even in the rain. Evidently tobacco was as hard to give up in the spirit world as it is in this one.

"A practical ghost," Stacy commented about his change of headgear.

"You see him?!"

"Of course not. He's your personal messenger, not mine."

"But those girls and that history professor, they saw the dolls with the poked out eyes."

Stacy sipped her beer and considered. Eagle-eye Joe strolled over just as she finished. "Why don't you steal some money from Galen's wallet and buy us all a round?" he suggested.

Stacy grinned. She had huge dimples and a broad, friendly smile.

"Sort of a finder's fee," Joe urged.

I tapped Galen's wallet in my pocket and thought about him ignoring me earlier that night. I pulled it out and took out three bills.

"A round for me too."

I pulled out another bill.

"And the tip."

Stacy took the wallet out of my hand and handed Joe a fifth bill. He nodded and left for our beers.

"So. Your shadow ghosts may be more of the doppelganger brand."

"I guess I hadn't thought of that."

"Sure. Leaving you a life-message. Do they appear at any specific occasions?"

I thought of the Dr. Seuss cat-in-the hat when I was ogling the woman's long legs the other night, but I kept quiet about that and said, "Well, this evening, right before I passed you on the sidewalk." I looked out to the porch.

Stacy motioned with her hands for me to continue. With its rain slicker and hat, the Sherlock shadow now looked more like an advertisement for cough drops. It scrunched its shoulders and leaned into the iron post and the rain.

"And the cowboy hat, it appeared in the bookstore when two girls were laughing at me because I'd hooked my hands in my blue jeans like Jimmy Dean or some street punk." I left out the Nazi helmet, which had appeared when I was berating a student worker for being late, at the insistence of my own boss, in a sort of trickle-down fashion. The student had started crying and quit one day later.

"Motif, I suppose the shadows and the hats make one, all right." Stacy placed her chin in her hand and stared at me. "But motive, moral? Is this doppelganger shadow a creature bent on making fun of you? Or is it several creatures? Or is it . . ." Stacy reached for my hand with simple sincerity. "You know, as long as you've worked at the University, I'm sure you could get some free psychiatric counseling." I blinked until she took off her glasses, cleaned them with a napkin and grinned.

"Bar jokes are the best, unless they're aimed at you," I told her.

She reached for my hand again. "Listen. This whole hot month, those two guys over there have scrimped on the air so much you'd think they wanted to chase off business." She looked back to the door. "The rain's let up and I've had it with this hot bar and this flat draught beer. You want to go to my place? You really are funny."

"This is the place where the woman was strangled and the dolls—"

"You think I'm nuts?" Her voice rose enough that several people and Freddie looked our way. "I broke lease and moved out. I live in a bungalow not four blocks from here."

So. So we left.

"Is he following?" Stacy asked under the second streetlight.

I looked back, not seeing anyone or thing until . . .

"Yeah. He's about a block behind. Staggering like he's drunk."

"This is another problem with your ghost story, its tone. A ghost or ghosts that change comic hats, that smoke a fat pipe, like maybe a bong filled with weed . . . not very scary or somber."

"Do ghosts have to be somber?"

"Poltergeists, you mean."

"Well, yeah."

Another streetlight approached. Or, I guess, we approached it. I saw light drizzle misting in its glare.

"The first time you saw one of these ghosts with a hat, were you scared? Do you remember what brought it on?"

Really? I hadn't slept with a woman since mid-winter and it was now August, and here I was walking an attractive, bright gal toward her "bungalow," and I'm supposed to dole out spirit-force details? In those same shifting seasons Galen had netted no less than five women I knew of. I'd heard their yelps and moans, sniffed their perfume, and at least twice had impaled a lost earring into my bare foot.

"The first one wore the Nazi helmet. That's all I can remember."

"That doesn't sound very doppelganger or very funny."

Doppelganger. Could that be true? Life-messages? Life-warnings? Change your lowdown ways or else? I shrugged in the dark as an apartment light winked out to our right. I swear that I could smell pungent Turkish Latakia pipe tobacco from my doppelganger's Cavendish pipe a full block behind. *We're going to have a fight at this woman's front door, brother*, I thought. *You aren't getting in with that stench, ghost or no ghost.*

"I don't guess it was. Funny, that is. None of them have been very funny to experience. It's only in the telling."

At last, at last, at last, we entered the bungalow—alone, together!—and she took off her zinc granny glasses and we made the wondrous warm beast with two backs.

Of course I was doomed to fall in love. No, I didn't spot a ghost wearing an inky dunce cap while holding a tiny Cupid's bow, but its warning wouldn't have mattered. My kersplat went mighty. And by next April Stacy had defended her Master's thesis and was accepted at the University of Pennsylvania's prestigious history department for its doctoral program. My kersplat went double mighty.

They say art imitates life. That's just a syllable plus one off. Art impregnates life. Six solar years later, Stacy got invited back to campus as an esteemed graduate who'd published an esteemed critical book with an esteemed press. I attended her talk and bought her book. I fully expected to see a ghost wearing, say, an inky Valentine's bear on its head, and I did. Yes, it cavorted a two-step behind her the entire time she spoke. If I'd had a pipe I could have used it like a conductor's baton to keep rhythm. But the anti-smokers had won, so no.

And no, really, on the inky bear hat, too. In truth, the last hat ghost I ever saw was on that rainy night, following with its stinking tobacco, its Fisherman's Friend rain slicker and cap, drunkenly dancing behind us.

"Great to see you," I said, walking up after Stacy's talk.

"Great to see *you*," she replied, shoulders thrown back. "Still at the bookstore?"

I wasn't even embarrassed to answer in the affirmative. I didn't mumble, shuffle, or glance at specks on the floor. I didn't recoil as if happening upon two gouged eyes. Yes, brilliant Stacy claimed hers was the perfect ghost story, but mine surely shares degrees of perfection. Motif: inky ghosts with changeable, inky hats. Mood: frivolous, practical, frightening, somber, and chiding, chiding, chiding. Moral? Ah, there lies the gem I came to see cut and polished before my eyes, even as I spoke with lustrous Professor Stacy. Moral: If the hats fit, go on and wear 'em. A perfect message from that mystic beyond hidden beyond our beyonds, a perfect admonitory doppelganger ghost story with . . . well, I guess therein doth lie a flaw, for no perfect finale has yet to manifest. But like everyone, I'm not exactly yearning for a finale. Am I? Are you, are we? So. My perfect ghost story will just needs wait. So. Please pass that hat.

THE WIDOW WITH THE HOOKAH

ALEN SWORE THAT HE'D SEEN a ghost in Naples, Italy, who sat on a balcony above a dockside bar, rhythmically rocking to piano music behind her, smoking a hookah, baring her breasts. If any male other than a sailor—what country the sailor hailed from didn't matter—looked up and huzzahed, her teeth would extend to fangs, her fingernails would twist to icy blue talons, and she would reach into that man's heart and rip a year or more off his life. One elderly grocer, Galen heard, had dropped dead in the street. But for sailors, she would keep rocking, and even caress them with a bare-breasted lullaby later that night in their drunken dreams. "It's true, I swear." He gave me a very un-Galenlike wink.

Galen swore to a lot of things, and you either appreciated the effort or went elsewhere.

This was an especially muggy Ohio Valley mid-summer Friday night, and though we'd shared houses together on and off for ten years, Galen remained older-brother intent on finding me some sexual relief, so a double date lay on the venue. Lexington was undertaking primal throes in gentrification, and we were headed to meet Galen's current girlfriend and a "very available, very hot" friend of hers at The Bungalow, a winery-seafood-dinery facing the courthouse. Turning onto the square, we heard two hoots that plummeted from raucous college boy shouts into pained, grievous howls.

Galen grabbed my elbow and twisted me around. "Don't look up. Or at least don't shout anything when you do. She's here, on the balcony."

"Who—" He yanked me again. I'd been lifting weights and had gained a good deal on him, but he still had some tug, so I shrugged in resignation.

"Remember a few years back when I told you about the widow ghost with the hookah in Naples?" He'd taken on his determined Cherokee look, crunching his brow and glaring, so I nodded. "Well, she's here."

"How here? Across the ocean? In landlocked Lexington, Kentucky?"

"I have no earthly idea how, but she's here. Same black raven's hair stacked in the same wispy, overflowing bun, same gold bandanna holding it up, same long tanned legs, same glittery red and yellow dress, same rhythmic rocking to a piano, same glowworm green emerald hookah—same everything. Did you hear those frat boys yelping, then howling like kicked dogs?"

I recollected the story he'd told me. "You're saying she just bared her breasts and took a year off their lives?"

"I'm saying that much off or more. You can look, you can lust, hell, you can wiggle your wong, just don't yell."

"What about those college girls? They're yelling. Is she going to—"

"Females can't see her."

"Why not?"

Galen exhaled through his nose as if I'd asked the sixteenth dumbest question in world history. Maybe I had. He let me go. I turned to look up at the widow with the emerald green hookah, and Galen hissed in my ear, "Keep quiet, keep quiet, keep quiet." Watching her rocking, I swayed, feeling dizzy and uncertain on my non-nautical legs. I ran the then current Italian beauties through my mind: Gina Lollobrigida, Sophia Loren, Annette Funicello. Well yeah, the Mouseketeer whose white Mickey Mouse sweater had outlined promising breasts to my once eleven-year-old eyes.

Smoke curled from the widow's hookah, a thick silvery smoke that bent its lovely back to reveal red spaghetti straps and whisper bedroom whispers. Ready to let out a boy-yelp, I inhaled, but Galen pinched my right arm, so I kept quiet. A nearby frat boy who didn't have the luxury of a guiding Naval hand yelled, "Whoo! Bare them titties!" to immediately gag and strangle, then slump onto a wood-slatted bench provided by the upcoming gentry for upcoming gentrification. His girlfriend rushed to slap at him and cry out, "Damn it, Danny! Gross!" It was almost as if the hookah widow were contracted by *Ms. Magazine* and Gloria Steinem to spread the good feminist gospel on Courthouse Square, Lexington, KY.

One look at Danny's face wiped humor and politics from my mind. A permanent worry line was threading his post-teenage eyes, as if he'd been fighting small business bankruptcy for nine years and was on the verge of throwing in the financial towel and suiciding his life insurance to survivors. His girlfriend spotted this same creeping line and moved from accusation to worry. "Danny? Danny?"

Galen followed my gaze and shook his head. "See?"

A chill rippled my shoulder blade, as if the widow were stretching to give a test run with her fingernails and slice off some spinal lifeline. "No damned worry about my mouth." I looked from Danny and his girl up to the balcony, which was wrought cast iron New Orleans style. The hookah widow stopped swaying to stare at me. The piano behind her tinkled, then thundered bass notes. In her light brown eyes I saw widening anguish and disbelief. I saw the roiling stormy sea that sank her husband's ship in the late 1800s. I felt the hands of neighbors on her shoulders trying to console her. I heard her screaming out at the Mediterranean, now mockingly calm. Then the piano's high notes tinkled again, and those eyelids lowered into bedroom temptation. Emerald flecks sprinkled to replace the ocean's demanding foam. Then Danny's girlfriend sniffled behind me.

"Wait, how can I possibly see her eyes from this far?" I asked the humid air, for our footsteps were falling well over a storefront away; in fact we were just approaching windows that promised the Dimpled Draught House would open "*Soo-oon*" in the fall.

"How do you think you can?" Galen answered. "She's a ghost."

The widow inhaled on her hookah, still staring at me. Me. Behind her, the piano lilted out the second-story window, like a circling white seagull, music from the French romantics. She kept inhaling, impossibly long and impossibly deep, and her breasts bulged impossibly huge and impossibly round, her eyes impossibly needy. Now we were nearly underneath the balcony. Her eyes *did* hold flecks of green, though mostly they showed light brown, a compromise Mediterranean shade, I supposed. She stood. A raft of perfume and hookah smoke wafted down atop various piano notes, undulating from note to note as if riding plump death-black seahorses.

"Pigeon watching?" a woman called out as I stumbled over some minor imperfection in the landlubber sidewalk.

"You really can't see her?" I yelped, dazzled by the emerald sequins on this new woman's bosomy blouse.

"You're the second guy who's asked me that. I think Lexington Water Company's dumped testosterone-laced LSD in its reservoir." She turned and laughed to a chestnut-haired friend, and they both sidestepped to enter ahead of Galen and me. We watched their legs and shifting buttocks. Neither of us needed the Water Company's prod.

As we entered the darkened dining room and bar, I spotted the busty emerald blouse moving ahead. To my left atop a wooden island, before an imposing mahogany bar, a huge saltwater fish tank full of clown fish and sea anemones glowed with placid orange and pink fluorescence. Then an octopus's misplaced seaweed brown tentacles writhed an interfering Scheherazadean dance. I'd never seen one in a tank, didn't know such was possible. It must have weighed a couple of pounds.

I tugged Galen's arm, distracting him from the chestnut-haired woman accompanying the emeralds. This friend wore a tight red skirt. "Don't octopuses live only in deep water?"

"Octopi," Galen responded flatly. "She's brought it here from Naples. Part of her act."

Of course.

Galen ordered a bottle of chianti in a straw basket. He was planning moves for me already. No frat-boy beer, no horsey-farm bourbon. I was to make a cosmopolitan *im-pres-sion* on this "very hot, very available woman." Sometimes I wished he would just let me lead my goofball bookstore life on my solitary. Though Galen ordered, I paid, and the bartender's maroon nails scratched the back of my hand as she scooted over a wineglass. A warning? A wanting? Or just a purposeful move for tips?

A clatter of dishes and eating utensils shoved into my head. But when I turned, the dining room behind was undergoing a lull, with only three couples contemplating menus. Still, all that clatter . . . as if the room were a shifting galley on a storm-tossed ship. Then heavy perfume and a mix of hashish and that god-awful pipe tobacco, Latakia, strolled the air over more seahorse piano notes. I remembered Latakia was a Cypriot blend. I guess that made sense for a widow from Naples. Had her sailor husband been a Greek? Not likely from the little I knew of Mediterranean history where countries kept to themselves except to war, thank you. The busty emerald-sequined woman, now at the bar, looked at me and laughed, but my attention focused on a sinew of silver smoke slowly descending the staircase. As if sniffing, the smoke encircled a waitress's head as she carried a dish of crab appetizers up the steps, their tiny orange pincers lifting in mortal resignation to afford some Kentuckian sea-faring pleasure. The silver smoke swirled to follow her up two more steps, then relinquished its interest in her for a lawyer I recognized, who was descending. He grinned and slipped a palm along the waitress's hip. With a backward twist, the smoke curled heavily about his face and sent him reeling against the wall in a coughing spasm. The waitress gave a disdainful look and continued her climb to Debussy's "*L'apres-midi d'un Faun.*"

"Did you—"

But Galen was hustling the chestnut-haired woman that the smartass emerald gal had come in with. We'd arrived an hour early just so he'd have time to do this, I'm certain. Get in some practice. If the Naples widow really was empathetic with *Ms. Magazine* and feminism, I couldn't understand how Galen escaped a double whammy of that silver smoke. But women seemed to love him, so I was missing something. This didn't surprise me—that I was missing something.

The lawyer still leaned against the stairwell's wall. He waved off a friend who tried to help him regain balance. His hair—it had a sharp silver streak running through it now, making him look like a raccoon. He touched it and recoiled. The tendril of silver hookah smoke wavered at the bottom of the steps, as if searching. Galen had left the bottle of chianti with me, and I hunkered as much as one can hunker behind a bottle of wine in a basket, as the smoke condensed into a rotating silver globe, as if forming a waterspout. The pianist upstairs had started playing again, forsaking the French romantics for "An American in Paris," its upswing more jazzy to get the early crowd moving. Three men climbed the steps straight through the smoky globe, two slapping it aside, one too tipsy to notice. But all three coughed vigorously and staggered. Another wait-

ress and a lone woman passed through without any effect. I
kept on relating that silvery smoke to the widow's hookah. I
even expected a face with succulent lips to condense in it, or
two baleful Mediterranean eyes at least. Had she really lost
her sailor husband in a storm?

Thunder sounded outside. Wait. There'd been zero-
percent chance of even showers. The huge fish tank before
the bar underwent a white flash, as if lightning were conducting through it. The grimy octopus squirted from a rock and
hung in the water, glowing purple. A mixture of ozone and
hashish wandered the room. Then I smelled a strong wave of
perfume.

"No pigeons in here to gawk at, so I guess you're doing
the fish thing?"

It was the woman with the emerald sequins. She stood next
to me, and in the room's dim lighting her emerald sequins
seemed to migrate up into her eyes.

"Your friend has cornered my friend, so I thought I'd stroll
over to test the waters with you. Stormy or calm, deep or shallow?"

Thunder again outside. "Stormy, I guess. And deep, since
I work at the University's book store."

"Ah, metaphor."

I felt dizzy from her eyes. She tapped the straw-covered
bottle of chianti, so I motioned for a glass from the bartender,
whose responding grin glowed eerily from fluorescent lighting underneath the bar. Both she and the emerald woman
staggered and the wineglass wobbled, as if the entire galley
once more shifted under heavy fifteen-foot seas. As soon as
the emerald woman filled her own wineglass, she jerked like
a puppet and began clapping her hands. Upstairs, the pianist
started a silly dance tune that sent my upper body mechanically bouncing.

"*Funiculi! Funicula!*" the emerald woman announced. Her voice had turned phlegmy. "Very popular when . . ." Thunder and a shout outside of "Show 'em both!" were followed by a strangled yelp that covered whatever the emerald woman said. She chugged her wine. I looked for Galen, but she yanked my arm, so I downed my wine, too. The octopus fluctuated from purple to violet to scarlet as the chianti bottle and I followed her up the stairs. She brushed aside the smoky globe—actually she extended her palm to push it aside as we climbed the steps. Was she taller, darker now? Had she donned a demi-bra exposing her ample cleavage? Had her eyes deepened with some long sorrow? Something about her was off.

The piano still bounced that silly song—a grand turnaround from the French romantics or even jazzy Gershwin. "*Funiculi! Funicula!*" Halfway up, I looked back for Galen—well, he'd find me and the chianti. On those steps I momentarily felt as if all the dining couples, all the meandering drinkers, and all the waitstaff below were staring at me in expectant silence. The silly piano tune ground to a halt, while the silvery globe at the bottom of the steps slowly spun. I stood, a courageous captain on a bridge, hoping to shout a belaying, saving action or at least offer hardy encouragement and moral support before the ship went under.

"Come on," the woman in emerald urged. I looked at her questioningly: surely something was off. But everything started up again, including "*Funiculi! Funicula!*" Had she doused herself with a cloying, glandular perfume? I followed, uncertain.

I'd never been to the top barroom here, and this one, well it couldn't possibly exist—not in Lexington, KY. It was more from Paris, France, year 2085. Strobes flashed amid scarlet lighting cascading from a flat black ceiling. The grand piano glistened a highly polished red, its lid propped open to hide the pianist. When we stepped onto the dance floor, hungry waves sloughed at my ankles, waves that glowed in fluorescence or maybe phosphorescence like Galen told me the ocean could get. What a strange special effect, part of me thought. How do they keep the water from trickling down the steps?

The widow with the hookah had her bare back to me, and though the glass doors leading to the balcony remained open, no street noise filtered through. The woman in emerald coughed and tugged at me, wanting to dance to the Italian *Funiculi! Funicula!* song. She banged her hips spasmodically and kept her face hidden, cast down toward the dance floor. Somehow she seemed taller. Entangled couples appeared, as if emerging from the walls, and red spotlights flashed, each spotlight revealing a limp man tugged by a brash wild woman with stacked raven-black hair. Dozens of couples. The women's hips swayed fulsomely under brightly colored peasant dresses, though their gaunt male partners performed only a clunky, half-hearted soggy rhythm in oversized dark slacks and white shirts.

"*Funiculi! Funicula!*" the emerald woman shouted. She was so much thinner, her skin and hair so much darker, and that perfume . . . she grabbed my hands and pulled me deeper onto the dance floor. One of the dancing men bumped me; he was sopping and left my right side wet and chilled. Waves splashed over my ankles now, alternately warm and icy. Another man bumped me, his eyes phosphorescent, unblinking, unfocused. He too left my back wet with water pooling about my belt. The perfume pulled me.

"*Funiculi!*" the transformed emerald woman shouted, keeping her heavily braceleted arms hiding her face. Her voice was hoarse, unlike the playful, lilting tease she'd had downstairs and outside.

"Funicula!" a nearby woman replied, tossing her head wildly so that her bun unfastened. Wet black hair stung my forehead.

The side of a barren mountain flashed in the center of dance floor, a frightening, too realistic hologram, with people riding a clanking elevated tram sharply upwards, dark-haired women in colorful blouses, rugged men with intent black eyes, their browned arms around each woman's shoulders, all of them singing loudly and actually swaying the tram on its rail as it ascended with metallic clanks. *Mount Vesuvius Tram Now Open!* a sign proclaimed. *"Funiculi! Funicula!"*

Thunder blasted. The women screamed, the men slumped. Red spotlights sent the hologram Mount Vesuvius skittering. The dance floor again turned animated and crowded. The woman I'd met downstairs—where was she?—my present dance partner no longer wore emerald sequins, but was dressed in the same brightly colored red, yellow, and green peasant blouse all the other dancing women wore.

"Funiculi!" she shouted. Her daring black eyes and thinly extending arms expected an answer.

Another woman tossed her hips into me, shouting the same thing.

"Funicula!" I heard a woman behind me shout. She must have slung her partner into me, for my back again got soaked as another rumble of thunder shook the floor underneath, the ceiling overhead. The widow on the balcony turned, cupping bare breasts in both hands and smiling, twisting her hips with seashore exaggeration. She let her breasts drop and motioned to me with both hands.

"Funiculi!" all the women in the room shouted.

I'd moved—or more truly, had *been* moved by the ever-multiplying dancers—so that I could see the pianist now. Though the same silly tune kept its same frantic pace, his motions came slow and limp, as if his body were caught in a silty underwater tow. Was it a recording? An antique player piano? Waves splashed over my calves, still with the same warm-cold alteration that you sometimes encounter in a lake.

The widow on the balcony bent backward to gaze at something. Had another frat boy shouted? She turned to face me. Her shimmery gown slit, revealing long, tanned legs and a hint of dark hair hungrily perched atop her mons. Motioning with her luxurious fingers, she stepped onto the dance floor. Yellow, white, and red flashed happily. The pianist stood, bowing from his waist with Old World exaggeration, though his piano kept rattling off the same song. *"Funiculi, Funicula!"* The widow waved golden tassels, not at me, but at him, her new husband of not even a year, promoted to *nostromo*, a boatswain in charge of the deck of a steel-plated warship in *Regia Marina*, the newly formed Italian Navy, now standing proudly in his dark blue uniform, she six months pregnant with what she knew would be a baby girl, all this just one year after the building of the funicular tourist ride up Mount Vesuvius and the composition of that silly *"Funiculi! Funicula!"* song commemorating the newfangled ride, so she gaily waved her tassels amid thronging yellow and white Mediterranean sunlight, dockside cheers, and then . . .

And then lightning flashed blue, orange, and horrid. Hard saltwater gushed to slap the piano; dancers were tossed like cows in Picasso's *Guernica*. I dropped the chianti bottle, which splashed and floated to bump into a sailor's corpse, dressed in the dark blue uniform of the newly formed Italian Navy, hitting his facedown head with a hollow clunk. The widow screamed, she screamed and stood naked, her arms lifting for supernal relief. Her wails overcame even the thunder, the lightning. A blood-and-water mixture gushed from between her spread legs, a maroon lump fell into the waves. The tide receded, washing the sailor, the lump, the chianti bottle, and the formerly dancing couples, rolling them all in limpid compliance, outward toward the four surrounding walls and the stairwell's opening.

The widow swayed. Her heels clacked on a dry dance floor. Shaking as if undergoing electrocution, she pinned her hair back and secured it with the golden bandana. She retrieved the hookah, which sat on the now glossy black piano. She gave a tentative puff, and, satisfied that the pipe remained lit, inhaled deeply. Exhaling, she stared blankly at the grand piano where a moonlighting professor from Kentucky's music department was playing "Maria," from *West Side Story*.

Someone behind me sang, quite poorly, "I just met a girl named Maria."

The widow strolled seamlessly though the few dancers on the floor—it was still early, just now dusk outside. Closing on me she extended the ebony mouthpiece of her hookah. "Hashish and wormwood steep the past, the ocean's floor steeps a sailor's bones. You should smoke this. We should dance forever, forever."

I looked down to see tidal water returning, seeping along the floor.

"Forever," she repeated. "Forever."

The water had yet to top even the soles of my shoes. I stomped to make a splash that gave me something to concentrate on other than the widow's breasts, her lips, her eyes, her perfume, her voice.

"Forever, forever."

Another stomp, and I considered: all those women dancing moments ago in their bright peasant blouses—they'd all looked just like this beautiful widow with her luxurious Italian hair and her Mediterranean complexion; her enticing long arms and her promising, whispering lips. And of course, her cleavage indicating milk-filled but childless breasts. But what of their gaunt male partners? All limp: young, old, Greek, German, British—or American. What of them?

The widow blew a stream of silver smoke my way. Its acrid forgetfulness reeled me forward. She smiled. Then another smell intervened from behind, a smell that indicated many animals had lost precious scent glands, many flowers pollens and oils. I turned to emerald sequins dazzling under the reflective, revolving globe.

"I lost you on the stairs. How'd you disappear? Your Cherokee friend—Galen?" I blinked and nodded. "He said to tell you that Cheryl and her friend can't make it tonight. Trouble with her sister or something. My girlfriend is in lovelust with what's in his pants. That leaves you and me, bub—if you can drag yourself away from pigeon-gawking." She gave a demure bat of her eyes, then brushed aside thick silvery smoke. "God, is everyone up here smoking joints mixed with cat urine? And this soppy, slick floor—a real lawsuit, just waiting to happen."

I felt a tap against my shoulder blade. It was the ebony tip of the hookah, I knew. I kept facing forward, facing the smartass emeralds. "Did you know that if you accept food or drink from underworld creatures, you become their slave?"

"You don't say." She gave a grimace, a sort of sweet one. "Book store stuff?"

"Maybe. I wonder if accepting a smoke counts, too."

"Well you're getting plenty of that up here. It's giving me a headache, along with that crappy piano. Ready to join the party downstairs? Just watch your step in this muck. How can the management—" She let her question go for another, "You game? My name's Sylvia."

"I'm with you, Sylvia."

I felt a fingernail slice at my neck, but hurried for the stairs. The silver globe no longer lingered at the bottom.

"You're bleeding," Sylvia commented as we started down.

I touched my neck to find it was so. "Better than drowning," I replied. "Lots better."

"Well duh," she answered.

I'll Be Home for Christmas

"**I** SAW HIM TODAY at lunch."

When I said this, Galen was carving a gargoyle out of a nine-pound chunk of maple. Already, the gargoyle clutched what looked to soon become a nude woman, limp in its only hand—its only claw, that is. Was the woman dead, dying? Whichever, the gargoyle appeared to be opening its mouth for a luscious, vengeful meal. Vengeful? Why did I think that?

Most gargoyles are hairless, but this one sported sprawling locks that glowed in orange sunburst following the wood's grain. It was the blondish nude woman who was hairless. The entire piece presented a bizarre departure from Galen's usual fanciful, big-eyed dolls that were proving to be such a hit in Lexington. Since Thanksgiving he'd forsaken them to work on this gargoyle, and even he couldn't explain why.

"I said . . . I saw him today," I repeated.

Galen was about to tap the chisel with his newly purchased black walnut mallet he was so proud of. Its wood tempered just the right hardness with just the right give, he'd bragged over the past month since buying it. He stopped before striking and looked up, then proffered both mallet and chisel in a confused gesture. "Saw who?" His voice hit a shrillness that bounced off the huge, useless basement heater.

"The person you've been talking about. Craig. Craig Jemison."

"That's not funny."

"I know."

The reason it wasn't funny was that Craig had drunkenly driven his fancy yellow Mustang from a party on a one-lane country road straight out onto Versailles Highway to create a four-lane disaster, killing himself outright and sending a Lexington family of three plus an Ohio couple to the hospital. Galen shook the chisel and mallet at me.

"I know it's not funny," I repeated. "I'm not making a joke. His pal, the guy working on his master's in anthropology, he came into the bookstore this morning right after we opened and told me he thought he'd seen him, too. Just this morning, riding around in that yellow Mustang. He was pale."

"He would be. He's been dead almost a year."

"Now you're not funny. I'm not talking about Craig, but Craig's friend, that guy in anthropology . . . I forget his name."

"Everyone does because it's a bi- name, a girl-boy name. But they're not going to be forgetting your name if you keep saying you saw Craig Jemison tooling around in his yellow Mustang. It was totaled, if you remember."

I did remember. The reason that Galen had been talking about Craig minutes before was that we were drinking some Stroh's bock beer we found in the back of our fridge. It was left over from October, and it was the very same seasonal brand Craig had been drinking one week before Christmas last year, when he totaled his Mustang by plowing through a stop sign half-hidden in fog, right onto Versailles Highway.

I wasn't lying about seeing Craig, and I wasn't lying that the anthropology guy—Lynn, that was his name—had dropped by the bookstore to tell me right after we opened this morning that he'd seen Craig driving down Rose Street half an hour before, just before his first exam started. Behind my desk, I'd shaken my head and looked up into Lynn's gaunt face—he was going to make a good anthropologist with that lean, tall look so he could peer over the veldt grass—and I'd blinked and nodded. Lynn had shrugged and left. But the more I thought about his serious thin face, the more my four morning coffees upset my stomach, so I'd walked out early to get lunch at

Omelet for U, where I spotted two of Galen's ex-girlfriends and none of mine. Could that be because I didn't have any? I'll not tell.

I'd drunk another coffee, eaten a hamburger with too much mayo, and onion rings with too much mustard. But on heading back to work and crossing Limestone Street, well there and then I'd seen that yellow Mustang and Craig waiting at the stoplight. He was rhythmically nodding his head, maybe to "Frosty the Snowman," maybe to Mozart's *Requiem*. He even turned to watch me. His eyes—I was that close—showed cloudy gray, not the bright blue they had been. He didn't smile, he didn't wave. In fact, he didn't even react when a turning car blared its horn, since I stood stunned halfway across the street. Craig's Mustang chugged onward, and something hit my back—a Coke can from the guy in the car that was trying to turn. I'd tripped and lurched toward the curb. When I looked up I saw . . . just traffic, no fancy chrome Mustang tailpipes.

I told this to Galen, who put down his precious mallet and the chisel and then looked out the window into the December night.

"Let's switch to wine. This stuff's ruining my head," was all he said.

My bock beer was nearly empty, so I stared into its eggy blackness and agreed. Bless those days when Medoc wine could be bought in America, and bought for around six bucks a bottle. We walked outside to sit under the exposed basement's awning and stare into the back yard. I lit a small mound of charcoal in a cheap grill. Its glow and the Medoc went a long way toward mellowing matters.

"I miss Louie, Louie," Galen said. "I've been thinking about getting a new dog."

"One of the women at work has a dog expecting."

Galen jerked, spilling red wine on the patio's glass table. "Did you—" he was staring at the space between the sorority behind us and the fancy house some history professor lived in, but he redirected conversation, saying instead, "Tell me about Craig again."

I did, emphasizing Craig's filmy blank gray eyes, adding that his knuckles gripped the steering wheel fiercely, as if he were on some secret, immortal mission. When I finished, Galen pointed to the space between the sorority and the fancy house, "A minute ago I saw a yellow Mustang drive by under the street lamp."

This was my cue to turn non-believer and I took it, commenting that there were lots of yellow Mustangs, even though there weren't. The color of choice for Mustangs back then and forever has been Courageous Red or maybe Menacing Black.

School—meaning the University of Kentucky—was letting out in three days. One more day of finals and two last days for the bookstore staff to wobble around shelving returned books and straightening beer steins and sweatshirts. It was unseasonably warm, which explains why Galen and I were sitting outside.

"Look," Galen said, pointing to the professor's house. A honey blonde co-ed was descending the back stoop, carrying out two bags of garbage. "He's slipping. Used to get pure blondes."

The professor, some hotshot with several books under his belt, had stolen Craig's blonde girlfriend a couple of years back. People blamed Craig's decline into alcohol on her absence, but I was never sure that Craig wasn't already heading his good time train in that direction. I watched the honey-blonde shake her beauteous self back up the steps and into the house. Damn if she wasn't in red high heels, maybe playing

Santa's helper early for the professor. Galen nudged me—was my mouth open-jawed? Probably.

"That's you fifteen years from now."

"What? A sex change?"

"No. A dirty old professor slobbering over coeds."

Well, Galen proved partly right, since I did become a professor. But the moral climate stiffened, and preying on young students drifted to verboten, so I became a dirty old professor in my noggin only.

The next day was Wednesday, last day of finals, and last rush for students selling back their textbooks, complaining about our buy-back prices. At least they were no longer threatening to burn the store down, as they had in the late sixties. Now I could even tell the more savvy business majors about supply and demand, noting that their professor had dropped the particular text they were selling. And we had a small Christmas tree by the register, which mostly calmed matters, though bringing on an occasionally snarky comment. Coincidentally, Craig's ex-girlfriend stopped by in the afternoon to sell her chemistry texts. I'd heard she'd switched to chemistry from anthropology after Craig died and after the hotshot history professor dropped her for an updated blonde coed. The guy ran through one a year, it seemed. Earlier, I had spotted her and her friend walking around the hallway, maybe waiting for a slack time in our book buyback line. And surprise, all her texts had been reordered, so she was going to leave a happy camper.

"Umm," I muttered, tabulating the money due her.

"That's exactly why I came here instead of going over to Kennedy's to sell these books," she said. "I want to talk with you." She looked at the red lights in the tiny tree, bit her lip, then looked at her friend, another blonde, for moral support. Her friend nodded and Sharon blurted, "Craig. I swear I saw Craig at lunch today, in his Mustang, parking it . . ." She stopped, but her friend took up the slack, saying,

"I was with her. I saw him too. Or I guess someone who—"

"No. It was him. Same yellow Mustang, same silly raccoon tail hanging from the rear view mirror."

The coon tail had been Craig's idea of a joke, a throwback to the roaring twenties. He'd shown me a sepia photo of his granddad and grandmom tooling around Cincinnati in a jalopy with one on their radio antenna.

Sharon stared at me. Her eyes were a beautiful blue, and I'd always carried a secret crush for her. Her lower lip quivered, so I bit my own in empathy, then said, "I thought . . . I thought I saw him at lunch yesterday. In the Mustang, I mean. And Lynn—you remember his friend Lynn—" Sharon nodded—"Lynn told me he'd seen him yesterday morning."

"He got out of the car," Sharon's friend added, "when we saw him."

"He just stood there, looking up at Rose," Sharon added. Rose was the anthropology building, though they were getting ready to move to a newer one. "I yelled out his name, and . . ."

"And he just turned and looked at us both," her friend said. "I mean just staring. Drugged out, or something."

Sharon buried her face in her hands with a sob. Two students were approaching to sell books. Sharon's friend took the money I'd laid on the counter, gave me a last glance, and tugged Sharon away. I stared at the Christmas tree's glowing red lights.

Thursday came and went. I didn't see or hear anything of the newly risen Craig, but Galen said he'd seen a yellow Mustang again, driving by the woodshop this time, and Sharon's friend came into the store, running to my desk and frantically announcing that Sharon had seen Craig from their apartment's bedroom window, pacing in the parking lot below, wearing a Santa cap. Her friend—Julie—asked if I would meet them that night at High on Rose as soon as I got off work. She stood there tearing at a Kleenex. I agreed. "Can you ask his friend who saw him, too?"

"Lynn?"

She nodded. The entire Kleenex lay on the floor by the time she walked away.

I called Lynn; rather, I called the anthropology department and left a message, since Lynn was a graduate student, which was where Craig could have been, since he'd earned nearly all A's before the affair with Sharon and the lecher professor. Then I called Galen, who was good with women, though a cynic about Craig. (He'd recanted seeing the yellow Mustang, saying he didn't know anything about cars, which he didn't, and that it could have been a yellow . . . Trans-Am? Camaro? Cadillac? I'd prompted, just to underline his ignorance. Yeah, he'd replied.)

Another girl—woman, really—showed up that evening at High on Rose, a friend of Lynn's who had also been a friend of Craig's, not in the romantic sense, but in the angelic sense of someone trying to save him from himself and his drinking. She'd seen Craig too, on the same night Galen had spotted the yellow Mustang on the street behind our house. So the witnesses were evenly divided, three males, three females. I made a private joke with Galen that maybe Craig's ghost was practicing holiday matchmaking. Galen didn't appreciate my humor. I guess I didn't either, since I took the joke no further with the other four.

Michelle was the third woman's name. And she was older, thirty-something, being a secretary in the anthropology department. She was the one who'd taken my call trying to reach Lynn and had relayed it. We six crowded into a booth and ordered a pitcher of beer, though Michelle ordered wine instead.

This got Galen's attention, along with her age. He had a thing for older women, and her dark hair matched his own Cherokee darkness.

Someone played Alvin and the Chipmunks on the jukebox and the owner Fred walked over to give it a kick, bawling, "It's too early for that shit!" Michelle and I laughed in commiseration.

What came of our high council? Well, all of us but Galen agreed that Craig's eyes were filmed over with a death pall. All of us except Galen agreed that he'd shown no emotion—no surprise, no anger, no joy—just a cold stare. Galen could be a contrarian, and this meeting brought out that aspect of his personality. "Look, it's the time of year," he insisted. "It's . . . what . . . a week away from when he died."

"One day," Michelle asserted. "He was killed on the seventeenth of December and it's the sixteenth today."

Oddly enough, her response got a look of jealousy from Sharon, who, I suspect, felt guilty she hadn't known the date by heart. Another owner, Joe Stearns, walked up to tell Galen someone wanted him on the phone. "The extra service will cost you a buck," Joe said. "Add it to my tip." He and my roommate didn't particularly get along. I got up to let Galen out, and when I stood I spotted Michelle's cleavage. Maybe I could take up older women, I thought, standing over her and staring a bit too long. Her lips twitched dismissively. Well, maybe not, I then thought, plopping back in the booth.

While Galen talked on the phone, Sharon wondered if Craig were trying to tell us all something.

"Like Marley in Scrooge?" I asked.

"Why not?" Sharon's friend Julie replied.

"Maybe your roommate's right," Michelle said, nodding back toward Galen, whose mouth had gaped as he held the phone to his ear. This gawping, fly-catching attitude was not a typical Galen reaction, I have to note. He was either tight-lipped and mad, or laughing and carousing.

"Right about what?" I asked absently, keeping an eye on Galen's oddball response to the phone conversation.

"That this all is just a case of mass hysteria, grief. Craig's death anniversary is approaching, we all miss him, and we all maybe feel guilty." Michelle gave the briefest of glances at Sharon to her left, but Sharon was staring wide-eyed toward the glass front door. I turned and caught a glimpse of what she'd seen, the tail end of a yellow Mustang. She started moaning and Julie put her arm around her.

At the bar, Galen yelled, "Go to hell! This isn't funny!" He slammed the phone down. Joe turned from pulling a beer to stare at Galen as he stalked back to our table. Galen was so upset he didn't notice Sharon's sobbing and Julie's consoling.

"Some asshole pretending he was Craig yapped that he wished he could be here with us all drinking and having fun," Galen announced.

This sent the half-full pitcher of beer sprawling across the table between Lynn and me, soaking us. It broke on the hard seat and Lynn's hand was gashed. He grabbed napkins to staunch the bleeding.

"Excuse us." Sharon's friend tugged Sharon from the booth. The two went to the women's room, a sort of no-man's-land, female friends assured me, saying some woman had Magic-Markered the wall with, "If Joe and Freddie had to piss in here, this rat hole would be a lot cleaner!"

While I dried off with napkins and Lynn pressed his palm to stop the bleeding, Galen blustered. Michelle tried to pin him down on exactly what the person on the phone had said.

" 'By Jiminy, I wish I could be there with the six of you,' is what he said," Galen sputtered.

This caught our attention, for "By Jiminy" was an out-of-date catch phrase Craig used, just like the raccoon tail on his Mustang was a silly, out-of-date fetish.

Galen returned our stares. "You think I don't know?" he asked, meaning of course the phrase was pure Craig. By this time, Lynn had used all the napkins, leaving a red pile on the table. "What the hell happened?" Galen asked, finally noticing.

Instead of returning to the table, Sharon and her friend Julie left after leaving the bathroom, though Julie stopped by long enough to collect their purses, look askance at the bloodied napkins, and suggest, "Maybe here Saturday?"

Galen was still in a huff from the phone call, the spilled beer, and whatever else, so moments later he left to go pound wood. Lynn kept grimacing and said he had final grades to calculate, since he taught as a graduate assistant, so he left also, dripping blood on the floor. Joe came over and gave us two more beers, on the house.

"One for you—" he nodded at me—"for putting up with your roommate. He broke a Christmas tree ornament slamming down the phone, to go with the pitcher that crazy woman who left broke here. And one for you—" he turned to Michelle—"for putting up with this bookstore guy and those two nutcase women." Joe swept the bloody napkins into a dirty bar rag. The broken pitcher stayed under the table.

For some reason, Michelle turned flirty as we drank the free beers. I never turn a flirty woman down, so an hour later we wound up at her room.

That was a surprise. I mean that she rented a room and not an apartment. She made good enough money—better than I did as a book buyer at the University's bookstore, damn it.

But she was insistent on saving for finishing her degree and heading for graduate school. Another surprise was the room itself: it was nearly a greenhouse, with a back glass wall that looked onto a second-story, covered patio filled with plants that came to leafy life when she flicked on the outside lights.

"Wow," was my post-hippie response.

When I turned, she was slipping off her blue high heels. This second "wow" I had sense enough to keep to myself.

Michelle had a wonderfully muscular body, though this was well before the health craze hit. She told me she wanted to be a physical anthropologist and dig. Well yes, muscles would come in handy.

We were rolling, tossing, twisting, osculating, and groping in her queen-size bed, trying different wrestling grips for maybe five minutes when a rapping sounded at those greenhouse windows that served as a back wall.

"What the shit?" Michelle said, her voice hoarse.

We both sat up, and when we did the outside light flicked on and the rapping turned insistent. It was glass-on-glass noise: a bottle of Stroh's bock beer tapping against a windowpane. Then the person holding the bottle moved away from the doorframe into full sight. It was Craig, smiling his crazed, half silly grin, his curly ginger hair glowing fiery in the greenhouse lighting. He wore a Santa's outfit and shifted his feet to grin wider, tilting the beer bottle at us in a toast. His mouth worked open and closed, saying something jolly it seemed, for his jaws worked like a cow chewing cud.

"Craig?" We both yelped this, puppies caught unaware by an angry tomcat. Angry? Why did I think that? The guy in the Santa suit looked goofball, a natural goodtime Craig. I heard a snap, and the greenhouse lights went out, and for sure I heard glass break, though all the windows remained intact. I slipped from bed and ran toward the door leading onto the patio. Right behind me, Michelle flipped the outside light switch, and I glimpsed a cottony trim against a velvety red that seemed to vaporize in the yellow light. Michelle's breast grazed my back as I opened the door, which scraped what sounded like glass across a parquet floor.

"Where's the other door?" I asked, scanning the greenhouse.

"There isn't another. This greenhouse sits enclosed over a double garage." Michelle was leaning close. I could feel her breath in my right ear, warm.

There was only one item out in that greenhouse that could hide a human or a human sized ghost in a Santa outfit, and that was an antique golden maple chifforobe. Michelle and I looked at it and then each other.

"Craig?" Michelle called tentatively. Her nails bit into my right arm.

"Damn!" I exclaimed, bending to my left foot, seeing brown glass scattered on the brown parquet. It was a broken bottle of Stroh's Bock beer.

"You're barefoot," Michelle quietly observed as I picked out a sliver of broken beer bottle and winced. "Wait. I'll get our shoes," she whispered. She returned with my tennis shoes. As I slipped them on I kept staring at the glowing maple, which looked fierce and harsh under the six light bulbs strung overhead. Michelle stuck something in my hand. A trowel. She held up a long flashlight like a club and nodded toward the maple chifforobe. We walked that way, tiptoeing. A scuffling came from behind the chifforobe, then a throaty voice crackled.

"By Jiminy, I miss everyone."

This phlegmy rattle sounded as we reached halfway across the maroon and golden parquet flooring. Michelle caught a potted flower to keep it from falling as I recoiled at the voice.

The flower's pollen stunk, and its odor clung to my skin like death.

"Craig?" Michelle called again.

A beer bottle rolled from under the chifforobe. I recognized a yellow Stroh's label flipping under and up, under and up. Stopping it with my foot I scooted it next to a plant stand.

"That professor—" a cough rattled out—"he dumped Sharon just like we all knew he would, didn't he?"

"Craig?" Michelle called in response to those words.

There was a bump against the chifforobe, another phlegmy cough.

"Sorry. I still bleed a lot. But it's energizing, everyone should try it." Another cough. "You know I warned her." The voice gargled from behind the maple, which glowed ever brighter, as if it had been given a saintly halo, or maybe devilish antlers of fire.

"Why? Why didn't she listen? It's not fair! I loved her!"

A cough. The chifforobe began shaking and scooting along the floor. Another beer bottle clonked on the parquet and rolled out, away from us this time.

"Yeah, everyone should try bleeding. It's a good thing to learn. She deserves just what I got! Just the same!"

The glowing chifforobe, all six by five feet of it, started to bleed, as if suffering some terrible disease of its pores—I mean its grain. A fog roiled from under it—the night Craig was killed out there in the country a terrible thick fog had risen, which obscured the stop sign, though of course the real problem had been all the beers Craig drank. Now this fog crept over the floor. Michelle and I backed away. A string of blue and red Christmas lights gleamed overhead.

Her phone rang and she ran inside to answer it.

"Craig," I whispered as her door caught on the broken bottle to stay propped open. "Sharon, she was just young and stupid and star-struck. Remember? He'd just had that big book published. The professor, he's the one who's guilty." I thought to move forward, but the chifforobe quivered like a magician's illusion gone awry. Blood oozed from under it onto the parquet.

"Energizing. Invigorating. A learning experience. I warned her. Her stupid friend warned her. Michelle warned her—"

Michelle, as if summoned by Craig's voice, came running out. "That was your roommate, Galen."

I only half-turned, afraid to look from the fog and the glowing, quivering, bleeding maple chifforobe. I raised my arms in question to Michelle—Galen? How? Instead of asking aloud, I stared stupidly at the trowel. Was I supposed to kill Craig all over again? Hack him and re-bury him in the many flowerpots around? Maybe in the poinsettias?

With a nervous glance to the chifforobe, Michelle said, "Sharon's friend Julie says that Sharon heard Craig calling her name outside their window, that he was rattling it and trying to get in. She told Galen that Sharon tried to slice her wrists. Galen's going over, but he wants me to come. He wants us to come. I've got the address."

"How did—"

Michelle gripped my arm again. "I guess Joe told him we left together. Galen dated my friend Amy so he got my number."

Of course. I was only surprised that Galen didn't already have Michelle's number—any way you want to take that. We took Michelle's truck—more physical anthropology material, I supposed, convenient to haul around mummies and tombstones and curses. The truck's cab smelled that deep iron smell of something freshly killed. I lifted my hands from stickiness on the seat, and while passing under a streetlight I could see blood on my palms and fingers. I wiped my hand on my jeans. By osmosis or empathy or something akin, my foot started bleeding again. It pooled in my tennis shoe.

"I cut myself back in my room as we ran out," Michelle said when I held up my bloody palm. "Something on the door grabbed my hip and tore right through my jeans."

"Jesus. Bad?"

"Well, not good. But I'm okay."

The weather'd turned cold over two days. A green Camaro skidded by us on black ice, making a half-turn, then continuing. "Do you think," Michelle started.

"Yeah, probably a drunken student."

"No. Do you think that people can go crazy after they die?"

"Ghosts?"

"Yeah, ghosts. Crazy ghosts. Like needing a psychiatrist crazy."

I stared out the passenger window. Did I spot snowflakes?

"Well?" Michelle persisted.

Galen's old beater Dodge pick-up with its dirty ivory camper shell was parked in the lot when we arrived. He'd won enough money to buy it last spring at the trots on a Perfecta bet. Blood smeared its driver's door, from window to the handle on down.

Julie and Sharon lived on the second floor. As we climbed, the outdoor iron steps rang metallically. Someone was playing Bing Crosby's "I'll Be Home for Christmas."

"Craig loved that song," I said.

"Shut up," Michelle replied.

"Wait. How could Craig get in a second story window?"

"Shut up," Michelle repeated.

As we reached the landing, yells and pounding sounded from an apartment's open door. We got there and saw Galen shouldering a second inner door, trying to break it down. His left hand was streaked red, and dried blood rivuleted his arm. It looked as if his walnut mallet had failed him and he'd caught his thumb badly.

"Some help!" he yelled, looking back at us and catching his left hand up with a yelp. "Sharon's in there!" Julie added, standing in the living room, bouncing on her feet like a kid. Michelle and I ran to heave against the door. Once, twice, and then our combined weight broke it down. The room inside lay pitch black. That phlegmy cough sounded.

"Sorry, I can't help it. But by Jiminy it's been good to see you all. How I miss this ol' brass bed. Good times." Another cough, and then blinds at an open window rattled. Moonlight seeped in, silver on the wooden floor to make a liquid puddle there sheen.

Julie screamed and turned on the room's overhead light. Sharon, in a blue satin slip, sat in a pool of blood against a brass bed, her arms at each side palm up, her mouth working like a dying fish's. A razor blade in her right hand tinnily clattered onto the hardwood floor. Blood spurted from her throat once, twice, then eased into gravity's slow trickle as her blue eyes stared blankly toward the open window. Julie screamed "No!" and ran to her, but tripped and knocked her head against the bed's brass frame, leaving a gash that sent her sprawling and dazed against Sharon, whose body slumped like a mannequin from the impact. Michelle ordered Galen to call emergency; she ran to tug Julie off Sharon, turning Julie's face away from the carnage. Insistent, the blinds clacked and rattled as wind outside howled between apartment buildings. I looked from Sharon and rushed to close the window.

When I did, someone stood in an empty apartment across the way, dressed in a Santa outfit. He tilted a beer bottle in a toast. Wind blasted and large flakes of snow began to fall. A winter storm was moving in. The forecast was for a white Christmas. It was something Craig always dreamed of.

Louie, Louie and the Blonde Hippie

E HAD BURIED LOUIE, LOUIE under a giant Dr. van Fleet rosebush that held a hundred or more green buds amid its thorns. In less than a month, the entire yard would be soaked in the perfume of its white petals.

I wrote "we," but Galen stayed possessive about the burial and insisted on digging the grave alone, though I did help carry Louie, Louie out, since he was a hefty Labrador mix that weighed well over a hundred pounds. Then, from the spare upper room in our two-story house, I watched Galen obstinately fighting roots, and I finally caught him slipping something from his work shirt pocket into the grave—the bone necklace and ring that had disappeared from my truck six years before? I couldn't make out. Anyway, he waved me down for the last words over Louie, Louie, and we both sniffled in our separate manly ways. Louie, Louie was an exceptional companion to not only Galen and me, but to the many girlfriends Galen encountered in his searching.

For nearly a year after that burial, Galen threatened to get a new pup. Intermittently he reported hearing a ghostly Louie, Louie whining, scratching, or digging in the back yard. I too thought I heard a dog making noise out there at night, and twice I found holes dug by the back fence. Louie, Louie had been quite the digger and he'd especially liked digging that spot. Galen would always joke that he was trying to get at the sorority house catty-corner from us. He even swore that Louie, Louie would pluck white roses with his teeth and lay them on the sorority's back patio.

Then, on Derby Day evening, a girl from that very sorority was raped and murdered. Her name was Dawn Carol, and she was a past girlfriend of Galen's, another one-month wonder, though this was one I'd gotten friendly with: she was the daughter of a Lexington surgeon, and an ex-hippie. Galen claimed that he knew her hippie days were over when he saw her on the street and she'd dyed her hair platinum blonde.

"Huh?" I said.

"You ever seen a blonde hippie?" He gave me his imperious high Cherokee blood look.

I thought about that for the rest of Sunday after we heard of her murder and decided he was right. The Lexington police weren't as agreeable. That very evening detectives came to our house to interrogate Galen as a past boyfriend, especially a non-fraternity one. Then on Monday, one of them cornered me just as I stepped onto our front porch, heading for work at the campus bookstore.

"How long have you known your roommate?" he asked, flashing his badge.

"We were in the color guard together at the American Legion Man o' War post before he joined the Navy." All that patriotism didn't impress the cop or his burr haircut in the least.

"He works at Hagan's Antique Furniture Repair," I added. "He carves woodwork. He's done it for four years."

This was the exactly wrong thing to say, since the young woman was sliced pretty badly, on top of being raped and robbed.

"Mind if I go in and look around your house?"

"I have to be at work half an hour ago."

"I can get a warrant."

I was shaking, but stood my ground. "You'll have to do that," I said.

He bent forward in cop aggression but walked back to his car and left. I promptly retreated inside to flush the two marijuana plants I'd harvested while fishing at a friend's pond.

Then I called Galen, who instructed me where to find his stash, which I was to flush, also.

While I rooted around for the weed and any stray paraphernalia, I smelled patchouli in Galen's basement workshop cum bedroom. I thought of Dawn Carol: a week before she and Galen parted ways, she told me I was one of the few guys she could talk sense with, one of the few who wasn't after her panties. I believe that was exactly how she put it: "after my panties." She'd kissed me on the cheek and I'd inhaled her patchouli and her heat. Before I got too carried away in her memory, I heard whining out in the back yard. I looked through filmy windows, but nothing. Turning, I faced a huge antique furnace that Hagan's probably could have displayed on the sidewalk to lure customers. It was staring blankly, and its hulking dull metallic somberness creeped me on top of everything else. The whining stopped, the patchouli seeped out around the loose windows, but the furnace kept staring.

I was glad to leave the house for work, only five blocks away on campus. As I walked there, the burr-headed cop passed me in his car, heading another direction. Why don't you find a lamppost to head-butt, I thought.

Back then, murders didn't happen eight times a week, even in a college town the size of Lexington, so everyone was upset. Turns out that one of the student workers at the bookstore knew Dawn Carol from the sorority. She underwent several crying jags during the day. I kept quiet about the police coming to question Galen and me.

That night, Galen told me that the same burr-haired detective talked with him during lunch hour at Hagan's. We were sitting on the back stoop drinking beer. The sorority fifty yards behind our house stayed still, though lights glared in every room. The van Fleet rosebush had started to bloom just since I'd talked to the cop and left for work that morning. I pointed at its two white flowers.

"That's what you smelled down in my workshop," Galen said.

I mumbled, *Yeah*, though what I'd smelled was hippie patchouli, a scent Dawn Carol had favored, if I remembered correctly. Hell, it was a scent every good hippie girl back then wore, and half the guys, too.

"London," Galen said suddenly, flipping his cigarette butt out in the yard like it was the all-consuming ocean. This was a crappy habit he had.

"Huh?"

"Jerry London, the dope dealer. She bought from him when she had chestnut hair and was a hippie. She complained that he always rubbed against her tits. She had huge cherry-red nipples under her no-bra blouse. I watched him stare at her like he was some drunk in a strip bar whenever she was in the Paddock Club."

The Paddock Club had been Lexington's premiere hippie bar, though those days were ending since Vietnam was well over and the brave Me-First 80s were facing us with a fetching, sardonic grin, *Come on, you know you want it, so go on and take it*. I stood and walked upstairs to retrieve two more beers. When I came back, Galen had begun carving. It was an effigy of Dawn Carol, he said. I watched two sorority girls out on their patio. One wore what looked like braids around her forehead and was dressed in a milk-pale hippie skirt, not the usual sorority a-go-go stuff. And those braids were more like White-girl imitation cornrows since they were not wound as small and as tight as the Blacks got them. Indeed, they were blonde I noted, but I kept my observation to myself, since Galen was so involved in his effigy. The girl with the fake cornrows gave a look our way. Galen huffed out something and when I looked back just the shorter sorority sister with coal black hair stood there rubbing her eyes. Someone called her and she went inside the brick sorority house.

"All that huff and puff brick didn't give Dawn Carol much protection," I commented.

"Cynicism doesn't become you," Galen replied.

We stayed outside on our patio for a couple more beers until Galen announced he had serious work to do. I climbed the outside stairs and then the inside ones, to look out my study's window as dusk fell. I was taking a French class on the University's dime since I'd become full time at the bookstore. Beckett's *Godot* made for sad and frustrating reading that night. I looked out to the sorority house—still only lights, none of the usual chirpy singing or shenanigans. Then I spotted a figure under a streetlamp on the sidewalk in front of that house. It was the woman with the milky-pale skirt and tight blonde braids. A large white dog joined her. She reached to pet the dog, but her gaze went directly to me—at least it seemed to. The French text before me swirled with Lucky's nonsense speech. I heard Galen curse downstairs; it sounded as if he'd hit himself with a mallet, something he rarely did, but then he didn't usually do woodwork after drinking.

In the morning, our paths crossed. Galen was scrambling eggs, being as cooking was his tertiary hobby after woodworking and women. He flipped a plate at me—an omelet with mushrooms, cheddar cheese, and green onions. Half of it spilled on the table.

"What's wrong?" I asked.

"London. I'm almost sure that sonofabitch did it. She bought from him."

"Did what?" I'd been playing twenty questions with Galen ever since we learned about Dawn Carol's murder. Today was starting no differently.

"Killed Dawn Carol. She always thought it was funny to lead him on and then short change him on the drug-money end too."

"Well, tell that damned burr-headed cop."

"I'm no snitch."

I scooped up the omelet and ate it, along with my first of a dozen cups of coffee and fake creamer for the day. I'd taken up smoking a pipe, too. I was young and invincible, what would it matter?

I'd gotten a promotion at the bookstore: I was now the trade book buyer. Sounds important, and I did handle a lot of money, but believe me, the salary was nowhere near commensurate, since this store was state-run. One of my jobs was to buy back textbooks. As I commented, hippiedom was dying, but the new, savvy me-ism loomed even worse. Complaint after complaint about the buyback prices of texts spewed out of otherwise seemingly responsible, well-groomed future citizens. Supply-and-demand meant nothing to them, even the business majors.

The buy-back bell rang and I strolled up to the counter. It was the girl with the braid around her face, holding an abnormal psychology text. I smiled, but she didn't respond. Her eyes stayed strangely filmed-over, as if she had cataracts at twenty-something. I gave her fourteen dollars for the book; it was going to be used again in summer session. Still no smile. The money lay between us on the counter.

"Thanks," I said, bobbing my head.

The money just sat there. I pointed at it. No response. I began to wonder if she were blind, but there was no dog, no white-and-red cane.

"Thanks. That's your money."

She turned away and walked out the door, leaving the bills on the counter. She was barefoot, I noted. Wearing a hippie tie-dyed skirt and barefooted.

"Miss? Miss!"

The cashier at the register looked at me. "That girl just left without taking her money," I told her.

"What girl?"

I looked from the cashier to the door to the counter. There was no money on it. I looked under the bin where we put books: there were only two math books and a freshman grammar text. But there was a smell: patchouli.

I pretended to not hear the buyback bell the rest of the afternoon, and I moved my desk's chair to concentrate on book orders. A list of French titles blurred in a comforting manner. I left work by the back door, avoiding the buyback counter altogether.

That evening, there was more activity at the sorority. Dawn Carol's memorial would happen tomorrow, Wednesday. A memorial without a burial since the morgue was holding her corpse as evidence. I watched half a dozen girls on their patio. Even from my distance, I could see that three of them were crying, the others offering comfort. Galen had a girlfriend over, so I sat hunched up on the higher stoop directly outside the kitchen, dealing with Beckett's *Godot*. The steps from the stoop led down to the back yard and the patio where we two had sat the night before. The house we rented was weirdly built, its front being ground level, its back jutting over a basement and the quickly falling landscape. The Dr. van Fleet now had three blooms. I thought about Galen's tall tale of Louie, Louie carrying roses to the sorority and gave a wry smile.

Night took forever to fall. There were just two sorority girls out on their patio now, which still had Derby Day decorations and wilting crepe paper hanging. A mist had set in, so

I couldn't see them clearly other than hair color and height. Blonde and black, about normal, was my observation. But one not so normal observation was that there sometimes seemed to be one girl, sometimes two, under the wet, drooping crepe. My butt was getting chilled from the stoop.

I thought I smelled weed drifting up toward me on that top step, but surely Galen wouldn't be smoking in the basement, what with that detective threatening to get a search warrant. That cop's not coming back, by the way, made us both nervous. Maybe that was his game, what did I know? I went for another beer, my third. The last sorority girls had gone in— well, not quite, since one stood on the patio petting a large dog in the increasing mist. Galen proclaimed that hippies couldn't be blonde. If that were so, then sorority girls surely couldn't pet large dogs. Through the mist I saw a flash. The lone girl had lit up a cigarette. Smoking in public? This was no sorority girl I knew. She and the dog walked around the brick sorority house to the sidewalk on the street, as if agreeing with my judgment. They stood there. I waved, even though I figured there'd be no response, what with the distance and the mist forming in the chill. She bent, however, to pet the dog, and then she did wave and the dog beat its tail on the sidewalk. Could I hear its thump in the mist? Who was I kidding? But then, didn't I hear it? And weren't the two of them under the same streetlamp as last night? And wasn't the dog yellow? Or was that the fog?

Screams erupted from Galen's workshop cum bedroom from his latest girl—I think her name was Denise. I watched as she ran out his back door, yelling "Asshole!" She looked up at me and flipped me a bird. Collateral damage. Then she was gone around the front of the house. I heard her throw something back, a beer can.

The next morning, Galen left early, disgruntled from last night's spat. It was his habit to go to the local breakfast dive, Omelet for U, after any lover's fight. I think he went there just to give a shot at picking up women. I brewed coffee and stared into the refrigerator at eight eggs and half a pack of bacon. No way I could handle cooking that. Stepping out onto the high stoop, I backed from the smell of patchouli. There was still mist from last night, and I gave a swipe of my hand to it and the patchouli smell. Below, by the rose bush, stood a blonde girl and beside her a large yellow lab that was the next best possible to a littermate for Louie, Louie.

"Galen's already left for work," I called, nothing better to say.

She turned. It was the blonde with the braids. She held up a white rose. I dropped my coffee cup twelve feet down onto the concrete below, where it shattered. When I looked from it, the blonde and the dog were gone. There wasn't even movement in the mist. I bent to look under the awning covering Galen's porch. Nothing other than the three chairs we kept there. I sneezed. Patchouli.

"Hello?" I called. "Hello?"

The mist cleared enough that I spotted one more rose on the bush. Four now. Well, five if she'd picked one.

"If you want your fourteen bucks, you know where to find me!" I shouted. I was shaking, looking down at the broken cup and still steaming coffee. I jumped up, put on a shirt and jogged to work, glancing over my shoulder as if the phantom girl might reach out with long, pearly nails.

That afternoon at the bookstore, Mildred motioned me over. Three women surrounded the sorority girl who knew Dawn Carol. This girl—her name was Janet—had just returned from the memorial service and she was showing pictures. The three women were cooing and comforting her. Mildred must have wanted me to do the same. Mildred had known Galen and me since we were kids collecting Matchbox Toys for my train set. Neither of us could do any wrong, hippie or no. So over I obligingly headed.

But the cornrow girl, as I'd begun to think of her, was standing by Kentucky blue T-shirts, holding them up before her. She had a white rose in her hair. Wide-eyed, I inhaled, wanting to run away and wanting to speak at the same time. Mildred called my name, so I kept up my original direction, tripping against the metal edge of a shelf.

"Such a pretty name," one of the women was saying as I neared.

"She's too beautiful to have been taken away so young," Mildred was saying.

"We were going to nominate her for homecoming queen next year."

Dawn Carol was fine looking, all right, though a bit short I remembered, so I didn't know about homecoming quality, especially in the bluegrass heart of this snooty thoroughbred state. But they were talking about a dead person, of course, so some *nihil nisi* was being spread like salve. Indeed, why not? Propriety is all right with me.

Mildred grabbed a photo from black-headed Janet as I joined them. "Wasn't she just stunning?" Mildred asked, pushing a photograph toward me.

The photo was of the cornrow girl, blonde hair and all. Yes, the cornrow girl was Dawn Carol, with her new blonde hair that I'd never seen. I began hiccoughing and jerked toward the T-shirts, backing into a shelf of fraternity steins. White roses fell from the ceiling, like huge hail in an approaching storm. One rose brushed my forehead and its thorn left a scratch. The cornrow girl, still standing by the T-shirts, plucked the one in her hair and held it out to me. She then motioned toward her friend Janet. When I looked to Janet standing beside Mildred a slash opened under Janet's right eye, another across her cheek down to her upper lip. Blood poured out. A full gash opened across her throat, and hot blood spurted onto my face, sopping my moustache. I knocked a stein to the floor where it shattered. Janet and Mildred and another woman grabbed me, their eyes worried, their grips sure, and their faces clear of cuts. By the T-shirts the cornrow girl still offered her rose. It was *her* face that was gashed. It was *her* face that was so freshly bloodied that it glowed under the store's fluorescent lighting.

"Your big yellow dog brought us a white rose this morning," a clear- but sad-faced Janet was saying when I righted myself from the shelving. "I found it when we were taking down the Derby decorations before the service. We didn't think . . ." She broke off into more tears.

Her brown eyes were wet and sincere. I looked from them to the T-shirts. Nothing.

Janet turned to Mildred. "Their dog used to bring us white roses last summer. We haven't seen it for nearly a year." Janet turned to me, "It has a weird double name . . ."

"Louie, Louie?"

"Yeah. Dawn Carol said that Louie, Louie sometimes met her and walked her to class. Even after she broke up with your friend."

Janet had a white rose in her hair that I hadn't seen, tucked behind her right ear. I knocked another stein off the shelf, but caught this one. *Where* . . . The floor was clean; no broken beer stein lay there. And Janet's face stayed perfectly clear, if you didn't count freckles, dimples, and make-up.

"Sorry," I coughed.

"For what?" Mildred asked.

At my age then, I thought hugging indicated a tryst was either taking place or very soon would. Nonetheless, I sucked up and gave Janet a hug, which caused Mildred to coo. Heading for my eleventh cup of coffee afterwards, I rubbed my left brow and startled at a small stinging cut there: a thorn from a falling rose?

Galen wasn't at the house when I got there. I thought about going out for a beer, but something held me back. Pozzo and Lucky entertained me as much as they did Didi and Gogo in Samuel Beckett's play. This is to say that they appalled me, as had the last five days. So I sat and pretended to read.

I smelled her long before I saw her. Patchouli, patchouli, patchouli. A combination of light steps and a silly romp were progressing up our house's inside stairs.

"Galen?" I called, even though I knew.

A brief flash lit the short hallway. She stepped into the study. This time her hippie skirt was an odd vermillion tie-dye, which had gashes of black flowing through it. Her blouse was an aged ivory, and she wore a black scarf about her neck. Louie, Louie—there was no doubting it was him now—padded behind her and walked over to lay a white rose on my knee. I reached to pet him, but she shouted,

"No! Touching would cause only sadness."

Louie, Louie backed away as if agreeing. I touched the white rose instead and received a prick for my reward.

"My little sister Janet is in danger," the dead Dawn Carol said. Her words came as puffs of mist, like what had filled the back yard for the last two nights. "You must convince Galen to talk." At this, she undid her scarf and blood gushed as if from an artery to spill over her ivory blouse, over Louie, Louie, and onto the worn Persian carpet. A black flash enveloped the room. I looked up from my hand and the white rose to see through the windows that the sun was setting. Where had time gone? The carpet pooled with blood. It still held warmth when I knelt and touched it.

Talk with Galen. But he outwaited me. I called both bars for faltering hippies, but he wasn't at either. Never say never, but I never knew phone numbers for any of the women he dated. So I walked downstairs to his workshop and left this note:

We need to talk about Dawn Carol. Louie, Louie left this.

I weighted my note down with a chisel and the white rose. The rose had blood spattered on it from Dawn Carol—that is, Dawn Carol's ghost and her ghost blood. Was it still on the carpet upstairs? I feared going up. Godot would just have to wait . . . some more.

Galen must not have come home, for I got up from the downstairs couch and had to make next morning's coffee. I did find a honeybun behind a can of baked beans on the back of a shelf, so at least that much was successful. I kept away from the back porch and headed to work on my usual path in yesterday's clothes. On Meadow Street a cop car flashed its light and pulled over. The passenger window went down and the burr-headed cop said, "Get in."

He handed me a coffee when I did and he pulled into the Campus Catholic Church's parking lot.

"We've checked you two out."

I was still looking at the coffee cup in half amazement, half suspicion.

"Go ahead, drink up. Lots of cream, no sugar, just like you take it. Like I said, we checked you two out. Truthfully, I've got bigger fish to fry than a two-bit marijuana bust." He nodded at my coffee cup again, so I drank some. He had indeed checked me out: it held the same ridiculous portion of fake cream that I used and no sugar. I nodded back at him.

"Miss Dawn Carol Baker hasn't been the only young woman raped and murdered in the fashion she was."

Not that I particularly knew the "fashion she was," but still, other murders were news to me, big news.

"A twenty-year old waitress the day after last Christmas. A UK coed last July Fourth. As active as your roommate is, I wouldn't be surprised if he'd slept with them both."

I remembered the coed from July Fourth, and I remembered that Galen *had* slept with her, or at least claimed to have when he saw her picture in the newspaper.

"We think this guy may be a serial killer getting more restless, but we're coming up with dead-end after dead-end. Hunches are all that's left. I have one about your roommate. He knows something, doesn't he?"

The cop had Cherokee brown eyes, just like Galen. He was about the age of Galen's older brother, the one who'd disappeared two years before. Galen had toyed with the idea of contacting Salvation Army, which evidently ran a missing persons file, but I think he was afraid to, afraid of what he'd find. And I agreed. Fully.

I looked out the car's window. Dawn Carol and Louie, Louie were standing on the steps of the church staring at us. Inhaling sharply, I spilled coffee on my leg.

"Hit a chord, did I?" the cop asked.

I lifted the cup to point at the church steps, but even as I did, I knew it was useless, for the two weren't even there for me to see now, though something white did lay on the brick steps. I didn't need 20-20 vision to know it was a rose.

"He's afraid of being a snitch."

The cop hit his steering wheel. "Damn it! July Fourth is coming up. Our resident shrink thinks a repeat is probable. Snitch? What, your roommate has some Eastern Kentucky hillbilly code of honor?"

"I'll talk with him. I will. One of Dawn Carol's sorority sisters works with me at the bookstore."

"Well, it just might be her who's next. Have you thought of that?"

"Yeah," I answered glumly. "Yeah. Yeah, I have."

"Okay," the cop said.

"Okay," I answered.

"Get on to work. Take the coffee with you. My name's on the bottom of the cup. And my phone extension."

I got out and the cop—Lt. Harrelson, I looked on the bottom of the cup—drove off. I waited a minute and then couldn't resist, so I walked to the church's front stoop. Ten years back, this was a New Age, ecumenical, Roman Catholic church under a vacuum-pressurized tent. Now it was a staid and dark red brick building with a crucifix on the roof and two on its double doors. Just a few steps away I clearly saw—a white rose.

The double doors melodramatically burst open, and a priest with purple trim around his black hat and cassock strode out, and my childhood upbringing strode in:

"Monsignor," I said, having gotten close enough to bend toward the rose.

"Don't. Touching would bring down harm!" He held a black leather book that I presumed was a Bible.

"She's a good ghost. She's warning me about—"

"I saw her and that hellhound. Spirits interfering with God's Providence cannot in any way or form be good. God's Providence must be fulfilled."

A rustling took place. The rose disintegrated into white petals on the sidewalk that slowly fashioned the name, "*Janet.*"

"She . . . Janet needs to be saved."

"Only God's Providence can save her." The monsignor had taken a step back on seeing the miraculous movement of the petals. "Hellfire," he whispered, pulling from the current ecumenical bag a bit heavily by leaning into Southern Baptist territory.

I bent for a single petal. It moved velvety between my fingers and dispensed a fragrance like patchouli.

"God's Providence," the monsignor hoarsely uttered as I walked away toward the bookstore, leaving him to bell, book, candle, and ranting.

Janet came in to work just before noon to relieve a full-time worker in what I referred to as our Dry Goods section. I wandered back to get a cup of coffee and on seeing her, handed her the white petal. "Pretend it's from Dawn Carol and Louie, Louie," I said. God's Providence be damned.

Tears welled, but didn't spill.

That night, I cornered Galen as he was stir-frying chicken and mushrooms. This was a planned attack on my part. I'd stopped at the liquor store and bought a bottle of French wine, hitting a bit out of my price range for some Medoc. This way-laid his Cherokee eyes.

I told him what the cop told me. I told him about Louie, Louie. I told him about Janet, Dawn Carol's little sorority sister. "She's cute," I added. "Black hair like yours." We both quaffed the Medoc, pretending we were Wall Street stockbrokers. Finally, I told him about Dawn Carol. I still hadn't gone upstairs to check the rug.

"What color was her hair?" Galen asked suspiciously.

I faltered. "She wore a braid, an African-American braid, all around her face. It was the jam." I threw in some on-the-spot slang to convince him.

"What color?" he persisted.

The oil he was using flared up and he pulled the pan off the fire. I checked the ceiling to make sure we weren't going to die.

"Blonde," I admitted. "But she had on three different hippie skirts and patchouli oil each time. And Louie, Louie was with her."

Galen grimaced and nodded toward the small bowl of mushrooms. I tumbled them in, leaning back in case there was another flare-up.

"Still changing clothes twice a day. But I knew she couldn't stop being a hippie down inside," he commented, shuffling the pan like he was cooking popcorn. "Okay."

"Okay?"

"Okay, I'll talk to the cop."

I immediately walked to the phone and called Harrelson, sending Galen into a panic. "I don't think he cares about marijuana," I said, "but save him a glass of wine. As a payback," I added, seeing Galen's disbelief.

Harrelson showed in an hour. I had to squirrel the last glass of Medoc away and open another bottle to keep Galen pretty much on the planet. This was just the opposite of what I would have expected: ex-Navy guy used to Shore Patrol becoming a bundle of nerves, naïve bookstore guy staying suave and congenial. Harrelson's eyes lit up when I put the wine in front of him. "Payback," I repeated. "I checked on you and you're a nice guy."

He grinned, gave toast, and Galen told him about Jerry London. Harrelson made a call on his walkie-talkie, then used our phone. He came back saying, "Camaraderie. We need more of it between divisions in the department. We could use some on the street, too." He finished the Medoc. "Damn, this is good," he commented. Galen's eyes narrowed as he looked at me. "My friend in drugs says this London guy is a real asshole."

"That's him, all right," Galen commented. Galen opened up about London rubbing against Dawn Carol before she turned blonde non-hippie, and her getting back at him by short-changing and taunting him sexually. I uncorked another bottle of wine. Galen just about buried his head on the table in disbelief. The three of us wound up playing Tonk, a card game Galen had forever been threatening to teach me. He and Harrelson, who'd also been in the Navy, took fifteen bucks from me by night's end.

And before week's end, Jerry London was in jail. That Saturday, I heard Galen shouting downstairs, "Louie, Louie!" I ran down. Galen stood on the back porch, arms akimbo like he was doing a go-go dance under his awning. It wasn't Louie, Louie, but a puppy that Louie, Louie could have easily sired. When the puppy saw me, he ran to the rosebush and plucked a white rose with his teeth and carried it to me.

"What are you going to name him?" I asked, smelling patchouli everywhere in intoxicating amounts.

"Blondie," Galen answered, gathering the pup's scruff. "Blondie, the true-blue hippie."

Ms. Sylvia's Home Cure

I's NOT LIKE YOU casually mention being stalked and hypnotized by a ghost, so it took a year for me to confide with Sylvia about the bewitching widow and her hookah. By then Sylvia and I were friends with benefits, though that phrase lay far in the future. What encouraged me to confide was a tit-for-tat. "Tit-for-tat" presents more untimely phrasing, because Sylvia disclosed that her early and overlarge breasts (Size 38-D) had provoked a "brash bitch" personality in both junior high and high school, in New Jersey and Kentucky respectively.

"I've toned it down. Now I'm just brash."

"Why'd you tone it down?" I huffed this out, since we were riding bikes and had just finished the last and steepest hill in Fayette County's reservoir park.

She pulled her honey-toned hair back to reveal a long white scar. I flinched and stopped pedaling, and she commented that maybe she'd tell me what happened some other time.

So, coasting our bikes down toward her pickup, I told her about the ghostly widow on the balcony of the Bungalow, the creature Sylvia herself had unwittingly saved me from last summer by walking on upstairs and then coaxing me on downstairs, even as that ghostly widow was mesmerizing me with her silk's voice, her pooling eyes, and her long, blood red nails. "If you hadn't come up," I told Sylvia, "I'd surely be joined in her legion of zombie substitutions for a long-before drowned husband." Sylvia looked at me askance, but I battled on, "I mean, you may not have seen them, but there were dozens of duplicates of her, and they were all twirling these sopping, adoring saps on the Bungalow's second floor, like in some ritual dance. Then you climbed the stairs, found me, and tapped my shoulder. I swear that a version of her dead husband was playing the Bungalow's scarlet baby grand before that."

"The baby grand was black."

"It was scarlet red until you came up. And remember how you complained that the wet dance floor was a lawsuit waiting to happen?"

"So then . . . you believe in ghosts," Sylvia said, dismounting her bike. She had fine strong legs, I must admit.

We began loading our bikes in her pickup, while darkness stretched tentative fingers. A university couple had been murdered here in the park two years before, which had caused the Metro police to double down on vagrants. It turned out that the murderer was a jealous ex working on a Ph.D. in chemistry. Whoops. Anyway, the park was supposedly haunted by the young couple. I figured Sylvia was referring to them, so I shrugged and searched about warily, wondering what ghostly shadow she'd seen.

"Well? You must believe in ghosts, then, right?" she asked again.

I shrugged again.

Sylvia laughed and hefted her bike into the pick-up. "Spoken with conviction, like a true bookstore bookworm." She plopped her plenteous breasts onto the side of the pickup's bed, bounced them, and grinned. "Listen, I know your love life is always burbling along like a mountain stream, but can you cancel your hot dates for tomorrow and come with me to my parents' house in Woodford County? That is, unless you planned on staying home to read science fiction and listen to the Cincinnati Reds on radio. Maybe you'll hear them splat out chewing tobacco on third base."

"I thought you'd dropped the bitch part from your double B act," I answered defensively.

"My good friend, you just naturally resurrect my double big B button." She shook her plenteous breasts and hair.

The upshot was that next morning we were once more in Sylvia's hot-red pick-up, heading for a farmhouse on a seventy-acre Civil War cotton plantation in Woodford County.

"You do know there was next to no cotton grown in Kentucky," I commented, reaching back for the Thermos I'd stowed in my overnight bag.

"Tell that to my dad. He moved down from New Jersey for a computer-engineering job at IBM. He and Mom arrived foolish rich, ready to believe any b.s. any realtor fed them. They just wanted a countryside getaway and a place to retire, simple and sweet.

"Then came complications. My mom was the first to hear creaking floorboards, opening windows and doors. My dad, ever the engineer, scoffed and installed ultra sensitive cameras, recorders, and finally, temperature gauges for what my mom swore were cold spots in the house."

Having passed the thirty stores in Versailles we turned onto a country two-lane. I spotted three crows perching atop a stone fence so old it must have been built by slaves, not uncommon for the area.

"There were three corbies, a-down, a-down," I half-sang.

When Sylvia looked at me, I said, "Peter, Paul, and Mary. Folk music."

"Bee-Gees. Disco. The Berlin Wall had fallen. Keep up with the times, bub."

"Now you're pushing my B button." As we passed the three crows, they stared with the infinite patience of that wise creature. "They can count, you know. They've done studies."

When that got no response, I asked, "So what happened with all the gadgets your dad bought?"

"They're still stored out here. But what happened was that they didn't disprove what Mom had been saying, but supposedly proved it. And then came an escalation."

"That doesn't sound good."

"It wasn't. Bloody knives, hangmen's nooses, smells. I think the parents would have suspected me since I was initiating my 38-D, double B state, but I'd been shipped to Granny's in New Jersey for the summer to see if she could do something with me. She couldn't, though all the boys in her neighborhood tried."

We were descending, heading down to the Kentucky River. My arm was hanging out the window, feeling damp already.

"Gotta go down before you go up," Sylvia said.

This provoked a blink from me, since Sylvia wasn't exactly a wordsmith. And then . . . was she talking about the surrounding landscape or about spreading her legs for the neighborhood New Jersey boys? Let it go, I told myself. "More crows," I noted instead. Then, "Look out!"

Sylvia slammed her brakes. A lanky man in a long black coat, despite the late morning summer mugginess, had emerged from surrounding trees to saunter across the road, leading a small white pig about the size of a fat cocker spaniel with a black leather leash and black hair surrounding its left eye, like a pirate's patch. The pig at least had sense enough to squeal, but the man just kept plodding.

"You ignorant, stupid—"

I grabbed Sylvia's arm before the man heard. He carried what looked like an antique single-shot rifle, and though it stayed pointed to the ground, his blue eyes turned to glare as if we had tread on his path, rather than vice-versa. His greasy Charles Manson hair didn't help matters. Then, plodding four more steps, once again ignoring us, pig waddling behind, he reached the road's other side. The pig's butt had a black patch of hair, too. Sylvia gunned the truck. I looked back to see the lanky man rolling a cigarette with a single hand, something of a feat in itself, especially as he paid rolling the cigarette no mind, but just stared our way.

"Most of the river rats who live around here are easy-going party folk. But now and then some turn prison-escapee scary. I keep Luke handy for them." She popped at the console between us and the lid sprang to reveal a revolver with a long silver barrel.

"That's Luke?"

"As in *Cool Hand Luke*. My home cure." She closed the console. "There's more I gotta tell you about my mom and dad's place." She checked the rear view mirror and so did I, but the creep and his pig and his rifle had slunk into the woods. Sure enough, we started ascending again along the road.

"The guy smelled like a walking country ham," I commented. "Or maybe it was his pre-salted pet pig."

"That's one of the smells my mother complained about. Cured country ham. She grew up in a Jewish neighborhood, so the smell made her queasy."

It turned out that the summer when Sylvia was staying with her grandmother, dead animals started getting plopped on her parents' front porch, back porch, inside on their expensive cherry dining room table, even inside their new double-door refrigerator. "Mom and Dad hired a security company—remember they were only coming here on weekends—but that didn't stop matters. By the time I returned from Granny Jenson's, Mom and Dad got unnerved and put the place up for sale. This was fine with my Double B personality, since I pined to stir matters in the local Catholic high school here in Lexington."

"It's been for sale all this time?"

"Yes and no. Eight years ago my dad started renting it out dirt cheap for weekend getaways, since no one from Woodford County would even look at the property to buy."

She slowed for a sharp curve that led onto a straight stretch with a cornfield on our right.

"Who dresses a scarecrow in black?" I asked, tapping my half-open window.

"Maybe that skinny jerk with the walking smoke-cured pig."

"Maybe," I said.

"It's not far."

Driving through Sylvia's 'not far' conjured a menagerie of animals. The crows now congregated in murders, that quaint term for a flock. Squirrels cocked their heads, skunks waddled out in front of us. Raccoons and opossums hissed. Two weasels slunk wetly in roadside ditches. I think I even saw the blur of a wildcat among some brush, but when I told Sylvia this, she poo-pooed my eyesight.

This farm too had a stone fence. Suddenly, the animals we'd passed as living now turned into carcasses. Four ground-hogs were slung over the fence, a tactic not unusual for rural Kentucky. It was something of an imitative magic warning, though never in this quantity. Then came skunks, raccoons— all the animals we just saw, even some rotting mess I thought might for sure be a bobcat, it too slung atop the stone fence. I rolled my window down and sniffed, expecting the stench of death. It was there all right, an undercurrent like soured bacon, permeating summertime air.

"You know, I wondered about some of those night animals out roaming back there on the highway in the daylight."

"Maybe they feel safer in daytime, you mean?"

That gave us food for thought as we turned into the farm. There was a motorized electric gate, and Sylvia entered its code, explaining that it was more of her dad's handiwork.

The long driveway's sides held young trees that topped out several feet over my head. "My dad hired someone to plant those when we first moved. They replaced—"

"Cotton?"

"Ha and ha. Field corn. I only saw withered cornstalks when we first came to look at the property with the realtor woman, and then again whenever we returned to pick up furniture and knickknacks. We came back in the daytime, just like now. My mother insisted it be daytime, and Dad sure didn't protest. They didn't talk much once we were here that last time. I thought maybe they were fighting, but Mom gripped Dad's arm and he kept patting Luke in its holster."

"Luke—oh, the gun?"

Sylvia nodded. I caught something on the right, a dark, lank shadow moving behind a line of trees.

"Do the river people come here? The river rats?"

"No one comes here. The pizza place we passed six miles back won't deliver here. Mom and Dad won't come here. They haven't been here in seven years. I hardly had enough time to mingle and gather gossip from the locals, but surely they think there's some bad weirdness associated with this place."

"So. So then why are we here, Sylvia?" I'd picked up that initial "So" speech habit from a woman of high, unrequited love, losing her but keeping her speech pattern. In more practical matters, the house lay ahead. It was a two-story affair, supposedly ante-bellum, though it didn't look quite that old to me. But who knows, maybe it was. There was the requisite balcony over the front porch, after all, and the exterior was white and in sore need of a paint job. And four pillars supported the balcony, though they were square and not grooved in the round Greek Acropolis style. Sylvia pulled into a gravel circle and stopped before the house's front double door. Two cast-iron, politically incorrect black jockeys held welcoming lamps on a cracked sidewalk that presented more of a grass-and-dandelion salad than civilized concrete.

"So why? We're here to make a point. That's why."

I stared at the jockeys with their shiny coal black faces and their exaggerated 'Yes, massah' grins. "Your dad sent you?"

She kept the truck running and rolled down her window to listen and sniff the air just as I had minutes before.

"God no. He doesn't know I'm here. He and Mom would have cardiac arrest if they knew."

"Well, someone knows, right?" I was thinking of the carcasses slung over the stone fencing and the lanky shadow I'd seen slinking among the trees.

"Lorrie. I told Lorrie. Did you tell Galen?"

"I don't see Galen that much because of Lorrie." This was true. Lorrie had taken the prize as far as keeping Galen enthralled, nearly a year now. She'd broken him up with Cheryl, which was fine with me, since I liked Lorrie a good deal more. She was studying to be a librarian, just a slow step away from a bookstore manager in my mind.

Sylvia was still sniffing the air, her nose working like a hound's.

"What do you smell? Blood? Death? An old Civil War battlefield?"

She grimaced and continued sniffing, then reached back for a holster, got out of the truck, and strapped it around her waist, then leaned in for the revolver and shoved it in the holster. "I don't know. Country ham, maybe." She slapped the gun on her hip. "There's another under your seat, if having one will make you feel better."

"I haven't shot a gun in ten years." I remembered shooting a ground hog with Galen and a friend. It felt stupid then and even stupider now with what we'd passed out front. Mean-spirited was the phrase that came to mind.

"Just offering," Sylvia said. "You know where it is, and it's loaded. Here's a spare key to the truck you can keep. Once we get everything out, I'm going to lock it and that gun in it."

I pictured the creep with the pig on the highway and that lanky black shadow threading among the trees. Taking the key, I looked at the silver gun on her waist, then pulled the blued snub nose from under the seat.

"Hell. Let's just try not to shoot one another, okay?" I held the snub nose in my palm and looked to Sylvia. "You have a holster for this one?"

She shook her head. "Just stick it in your pants and try not to blow off your nuts. I would be so sad." She stuck out her tongue.

"Sadness is relative." I wound up shoving the revolver into the back of my pants, figuring maybe the bullet would travel harmlessly down the crease of my sweaty butt.

Once inside the house, we again both paused to sniff. The smell of old, old, old and empty, empty, empty was all I could conjure. But Sylvia was right: Maybe country salt-cured ham underneath. And while I didn't exactly feel ghostly cold spots, the house was cool—from the tall ceilings and the surrounding shade trees, likely. I gave another sniff.

"You realize we've both used our noses as much as our mouths since we arrived," I commented.

"Ooh-la-la, such an offer." Sylvia gave her hips a double twist. Something hollow shattered in the back when she did. She set down her suitcase and pulled out Luke. I felt a trickle of sweat heading for the snub nose pointing at my butt. The hell if I was going to pull it out to keep Luke company, though.

We moved in tandem past the stairs and two very amateur paintings of Civil War officers with the requisite glaring eyes, frowns, and moustaches. Sylvia thought renters had left them. Then we passed by two rooms with closed doors while heading through the house toward the rear, where the crash had sounded. There was a spacious kitchen with a built-in refrigerator and oven and a fancy butcher's block table. No renters had left those. We walked outside onto a breezeway connecting to what once must have been a freestanding kitchen detached from the house to prevent fires. Its open door emitted the century-old smell of smoke. It also swallowed any light and looked forbidding, like the jaws of a junkyard pit bull. I thought I saw something pale swaying inside, when Sylvia said, "There!"

To our right, on a flagstone patio, lay the source of the crash: an overturned clay churning pot. A small pig was rooting in it, eating something. My eyes watered from a sudden combination of smoke and salty, greasy ham.

"Lorrie!" a voice yelled. It was the lanky man, still in his long black coat, still holding his single shot antique rifle. He looked up at us. "I been chasing her half a mile. She got off her leash. Sorry about your pot there. I'd pay, but I don't got no money."

"She's your pet?" Sylvia asked.

"Pet? Hell no. Me and the family's going to eat her next Sunday night, a week. You and your boyfriend be welcomed to come, if'n you be staying that long." He grinned, though I couldn't see any teeth, only his bright blue eyes poking pale skin.

"You know how to shoot that thing?" he asked Sylvia.

She turned, cocked the firing pin, and shot, hitting an old can in the weeds about thirty yards away.

"Dang! You might be related to my old lady. Gotta go now. Sorry about your crockery. Come along, Lorrie!"

When he put the leash back on the pig and kicked it, it stopped rooting to follow him with a squeal. We watched him enter a clearing in the trees, which descended, leading down to the river no doubt. His black hair lifted in a greasy breeze and then he was gone, though the pig's squeals still climbed to reach us.

"He's going to eat Lorrie?" I asked.

"Why's his pig named after my roommate?"

I stared back toward the clearing where the man and pig had descended. "Chance," I said, though I wasn't sure I believed that. I walked over to the tin can she'd shot. It was Campbell's tomato soup, the label barely clinging through the years and weather. I thought of Andy Warhol and fifteen minutes of fame and spotted a nearby refuse pile of old cans and bottles. Picking up the can, I admired the hole through it and carried it to the pile.

"Jesus," was my comment, for three rotting skulls topped the rubbish. They looked like dog skulls, their canine teeth ridiculously long and sharp, hair and skin clinging about them. Shreds of a leather collar lay under one skull. I looked back for Sylvia, but she was unlocking the side door to the garage. She turned and motioned for me. "Let's unpack Dad's hi-tech snoop equipment," she called.

I walked over and entered the garage. Sylvia was busying herself with the first of three small crates, reading instructions stuck inside its lid. A barred window on the far wall let a beam of sunlight shine through like in a medieval picture, except there was no kneeling saint illumined by angelic, grace-filled dust motes. Beside that window stood a pink refrigerator.

"Abandoned refrigerators are a bugaboo of mine," I commented.

Sylvia looked up from the instructions.

"I mean, who knows what could be inside."

She grimaced and strode over. If she'd had on red heels there would have been some mighty clacking even on the crumbling concrete floor. As it was, her tennis shoes slapped out pitilessly. She yanked the door open and let out a scream. I rushed over to see her gawking at . . . the pale pink, empty insides of the refrigerator that was evidently plugged in, for its light was on.

"See? That's why we're here. To bunk all this ghost business." She bent and rubbed her hand over the empty racks and even stuck her head in, twisting to look up. "All clear, except for some spirit world mold."

She strutted back to the first box and began emptying its contents on a table. I peered into the refrigerator she'd left open, unsure whether I was relieved or angry. Either way, I wasn't going to stick my head in like she had. Besides, she hadn't opened the freezer section, which stared at me ominously. Other than the refrigerator, the table, and the three crates, there were two small green metal cabinets on rollers and a larger one about my height, all of them closed. After Sylvia's theatrics over the refrigerator I wasn't about to comment on their potential. One more filmy, barred window lay on the garage's east side, and already the sunlight was lessening in it. The afternoon was moving on.

"*Funiculi, funicula!*"

"Sylvia!" I yelled, turning to see her tick-tocking her upper body while clinking two hand-sized metal tripods against one another. "Sylvia, stop!"

Giving one last clink she looked at me with a shrug. I rushed to the table where she'd laid out a dozen of the small tripods.

"What?" she asked reasonably enough.

I looked into her eyes: it was Sylvia, not some revenant Italian widow capsizing Sylvia's soul by singing a ridiculously hypnotic song. I picked up one of the tripods. "So. What are these for?"

"No, bub. Explain your panic. Don't change the subject."

So I told her about the hookah widow singing that same silly song, trying to hypnotize me on the Bungalow's dance floor. I didn't tell her about the widow seeming to shape-shift into Sylvia herself—or maybe that was just delusion on my part?

"Is she still down there at the Bungalow? On the balcony?"

I shook my head. "Galen says there must have been a junction of weirdness that summoned the ghost widow from Italy that night."

"A junction of weirdness," Sylvia repeated. "That's what I think was going on here fourteen years ago when my parents bought this place. I think some damned hillbilly family wanted the property but couldn't afford it, so decided to make my mom and dad miserable. They made me the happiest teenager on earth, since I sure didn't want to spend my weekends here in silty river boondocks outside a rink-dink hillbilly town. But now, well, that seclusion holds at least partial attraction."

A glaring face filled the far window, and blood spattered its upper pane. I saw this over Sylvia's right shoulder. It looked as if some whiskey-headed hick glared in just before a suicidal bird flew full tilt into the pane. Sylvia saw my alarm and turned. When she did, the window morphed back to its patina of friendly dust.

"Did you see something?" she asked.

"A cardinal flew by." When you're lying, it's best to toss some off-the-wall detail. But then, of course, you shouldn't be lying to friends.

Sylvia tilted her head then held one of the tripods before me. "These are motion sensors. They work on a beam of laser light that sends back a signal when it gets broken by any physical object. I don't guess they'd do any good for ghosts, though your hookah widow might prove an exception with her physique. Breasts have a way of doing that." Sylvia grinned and indicated the tripods. "There are twenty of them. Takes two to dance in teamwork, so that makes ten spots we can install them for the night."

I took the thin-legged metal instrument from her and plinked it with my fingernail.

"What kind of bird did you see in the window?"

I blinked. "A . . . uh—"

"You shouldn't lie to friends."

I sighed. "All right. It wasn't a bird. I thought I saw face, then a splat of blood, then both went away. Maybe it was the wind shifting leaves."

"That's what my mother said she saw lots of out here. Staring faces, blood, dripping or in splatters. But they'd disappear when she walked near. If my dad hadn't used all these instruments, he likely would have had her . . . well, not committed, since they love one another, but something. Called in the analysts and the Zoloft or whatever they prescribed back then."

Giving a last glance at the window, we turned our attention to the gizmos Sylvia's computer whiz dad had concocted. Besides the ten motion sensors, there were three ultra-sensitive temperature gauges with built-in recording devices that could measure changes as little as three degrees Fahrenheit. There were four movie cameras with night film. All these connected by radio wave to an electronic console with battery-pack backup, which filled a pink suitcase to match the pink refrigerator. Last, there was a Geiger counter. Sylvia and I both shrugged at this item, but read the accompanying typed explanation her father left:

Some Duke University paranormal investigators conjecture that what turn of last century investigators labeled 'plasma residue' from spiritual manifestations might be radioactive decay. To cover all bases, I procured this Geiger counter. Maybe a grandson will find it a fascinating relic of Cave-age science.

The Geiger's actual instructions were pretty simple: turn the switch on, leave promptly if the clicking gets too loud and too bunched together.

"Aw," Sylvia said. "A grandson. My sentimental, computer engineering dad."

"Your sentimental and practical computer engineering dad," I replied, placing my finger on the advice to skedaddle if the Geiger became too lively. "So. Did any of this work?"

"My mom says this equipment is what convinced Dad to abandon the place. There were recordings of cold spots. And the cameras would catch shifting gobs of light, bloody carcasses that would appear, but the motion detectors wouldn't get tripped."

"Sounds as if the ghosts wanted to have their cake and eat it too."

"Meaning?"

"Meaning they can kill animals and dump their carcasses, but they don't constitute enough matter to trip a motion detector."

"Lord, I believe, help my unbelief."

"Exactly."

We spent the next three hours placing the cameras and detectors about the house. "Too bad Dad didn't buy a smell-o-meter," Sylvia commented.

"Salt cured country ham?"

"You got it." She sniffled and looked about the hallway we stood in. Had the two paintings shifted askew? I walked to straighten one. The Confederate captain or whatever-he-was smirked.

We decided to sleep in a second floor bedroom that accessed the balcony.

"An escape hatch is always good," I commented while leaning over the balcony's rail. "Though it's a double edged sword, since it offers one more access point to us at night."

"That's what Luke's for. In case some ghost shimmies up one of those pillars."

At the mention of Luke, his cousin the snub-nose delivered a pinch to my butt.

Late afternoon came on. A murder of crows lifted from a clump of trees in the distant area where Sylvia said the bend of the river lay. Already, fog was rising from there. When I asked Sylvia if this was normal, she replied she had no idea, giving me something of a bookstore, bookworm shrug.

Since neither of us were particularly good cooks, we'd bought weenies and buns and canned chili. I carried a bag of charcoal toward the stone grill, half-expecting the charred carcasses of the three dogs or coyotes. But the grill was nearly pristine. Soon enough we had coals lit, after I double-doused them over Sylvia's feminine sprinkling of lighter fluid. Sylvia commented that I was a real caveman, to which I returned my bookstore, bookworm shrug. While we'd remembered tongs to take the hot dogs off, I realized we'd forgotten an oven mitten the moment I placed the canned chili over the coals. Sylvia thought there was one in the kitchen so she went in.

While she did, I inhaled the surrounding quiet, thinking I could get used to this in contrast to even small city Lexington's hustle. I looked up to see that two of the house's six back windows on the second story were open. Sylvia's dad needed to vet his renters more closely or the place would turn into mushroom and mold.

Sylvia walked out with two oven mittens. "My mom's right," she said, handing them to me. "The whole time I was searching the kitchen drawers I felt like someone was standing behind me."

"The empty house phenomenon," I said. "Just like the abandoned refrigerator phenomenon."

"I guess. And that damned smell of country ham. I also heard noise from upstairs, like someone was opening a window."

I glanced up to see all six windows now closed. Not only that, but shapes filled each window to look down, all wearing those long black coats the creep with the pig wore. Women, teenagers, and men. They quickly backed away.

"Two of those windows were open when you went in." I motioned with the tongs I had remembered. "Now they're all closed. And . . ."

Sylvia turned around to look up. "And," she prompted.

"And I swear I just saw faces looking down from all six windows."

Sylvia slapped Luke and looked up. "Well," she said, "Let's find out."

Sylvia's father's doodads worked with miniature transmitters. We'd kept the pink suitcase console nearby on a picnic table. After looking at the now empty windows, we walked to check the console. Nothing had triggered any receivers. We'd tested the sensors, so we knew they worked. We looked back up at the empty windows.

"Lord, I *don't* want to believe, so help my unbelief," Sylvia commented. "I guess wind or simply chance could have knocked those windows closed."

"And the faces?"

"Your empty house phenomenon."

I shrugged. Sylvia returned my shrug, but I noticed that she removed a box of bullets from her handbag and replaced the single spent cartridge from shooting the tin can with a live one. We then turned to the serious task of gourmet cooking, managing not to burn the hot dogs. We'd done a fair amount of work that afternoon, so we nearly finished the pack.

"Suppose," I said between munches and watching the sun set, "suppose that Galen's right about randomly gathering influences . . ."

Sylvia guffawed. "You're saying that Galen's another Jung?"

I don't know why Sylvia's saying this surprised me. Her sometimes brusque manner covered the fact that she had majored in anthropology and taken a minor in psychology to wind up working in a vaguely related job as docent for the state historical society's Mary Todd Lincoln museum by dint of her outgoing personality.

"I wouldn't go that far. But maybe he's onto something."

"Your point?"

"What if the two of us are randomly gathered influences?"

"His—what?—junction of weirdness?"

That bulb got planted in the back of our minds like a black tulip as we drank beers and watched the sun set, then toted the pink suitcase and Luke and his snub-nosed cousin upstairs to the spacious bedroom.

Sylvia's mom and dad had carried the rental amenities only so far, so there were no TVs to watch, no stereos to play. The house was situated in the boondocks anyway, so even Lexington's two TV stations were a bit out of range. Remembering this, Sylvia had packed a transistor radio from her teenybopper years. She pulled it out and turned it on. The Versailles station was playing country-rock, a vile mixed form if ever there were one. She found WVLK from Lexington.

"AAAH—AAAH—aaah, Stayin' alive" banged out, already an oldie. Sylvia twisted her hips and I joined in, in my bookstore, bookworm manner. Luke's cousin, the snub nose, rubbed the wrong way, so I placed it on a dresser, facing the door, which we had locked from the inside. I grimaced at my face in the dresser's dusty mirror but smiled at Sylvia's rotating hips, which almost made the mirror shine.

One thing led to another. Soon enough it turned dark outside and soon enough we were snuggling on the bed, even though the station's music kept its frantic disco pace. Sylvia was the world's softest kisser, I'd discovered months before, so I was happy to continue slurping, though boys will be boys and her 38-D breasts soon caught my attention. I palmed one, moving toward its already hard nipple.

But I stopped, because a cloying smell of cured ham filled the room. If you've never been in a homespun curing room, count yourself lucky. Salty pork and grease molecules shove out half the oxygen, while the other half gets shoved out by moldy smoke. That's what filled the room—enough to hurt my throat.

And with that smell, the room's lights went out. This left the console spewing an odd green, which started blinking, casting on-off glows against the plaster walls and ceiling. Still shoeless from dancing, we got off the bed, each giving a yelp of surprise at the floor's coldness. We ran to the pink suitcase. Eight motion sensors indicated intrusion. The only two that didn't were the one for our balcony and the one just outside our door. There were only four temperature gauges; we'd placed them where Sylvia's mom had complained of "cold spots." All four registered drastic negative drops, making us more aware of the cold floor. I went to the bed and put on my shoes and carried Sylvia's to her, as she stayed bent studying the console.

There were only four security cameras, since they came expensive, even for Sylvia's parents and their money, even for her dad and his tech savvy. We'd placed one outside the back door, one outside the front door, one in the hallway outside our door, and one facing the door to the cellar. The one outside our door flickered, revealing the hall filled with incandescent, vaguely human-shaped blobs, nine or so. They had heads and shoulders, but no connecting neck. And amorphous arms, no legs. The center of their heads glowed brightest. Sylvia placed her finger onto one glow.

"That's where I'll shoot the sons of bitches."

The screen emptied. A bumping hit against the door. We looked at one another. Sylvia stood back and aimed about shoulder height and nodded for me to open the door. When I did, the lights came back on and the small pig from before ran in, dragging its black leash.

Sylvia didn't fire, but steadied her gun against something I couldn't see on the door's other side.

"I was hoping you'd shoot it, save me and the clan that trouble."

I didn't even need to peep around to know it was the hillbilly creep in his drenchy, smelly black coat.

"You raise that rifle, you're a dead man," Sylvia said.

"I'm already that. Dead, dead, dead."

A hiss sounded, like air being let out of a balloon. The pig turned to face the door and began squealing. I peeked around to see an empty hallway. Looking at Sylvia, I pointed to indicate I was going to turn on the hall light and she nodded. The pig collided with my feet as I did, nuzzling me with a small tusk that half tickled, half pinched. As I flipped the light switch, I caught a black form heading down the stairs. Now I wanted

the cousinly revolver. I walked backwards and fetched it. The
console stopped blinking, but the pig kept nuzzling my ankle.

"I saw something heading down the steps."

"Everything on the board has returned to normal."

Sylvia and I spoke at the same time. The pig gave up trying
to get my attention and pitty-patted to Sylvia.

"Well, you're real enough," she said, addressing the pig,
which looked up at her expectantly, awaiting a caress or tidbit.

We walked downstairs, guns at ready—at least Sylvia's was.
I suggested I walk first, since she was the one who knew what
she was doing with a revolver and I feared I'd shoot her back
or my foot—the gun was certainly out of the crack of my butt
now, so at least my rear end was safe. The pig stayed next to
Sylvia, snorting calmly, rhythmically. Since it weighed a good
deal less than 50 pounds, I supposed it was youngish.

The front door looked secure. In movies I'd seen where
people placed bottles on doorknobs or glued wires that would
break if the door opened, and I wished I'd thought of taking
either precaution. But then, we had high tech, didn't we? All
of Sylvia's dad's contraptions plugged in to extension cords
with that bank of back-up batteries? As we walked toward the
kitchen and the back patio, the pig once more began squealing. A young woman in a black coat pointing a rifle at us
sifted downward from the ceiling like dust. Sylvia fired and
the woman dissipated onto the floor, leaving a gummy black
residue the pig snorted at, clacking its hooves on the hardwood.

I gingerly toed the residue with my tennis shoe and had to
fight to get my foot back, it was so sticky. The tip of my tennis
shoe let off acrid smoke and the little pig's nose crinkled as it
backed to stand near Sylvia again.

"Good boy," I assured the pig.

"Good girl," Sylvia said. "Lorrie, remember?"

Whichever it was, we both liked its comforting snorts. I looked up at the ceiling: the house seemed more pre-Civil War to me now, as the ceiling was at least twelve feet high. There was a ceiling trap door about ten feet from where we stood, between the two bedroom doors before the kitchen. But the woman's black form had descended from directly over us, not from it. What to say? Magic is when you're filled with wonder; horror is when you stop thinking. I looked from the ceiling to see Sylvia once more replacing a spent cartridge with a live one she'd pulled from her bra. Size D was working in her favor. She tossed me the spent cartridge.

Lorrie the pig was snorting now, rooting at the baseboard, which it sniffed along, heading toward the kitchen. But she stopped at the door on our right. She began bumping that door, giving out small cries amid snorts. If I'd been in a thinking mode, I would have thought, *Too much like an abandoned, closed refrigerator*. But I wasn't. Sylvia, however, was:

"That's one of the rooms with a motion detector. It's one of the rooms that indicated motion." She stood back, once more raising her revolver. I obliged by repeating what I'd done upstairs, flinging the door open, except this time I too kept my gun at ready.

We stepped in and I flipped on a light switch. The room's stench knocked us back. In piles around the room—on the white coverlet bed, on the dresser, on the bedside table, on the small walnut secretary—lay human bones. Like the dog or coyote bones topping the rubbish heap, these still had flesh clinging to them. Seven or more human skulls stared back, some with splotchy hair still attached. The pig had stayed outside and she began squealing. Sylvia turned in time to fire at a young man pointing a rifle at us. He dropped down as before, leaving a gummy black residue outside the door.

"Noooooo!" echoed about the hallway.

The stench in the room was gagging, so we exited, stepping over the man's tarry substance. The scream of "Nooooo" kept sounding and I placed my hands over my ears, as did Sylvia. Then I slammed the door shut. Immediately, both sound and smell disappeared. Even the leftover stench clinging to our nostrils and our hair left. The smell of old, old dust silently clung once more to the air. I glanced at the two amateur Confederate paintings on the hallway's wall, with their no-nonsense Hey-we-really-won-didn't-we-boys looks. I flipped them a bird.

Sylvia bent, since Lorrie the pig was pushing something along with her snout. With a snort, the pig left it by her shoe. It was a grimy Confederate Civil War cap, with everything from spider webs and leaves and dirt to probable bloodstains. It was embroidered, so it had belonged to an officer. I looked to the paintings again. The younger man on the right wore a cap just like this one. In both paintings, I saw resemblances to the creep who kept showing up. Sylvia did too, for she said,

"The one on the left is father to the one on the right. They both look like the creep with those eyes and those sallow cheeks."

Dead, dead, dead, echoed in my mind.

"Did you say that?" Sylvia asked me.

"I . . . I don't think so."

"Your revolver is cocked." She pointed at the blued snub nose. "Be careful where you point it."

"How do I change that?"

Sylvia snorted and took the gun from me and showed me how, pulling back on the hammer while holding in the trigger, then easing the hammer.

"Where's the safety latch?" I asked when she gave it back.

"Revolvers don't have a safety. How'd you even know to cock the hammer?"

How? Truth was, I didn't know. I'd only shot a rifle and shotgun before. And truth was, I didn't remember cocking the hammer or saying *Dead, dead, dead.*

"Maybe you should keep both guns," I said weakly, recalling Galen's comment about a junction of weirdness.

A dry laugh echoed from the kitchen. No, it was from upstairs. No, it was from the back porch. No, it was from the room we'd just been in.

"Fuck you!" I yelled. I cocked the hammer and fired at the closed door.

There was a clatter and Sylvia inhaled. Looking to her closed eyes I realized I'd screwed up a big law of gunmanship: Don't fire unless you see your target. Still, I felt certain I'd done right, so I opened the door and saw that I had: another pile of steaming black tar lay just over the threshold, opposite the one Sylvia had shot. There was a small difference, and that was a Civil War sword lying on the floor, just like one of the two that the Southern dandies outside on the wall held.

Now the house filled with wails and screams. Windows rattled in their frames. Lights flickered on then off, and a deep taste of iron blood and a smoke that smelled horribly of burnt fat and flesh filled the hall, swirling as if the walls themselves emitted it.

"Dead, dead, dead! Die, die, die! Meat, meat, meat!"

These shouts echoed while the lights flickered, accompanied by crisp snaps indicating shorts in the wiring. Was the entire house going to burn? The black pitch puddles inside and outside the door began to sizzle.

"Dead, dead, dead! Die, die, die! Meat, meat, meat!"

Both paintings fell, splintering their frames.

"My husband! My son! My husband! My son!" This replaced the previous shouts. Lorrie the pig began squealing mightily and we turned to see a blood-spattered dirty white dress de-

scending the stairs carrying a rifle pointed outward. Once the figure reached the small landing, it and its rifle turned toward us. Sylvia fired. So did the specter in the dress, and my shoulder jerked back—I first thought from my gun's recoil, then realized I hadn't shot. I was hit. Three more blood-spattered dresses descended. Sylvia didn't wait for them to turn on the landing before she fired. Lorrie had not stopped squealing.

I felt my shoulder burning. It smelled like food. *Dead, dead, dead.* I felt my thumb cocking the firing pin. Underneath her Bee Gees flowery T-shirt, Sylvia's flesh smelled. *Food, food,* I thought, *meat.* The smell of her blood, my blood, ran through me like dark chocolate, like cured ham. I raised my revolver and aimed at Sylvia's honey blonde hair. Lorrie the pig kept squealing and Sylvia fired again, bringing down a boy with a rifle to create another puddle of steaming tar dripping down the steps. A young woman fairly oozed down from the chandelier over the door to point her rifle and grin hideously. Several of her teeth were missing. As she nodded at me, her brown-stained, blood-stained dress swayed hypnotically. Her teeth turned bright and immaculately white, her lips turned plump, kissable, and scarlet. My finger tightened on the trigger.

"Bookstore, I love you, but shoot!" Sylvia shouted.

I moved to fire at her—not Sylvia, but the thin hillbilly ghost with the rotting teeth and the swaying dress—somehow connecting and dropping her to the ground, once more to form a puddle of steaming tar. Two seconds, three, then all the puddles fried into ashes. I thought I heard church bells from when I was a kid. I inhaled the clean, fresh air of freedom. No more ham.

Sylvia was fumbling with her bra, trying to reload. She dropped a bullet on the floor and cursed.

"There won't be any more," I said.

"How the hell can you know?"

"I just know."

She made a face at me and kept loading the three bullets she had, then stooping to gather the one she'd dropped even as Lorrie the pig nudged it toward her tennis shoe.

But I was right, though I didn't know why I was right. Was it some shade in the young ghost woman's eyes when I managed to shoot her and not Sylvia, like her intruding, panting will had urged me to do? Was it the cessation of squealing from Lorrie the pig? Or my perception that lightness played the air, when in fact the air stayed as dusty as it had been? Or the lights staying on, as bright or brighter than before? Or the suddenly calm, non-beeping console upstairs? Or the tar cooling and turning to dust? Ashes to ashes?

No, it was the absence of that cured ham smell that convinced me.

"We need to—" Sylvia stopped on seeing my shirt spattered with blood. Lorrie began bumping the same door behind us, cracking its frame. She looked back with a snort. Now, now I felt pain in my shoulder, and lots of it. My initial shock was over, I was nauseous, still I nodded at Sylvia and stepped to open the door. There was no need for her to fire, though, for the room was antiseptic; no powder, no black steaming tar, no skulls, no bones, no stench. A large pink doily glowed atop the dresser. All that was left from before was the sword on the floor, which Lorrie the pig nudged toward me.

Grimacing, I fell against the wall to catch my breath. Lorrie kept nudging the sword until it touched my foot. Bending to lift it, I nearly blacked out from pain. Its steel was polished, not rusty and tarnished.

"Goddamn, this hurts!" I yelled, slapping the flat of the sword to my shoulder. A wad of dried blood expelled a Minie ball, which hit the floor with a leaden clunk. The sword felt like a mother's comforting hand, so I pressed it to the wound.

My shoulder warmed and tightened, skin stretching like a balloon to nearly heal, leaving a grandly red, grandly tight hot bulb of flesh. The sound of crinkling, like a grill filled with chicken spattering and burning wild, filled the air. The powdery, tar-colored granules all around us disappeared in small, bouncing pops. Music from the transistor radio upstairs drifted down, that jaunty Beatles' song, "When I'm Sixty-four."

I didn't think I'd ever see Sylvia cry, and of course I didn't. But guess what? My bookstore, bookworm eyes got pretty wet. "Let's go up with the music and that console," I suggested.

"Let's go up where I left the box of cartridges," Sylvia replied. She held the partly flattened Minie ball in her hand. "Damn, these things are nasty. Seventy caliber, at least."

"That's my girl."

The Beatles sang on, and plenty of other oldies played as we sat on the bed, but Lorrie the pig and the console stayed quiet, with Lorrie keeping atop Sylvia's feet.

The moment dawn even thought about stirring, three sheriff's cars with lights bubbling pulled around the driveway, surrounding Sylvia's red truck. A lanky man got out, looked inside Sylvia's truck, then twisted two perfect 180's to assess his surroundings, using a large black gun as a compass point. From the other cars four men emerged, two with shotguns, two with pistols. Their tan uniforms looked comforting. The lanky man whom I presumed was the sheriff glanced up and saw Sylvia and me waving. He nodded and reached inside the car to pull on his hat. The black gun had not left his hand.

"You Ms. Barnes?" he shouted up to Sylvia. When she answered in the affirmative he said that her roommate and her parents had called him. That neighbors had reported hearing gunshots.

"We shot them. We're okay. Do you want to come in, or do you want us to come down?"

"I've never been inside, if you don't mind."

"Not a bit."

I saw him through the camera over the front door and inhaled sharply, but Sylvia was already on her way down. Though not the spitting image, he certainly resembled Lorrie the pig's former—so I hoped—owner. I caught up with Sylvia and told her this. She stopped on the steps and inhaled freedom air just as I had after I shot the young female specter. "It's okay," Sylvia replied. "You're right, its over."

When we let the sheriff in, his four deputies stayed outside shifting from foot to foot. The sheriff looked askance at Sylvia's holster and her grand silver revolver.

"I've got a license to carry."

He shrugged. Then he looked at the two paintings on the floor. "So you're telling me the two of you were target practicing in the middle of the night?"

"Yes."

"No."

He bent to look at one of the crumpled paintings, keeping an eye on Sylvia and her gun. I'd left mine upstairs, glad to be rid of it.

"My grandmother was right," he said, nodding at the two paintings.

"Beg pardon?" Sylvia asked.

"My grandmother told me that her pregnant grandmother ran away from this place. That a group of Confederate soldiers and their families lived here and waylaid boats down at the river. That people were petrified to come near, that the renegade soldiers were cannibals, that they ate the people they robbed on the river after hanging them to cure like so much pork. Tell you the truth, I wasn't excited about coming here before dawn. No one comes here. It's too damned creepy."

"It's haunted," one deputy called out from the porch. "My fiancée's oldest brother disappeared around here."

"There've been others," the sheriff added.

"I think we stopped all that last night." Sylvia patted her revolver. "My daddy's home cure. Do you want to come upstairs and see?"

The sheriff turned, "Tommy, you and Wayne stay here. Gary, you and Billy come on up with me."

When we got to the bedroom the three of them oohed and ahhed over Sylvia's dad's electronics, snorting and pointing at the screen displaying the two deputies scratching their butts on the porch. We then showed them the sword and the cap, which got Lorrie the pig shifting nervously from hoof to hoof.

"That pig saved us," Sylvia said.

" 'Smarter than a hog,' my granddad used to always say. I know a couple who keep two for pets. They make good pets, if you don't have dogs."

"I don't," Sylvia said, "just a boyfriend who acts like one." The three men chuckled at my expense, no doubt admiring the bounteous breasts before them.

I picked up the embroidered cap and pointed at the sword, which had tarnished and pitted greatly since it miraculously healed my shoulder just hours before. The Minie ball was on the dresser, and Sylvia handed it to the sheriff. "We're not asking you to believe, we're just going to tell you," she said, punching at the Minie ball in his palm.

"Hell, I'd believe anything you said about this place, as long as it wasn't good. The sheriff before me ran that realtor woman out of the county after she sold your dad and mom this place. It had done just fine being left alone for twenty years.

It was only whenever people moved in permanent-like that trouble always started."

We told them about meeting the man on the road with Lorrie the pig, about how he came nosing around, and how we set up the security devices.

"And the shots?" the sheriff asked.

"Show him your shoulder and the shirt you were wearing," Sylvia insisted.

The bloodied shirt was in the trash. I lifted it up and a deputy inspected it. Then I took off my clean shirt: a shiny red inflammation the size of someone's fist covered my chest and shoulder. The sheriff touched it and I winced. Sylvia pointed to the Minie ball still in his hand.

"You're saying—"

Sylvia and I nodded. His eyes narrowed and he whistled.

"You know, someone got one of them Catholic priests out here after World War II. That's what my daddy told me. Popish exorcism. Didn't move matters any bit more than a good chicken-eating, hand-layin', foot stompin', mouth hollerin' preacher had." He looked to Sylvia, who was petting Lorrie, and he nodded at the silver revolver on her side. "I'm a great admirer of the home cure myself. Which is why, I guess, we do kindly need to check around, despite me believing your tale."

So the five of us walked around the house and the garage and the grounds. The skulls still atop the trash pile were dog skulls, we learned. The sheriff said there hadn't been coyotes around for ten or more years. "Maybe they all got ate up," he offered, shaking his head. He gave a look back at the house and shivered.

"Okay, young missy, we're leaving. You call your momma and daddy, and your roommate, you hear? And you take care of your little oink friend there. And you—" he just shrugged looking at me.

As the three cars pulled off much more sedately than they'd arrived, I leaned to pet Lorrie and said, "You're wrong, you know, about that pistol—"

"Revolver."

"About that revolver being the home cure."

"Oh?"

"Yeah, the real home cure came when you called me 'Bookstore' and said you loved me and I better shoot." Of course I didn't mention that I almost shot her instead of the thin hillbilly ghost.

"Aw." She stopped petting Lorrie to blow me a kiss.

"You can't call it Lorrie if you're going to keep her."

"Lorrie and Galen got engaged last week. Didn't Galen tell you?"

Part of me wanted to drop to my knees and ask her hand in a double marriage ceremony, but then part of me wondered about Galen's junction of randomly gathering elements—could that be Sylvia and me?

"Of course he didn't tell me. Hell, call her Galen. No one knows whether it's a male or female name anyway."

"No," Sylvia said. "Her new name is 'Hambone.' "

Truly Mine

IF I COULD LAUGH and bend time, if I could pen these my notes down a century and more ago, I might begin: *It was deep winter. My young maidservant had just left my room after adding a log and stoking my fire. I remained alone, vigorously investigating my tome of Rosicrucian lore, when I heard a tapping at my bay window behind me and turned to see* . . .

Even, I suggest, if I were still laughing and bending time, still writing my experience a short—as the life of mountains, not humans, flows—fifty years ago I might begin on my new electric typewriter: *It was deep winter. The quiet outside my farmhouse indicated that my county's snowplows were flummoxed by last night's stormy onslaught. I was coaching my Ph.D. candidate in psychic studies through the final throes of a dissertation at Duke. While none of my spoons had been telekinetically bent, an interesting core of data surrounding the extrasensory abilities of the human mind in altered states presented itself. My candidate had departed my cozy den for a four-wheel drive to brave the roads one short hour before, so I was amazed to hear a rap at my front door. The rapping at my door persisted. Reluctant, I shambled over to see* . . .

But it was now, and it was muggy summer. I had just left my late afternoon class and my recalcitrant upper-class students, whom I had spent one hour trying to convince that Hamlet Senior's ghost may have existed in quantum state like Schrödinger's cat as both graveyard emanation and psychic discharge from the young prince himself. I had to translate several of my terms, including my spryly ambiguous kitty-cat.

It was, as I mentioned, summer, my favorite season. My age had left me with distaste for air-conditioning, so my car window was down as I flipped my turn signal and approached my driveway to my house. I stepped out of my red Nissan Altima to open my farm gate, whose metal emitted an odd chill to my right hand. I concluded that a localized thunderstorm might be approaching my gentleman's farm, for the sky was vaguely overcast. The sky wasn't mine, I realized in disappointment, or I'd have it glowing bright blue.

Getting back in my Altima, I heard some oldie-goldie station playing Grace Slick's "White Rabbit." I must have knocked against my car's console, for I'd been listening to my CD of *Hamlet*, wishing I'd simply played it for my students instead of lecturing futilely. I got out, closed my gate, using my warm left hand, and I drove toward my house, a white, two-story affair from the age of money in America; that is, the Roaring 20's.

A figure was standing on my lawn. Where were all my six watchdogs? The figure was a young man's. He lifted a bottle of what looked like red wine and tilted it in invitation.

My right knee had been throbbing all morning and then through my lunch and then through my lecture. Now it didn't hurt. What's more, my shoulders turned fluid with youth, no bunching or scraping, no popping. The figure ahead grinned and tilted the bottle once more. I'd stopped my car without thinking. Recognizing my good friend Galen Kingsbury, I quickly pulled forward on my winding concrete drive.

Galen, I should step out of my scaffolding and say here, was as dead as King Hamlet. More precisely, he was as dead as Charles Dickens' Scrooge's Marley, he was as dead as a doornail. But I didn't think this then, for my brain had bounded back to a supple time, so my foot happily pressed my Altima's gas pedal, and I edged beside the young man standing there on my front lawn. Indeed, I bounded out of my Altima as if I too were a chirruping youngster.

"Galen!" I called.

He couldn't answer because he was lighting a great black cigar. Where had the wine bottle gone? Ah, resting on my landscaping rail tie, there it sat. Galen puffed at the cigar in that jaunty way he always had, twisting it as if to pass judgment on the cosmopolitan job he'd done firing it up.

"Galen," I said again, grinning and bending for the wine. Then I stopped. There in my very yard, the air around Galen and the wine bottle took the same penetrating chill that my farm gate had conveyed.

"You're dead," I think I said, glancing up with my two eyes. "As a doornail." Did I add this, or did Galen respond?

I looked down at the wine, which was a Medoc, our favorite, not only for the taste but because it was Edgar Allen Poe's favorite also. What other prompt could an ex-Navy man and a cackling college caballero need? A fresh stogie lay beside the wine bottle, black, oily, and inviting. As I reached for both, I remembered that I'd made it to my class that morning and that one of my professors had rattled on about Hamlet's dad, the ex-king, being a cross between a real revenant and a psychic emanation of Hamlet's subconscious. A student had raised her hand and asked what "revenant" meant. I was glad she did, because I didn't know, either. With an academic smirk, the professor explained that it was simply another word for ghost, with the added implication that the ghost had returned on business, if you will. "Aren't all ghosts back on business?" the student had countered, erasing the professor's smirk.

"Galen," I said again, regaining my own professorial hauteur. Yet I remained bent and my hand remained vacillating between the cigar and the wine, both soon to be mine. Pungent smoke breezed downward—I supposed that Galen had exhaled in my direction. And I could smell the wondrous wine. How long had it been since I'd quaffed Medoc? That wine's price had escalated like a war and moved well out of reach of my paycheck, professorial or not.

"Galen," I called again, addressing the lace-up work boots he always wore, in imitation I always supposed, of his dead older brother. The right boot's yellow-corded lace needed tying. Should I point this out before he tripped in my yard, or over my railroad tie? Can ghosts trip?

A family story of the Kingsbury clan was that Galen's dad, who'd died relatively young, had intermittently been called by a fetch, a revenant, if you will, who undertook the form of a long-before murdered mountain child. The ghostly visitations continued for eleven months, until the dad's death. I pulled back and studied the scuffed tan boots, the loose yellow cord, the bottle of Medoc, and the black cigar. No! No, no, no! I, as being among the healthy and living, could not, would not be tripped up by either a yellow bootlace or some folkloric hillbilly mountain trick.

"No!" I shouted. "No! Leave! Take those props and don't ever come back! Never!"

I raised my head—*my* head!—to encounter billowing smoke. The smoke expanded, like fog rolling down a mountain, ubiquitous, unrelenting, hugely obnoxious, and disastrously thick. Its tendrils brushed my cheeks and stung my eyes; then coiled to embed in my beard—*my* beard! What I took for Galen disjunctured into thousands and thousands of black gnats, spiraling like newborn galaxies, only to swarm away and disappear. The sky remained vaguely overcast. I straightened and stood. I stared at the olive-green leaves of an imposing oak near my house. Was that a squirrel's nest curling about itself on a higher limb? A crow cawed just over my fence line, then one of my six watchdogs barked from my back yard. On my landscaping tie at my feet lay a discolored cigar stub— *my* stub!— from months before, from early spring when I'd tried planting my strawberry plants that never took. I swayed as my gristle disjunctured and my bones loosened. Decaying below, its Honduran tobacco unraveling on the weathered landscaping tie, the cigar stub stared . . . black, intent, patient, and waiting . . . for death, my death—the one and only thing truly mine.

Joe Taylor has had three story collections published (*The World's Thinnest Fat Man*; *Some Heroes, Some Heroines, Some Others*; and *Masques for the Fields of Time*) and a matching number of novels (*Oldcat & Ms. Puss: A Book of Days for You and Me*; *Let There Be Lite: How I Came to Know and Love Gödel's Incompleteness Theorem*; and *Pineapple: A Comic Novel in Verse*). The linked stories from this collection have appeared in several magazines, including *moonShine*, *Jitter*, *Weird and Whatnot*, *Steam Ticket*, *Red Dirt Forum*, and *Cleansheets* Review (online). He has edited several story collections, including *Tartts One* through *Tartts Seven* and *Belles' Letters*, and he has a novel forthcoming entitled *The Theoretics of Love*. Several completed novels are floating around in electronic ether. He presently is putting the finishing touches on a second comic novel in verse, *Back to the Wine Jug*, which features a resurrected Victoria Woodhull, J. Edgar Hoover, Diogenes and his faithful hound Pluto plus that ever-present but not so effective lantern that shines in eternal search of one honest (hu)man. Taylor and his wife Tricia house 15 stray dogs, which almost matches the number of years that he has directed Livingston Press at the University of West Alabama—over 25.

Printed and bound by PG in the USA